The Ot

Of Solitude

By Val Manning

Dedications:

This book is dedicated to the memory of those innumerable brave women who played their part in WW2.

Many thanks also to Jenni, Joyce and Julie for their enthusiasm and honest feedback during the redrafting of this book.

Acknowledgements:

The following three books (all published by Elmont Publications – The Working Waterways Series) provided the inspiration for the historical element of the novel:

Eily Gayford "The Amateur Boatwoman"),

Emma Smith (author of "Maidens' Trip")

Susan Woolfit (author of "Idle Women").

I also owe much to DH Lawrence and George Eliot for their early influence on my taste in fiction and for the quotes at the start of each chapter.

Table of Contents

"She thought it was part of the hardship of her life that there was laid upon her the burthen of larger wants than others seemed to feel – that she had to endure this wide hopeless yearning for that something, whatever it was, that was greatest and best on this earth." George Eliot (The Mill on the Floss)

At Buckby Wharf on a cold December morning, the still surface of the canal was a picture of tranquility. Reflections of the streaky wisps of cloud in the pale blue sky merged with the faint mist above the water, creating a sense of mystery and romance. Alongside the canal a row of terraced cottages, each with a lovingly tended garden, looked on silently, their small upstairs windows like sleepy eyes observing the passing ducks. There were few boats on the move at this time of year; those that were still occupied were moored close together along the towpath, cratch covers pulled tight against the damp air, with only the wood smoke curling from their chimneys to indicate that there was life aboard. In the pretty locks, with their freshly painted black and white gates, it was impossible to tell the depth of the water or to guess the extent of the danger lurking in the invisible strong currents below. The serene stillness gave no inkling of past tragedies or the terror that may yet be encountered within and beside these waters.

Many miles away from this picturesque location an argument was raging between a mother and her daughter.

"Jessica, when will you learn to stop being so impetuous? You can't give up a perfectly good job and go and live on a long boat!"

"It's not a long boat - it's a narrow boat, and lots of people live on them." Jessica's mother's reaction was to be expected, but then Barbara had no idea how awful Jessica felt every Sunday night with the prospect of another week ahead of her. The butterflies would start mid-afternoon and by bedtime she would be sick with apprehension. Every Saturday was spent marking children's work, planning and preparing for the week ahead, leaving no time for a social life. Jessica knew there had to be more to life than this unrewarding treadmill from one term to the next. Longer holidays didn't compensate for the hard slog, as she invariably found herself going down with a virus as the term ended, resulting in most of her holiday being spent recovering. Jessica had heard other teachers talking of the buzz that they got from the job that made all the hard work worthwhile. But Jessica had yet to experience such a buzz as all she could think of was how to survive. She wanted more from life than this - there just had to be more than this. It was as if her real life was on hold and she was just waiting for it to begin. Life was all work and waiting. What made matters worse was she was uncomfortable with her colleagues at the school. Even though it was her second year at the school she was still very much the outsider. She often suspected they were gossiping about her unprofessional behaviour. She had no idea how they could possibly have discovered her guilty secret since she and Steve had always been so careful, yet they acted as if they knew. There was always an empty chair next to her in staff meetings, she observed.

"But what will you live on? You can't give up working." Barbara's tone of voice reflected her impatience with her troublesome daughter. Jessica sighed as she started to reassure her.

"Mum, I've done the sums, and with what Auntie Joan has left me, as long as I don't go crazy when buying the boat and I am careful how I spend my money, I can afford to live for at least year without working. My time at college taught me how to economise. I've managed to pay off my debts and even save a little. If I'm not working I won't need any smart clothes or a car so I can manage on very little."

"But you could put down a really big deposit on a house with that amount. You can't just fritter it away."

Jessica had no brothers or sisters and as a child growing up in the Staffordshire village of Alrewas she would have had little to do in the long Summer holidays. So she had always been pleased to spend time at Auntie Joan's house on the other side of the village. Auntie Joan (who was in fact her great-aunt) was a teacher. She was unmarried with no children of her own and was more than happy to look after Jessica in the holidays while Barbara, her niece, was at work. She took great pleasure in spoiling the funny little girl who used to hate wearing the pretty dresses her mother bought for her and had been known on occasions to tear them on purpose. When she became a teenager, it was Auntie Joan who had finally persuaded Barbara to let Jessica have her beautiful dark hair cut short and to resign herself to her daughter's preference for jeans rather than dresses.

Auntie Joan's house was a little cottage close to the Trent and Mersey Canal where Jessica spent many hours of her childhood on the towpath watching the ducks and swans and waving to passing boats. They would sometimes take a picnic and walk to the busy Fradley Junction and Jessica learnt to read the names of the many boats that were moored there. She loved to hear Auntie Joan's stories about the boat people and much to Auntie Joan's delight she would sometimes pretend she was leading a horse along the towpath, encouraging it to pull the imaginary barge and feeding it with oats. Auntie Joan had a great love of history and explained to Jessica how and why the canals had been built and how steam trains had replaced the old working boats. As well as the history of the canals, Auntie Joan taught her about the local history of her village; how the river used to flood and how the name of the village, Alrewas, came from the words Alder Wash. She also taught Jessica the names of the wild flowers and trees, and how to tell the difference between a swallow and a swift. As Jessica grew older, Auntie Joan had encouraged her to read extensively and to share her passion for authors like George Eliot and D.H. Lawrence.

Sometimes Auntie Joan would read to Jessica extracts from a diary she had kept while she was working on the canals during the war. There were many things in the diary that Jessica could not understand and her aunt would frequently stop reading to explain patiently to her niece the meaning of technical words like "cratch", "top-planks" and "rigging-chains". There was one such term that Jessica found particularly amusing. "I thought "winding" was what you do to babies," she said.

"Yes it is, but this is nothing like that. When you have a seventy foot boat travelling along a narrow canal you can't just turn around anywhere. You have to go on to the next winding hole, where the canal is wider, put your front end into the widest part and shove your tiller over as far as it will go to help you turn. Sometimes we got stuck in the mud and one of us would stand on the bow of the boat with a long pole and help push the boat round. It wasn't easy," Auntie Joan explained.

Despite her inability to fully understand everything her aunt told her, the diary extracts gave Jessica a good understanding of the hardships her aunt had endured. With bedbugs and freezing cold weather, a bucket for a lavatory and six o'clock starts, working on a boat was not as romantic as it had first sounded. "Didn't you ever get frightened you would fall in?"

"No, I was much younger then and quite nimble, so I wasn't too scared. A friend of mine went to work in a factory instead of coming on the boats with me. She said she was scared she would fall in and perhaps she would have done as she was always rather clumsy. She went to work in one of the munitions factories in Coventry instead. I was only properly frightened when we had to unload our cargo in London in case a doodlebug landed near us. Luckily, by the time I went to work on the boats the main bombing of the cities had stopped but those damned doodlebugs terrified us."

Auntie Joan would never let Jessica read the diary herself as she said it was private. On one occasion, Jessica had tried looking over her shoulder to read the extract with her but she had not yet learned to read joined-up writing and could make no sense of Auntie Joan's straggly letters with their big loops. There was one story in the diary that Jessica loved to hear and she would ask her aunt to read it to her over and over again. She enjoyed the excitement in Auntie Joan's voice as she read aloud.

"November 4th 1944. We lost our cat Winston today. It happened at the top of the Long Buckby flight where the locks are very deep.

Winston suddenly jumped from the butty to the motor - we think he must have spotted a mouse. At exactly the same moment as he jumped, Joyce (who was on the tiller) let the boat crash into the gates at the end of the lock. This made the boat bounce backwards and a small space was created in the middle. That's where Winston ended up. The boats moved back together again and the small space was gone. Joyce screamed and tried to push the boats apart but they were heavy with cargo and the currents were so strong she just couldn't budge them. Annie and I couldn't help her because we were up on the side of the lock. We were frightfully upset, thinking Winston must be either squashed or drowned. But then by some miracle Winston appeared in the water at the stern. Even though the currents were throwing him about all over the place, he managed to get his claws onto the rope fender and Joyce pulled him aboard. He shook himself all over and gave her a haughty look as if to say, "Why did you do that?" Afterwards, Joyce said she should have cut the engine because if Winston had got caught on the propellor he would have been cut to pieces. But at the time we were panicking so much that none of us thought of it. Winston doesn't seem to be any worse for his adventure, although he is now sitting in front of the fire trying to look wounded so that we will give him some more milk."

Jessica's had never enjoyed a particularly close relationship with her mother and she suspected that she had always been something of a disappointment to her. So when she had problems, it was often Auntie Joan she turned to for advice and support. Often, but not always, as there were things in her private life of which she was too ashamed. When she had started her teaching career, she had told Auntie Joan how hard she was finding it. Auntie Joan had understood the difficulties she was

10

experiencing and could fully appreciate how tired Jessica was feeling. She had sympathised with her when Jessica told her about the long hours. "With all the lesson planning and paperwork you have to do now, I don't think I could have done what you have to do," she had told Jessica.

"It's the constant assessment that's the real killer Auntie Joan, and having to keep records of it all."

"Well, don't think you have to keep doing it. Remember, you need to have a life of your own as well. I'm looking forward to the day when you make me a great-great-aunt. If you don't get out there and live, how will you ever find Mr Right?" her aunt had admonished her.

"Oh Auntie Joan, there are lots of things I want to do with my life before I settle down and start having babies."

"Well get out there and do them whilst you can." Jessica had smiled and nodded, wishing she could tell Auntie Joan that she had found Mr Right but he already had a wife and children. Gently taking hold of Jessica's shoulders, Auntie Joan had turned her around to face her and earnestly entreated, "Promise me this. Whatever happens in your life, you must always remember to follow your dreams."

This was the last conversation she ever had with Auntie Joan and at the time she could not have known that her great-aunt would bequeath to her the eighty thousand pounds that would buy her freedom. She also had no inkling that Joan had any trouble with her health so the massive heart attack that had killed her came as a terrible shock. Throughout that awful service at the crematorium, Auntie Joan's last words kept repeating themselves around her head. "Follow your dreams, follow your dreams, follow your dreams."

The Narrow Escape was every inch the status symbol; her 60 foot length gleaming from the intricate rope work of the bow fender to the spotless brass tiller handle. The blue and cream paintwork was flawless, the shiny brass fittings without the tiniest spot of tarnish. The ornate lettering and decoration had taken the sign-writer over two weeks to accomplish and was a stunning work of art. "Jo, Mr Sheridan will be arriving this afternoon to collect The Narrow Escape. Can you bring her up from the workshop for me and put her beside the office please."

"OK Dad. A glass of bubbly tonight to celebrate, I think?" Joanna was pleased this day had come at last. Her family had been building boats for generations but there had never been such a difficult customer. He was forever on the phone, checking up on progress and changing his mind about the finer details. She could not remember a boat ever having built to such exacting standards.

An experienced boater herself, Joanna skilfully steered her way through the other boats around the entrance to the workshop. She slid The Narrow Escape gently into place beside the marina office and after tying up carefully on the bollards she could not resist taking one last look inside. Stepping briskly down the three steps to the rear cabin, she gazed in wonder at the immaculate interior. Wooden blinds, solid wood flooring and light oak fittings were complemented by the plush fabrics of the sofa and armchairs. There could be no doubt that only the best would do when this particular boat had been fitted out for Robert Sheridan. It was a reverse layout, with the main living area at the rear and the bedroom with its fixed double bed at the front. Every inch of space had been painstakingly planned, so the galley contained a washer dryer and freezer as well as the usual fridge, microwave, hob and cooker. The diamond blue corian work surface and sink positively glowed with sophistication. In the lounge area, more home comforts were provided by the huge 3D television set, complete with surround sound. Of course, all these appliances demanded a highly efficient electrical system with a bank of batteries and twin alternators to keep them fully charged. The Beta 50 engine was the latest model, quiet-running and fuel-efficient, hidden away beneath the deck of the cruiser stern. Joanna left the boat and returned to the office, wondering if Mrs Sheridan would appreciate what a gem of a boat her husband had purchased.

As the Lexus slid smoothly out of Newport Pagnall services, Zena Sheridan whispered a silent prayer of thanks for the invention of SatNav. Remembering the very early days of their marriage when her navigational skills had been put to the test, Zena appreciated being able to sit back in the soft leather seats without having to pay attention to where they were. Not that Rob had ever shouted at her in those early days but he had a way of fixing his mouth that left her in no doubt that she had disappointed him. Rob always drove when they went out together. She was by far the better driver; of that she was certain but on the few occasions when Rob had allowed her to take the wheel there had been such an atmosphere in the car that she had long given up this particular battle.

Rob was impatient to reach the boatyard. He had been planning this purchase for the past five years. He had taken a number of canal holidays with his old college friends while the children were little and he planned frequent escapes to his new boat to balance the stresses of his increasingly demanding job. In the current economic climate he reasoned that he would do well to invest his money in a boat rather than leaving it in the bank. Zena had not accompanied Rob on his previous canal holidays as her husband considered their two sons too young for a waterside environment. On the single occasion that Zena and the boys had paid a visit for a day it had been a nightmare keeping an eye on Lawrence and Zac as they charged around the boat and along the towpath. So Zena had told him she fully understood his decision that it was best for her and the boys to stay at home. And these holidays without Zena had provided him with opportunities to have fun of a different kind. He and his friends would never tell their wives and girlfriends what they got up to. "What happens on the canal stays on the canal," they had agreed. As the years went by, Rob's group of college friends had dwindled and the boating holidays had become a thing of the past. Rob had worked hard and done well and now it was time to enjoy the rewards of his labour. With both Zac and Lawrence away at school he was finding his home life comfortable but boring. Although Zena was always compliant their love life was rather mundane. So when she expressed an interest in coming boating with him it seemed a good way to put some novelty back into their life. The Narrow Escape was the boat he had always dreamed of and while Zena may not be as exciting as the girls he had met on his earlier boating holidays she would at least be available every night. The fact that she was also a superb cook was an added bonus and he had designed a galley that would do justice to her culinary skills. Nevertheless, he had decided that they would eat out sometimes to give her a break. There had been a tricky moment last year when Zena had suggested she might like to go out to work once both boys were settled in boarding school. Fortunately he had talked her out of the idea; it would have been impossible to organise free time on the boat if they had to work round her commitments as well as his. It was only an hour's drive from home to the marina he had chosen so they would be able to get there as often as the opportunity arose. As a partner in the firm he now had more holiday entitlement and more choice about when he took those holidays. He could put in extra hours in the winter when the boat was out of action and in the summer he could keep in touch with the office by email, phone and video-conference; that meant he could be away for a few weeks at a time.

Rob was impatient for the boys to start their long summer holiday. It would be such a great adventure for them now they were old enough to help with the locks and the steering. He adored his sons and wanted them to have all the experiences he had enjoyed as a child and more besides. He could still remember the day his father had first taken him fishing and had decided it was time for his boys to have their first lesson in the art of angling. But they would have much better equipment than he had since the world of fishing tackle had moved on since he was a boy. There were some seriously expensive rods available now and he could afford to buy the best. He had already started to research what he needed to buy; for the boys simple float rods would be enough, and for himself he fancied trying an angling pole. Then of course he would need to buy reels, floats, tackle box etc. Rob was looking forward to choosing and buying this equipment; now The Narrow Escape was built he was in need of another new project.

Having been so lost in his plans for the future, Rob was pleasantly surprised when he heard his SatNav telling him, "You have arrived at your destination." His smug face broke into the most self-satisfied smile as he drove through the gates and down the long drive to the marina office. "Here we go, love, we've arrived at the boatyard. And if I'm not mistaken, I can see The Narrow Escape outside the office. Doesn't she look fantastic?" But Zena was fast asleep in the passenger seat.

"Well, my driving can't have been that bad," he muttered. "The way she talks, I'm amazed she could even take her eyes off the road." Rob looked at his wife. Even asleep, with her mouth slightly open, she was beautiful. Unlike so many women who let themselves go after they had babies, Zena had kept herself in good shape. He congratulated himself on his decision to pay for her gym membership, including the personal trainer who motivated her to attend regularly. She had excellent fashion sense and used her monthly clothing allowance to good effect. She looked great in whatever she wore, from smart cocktail dresses to the new outfits she had chosen to wear on the boat. He missed the long blond hair of the girl he had married, but had to admit that her cropped style suited her and she kept it neat with regular trips to the stylist. He had known from the moment he first saw her that despite her dreadful background she had the potential to be the ideal wife of a successful lawyer. She was stunningly beautiful and graceful, and he had found her naivety so endearing. All he had to do was to get her away from her chavvy family and give her the guidance she needed. He had lavished her with attention and presents that no young girl could resist. She had been swept off her feet by him, enjoying the envy of her classmates on the few occasions he collected her from school in his father's smart BMW. As a new recruit at one of the big London law firms, it had been easy for him to impress her parents and persuade them to put aside their doubts about the age difference between himself and Zena. When he proposed to her on her seventeenth birthday, her parents had readily agreed that going to college was something she could always do later. They set about organising the dream wedding for their daughter, towards which his parents had of course made a very generous contribution. He had chosen well; she had always been the dutiful wife, attending business functions and hosting dinner parties for important clients with decorum and good taste. He had watched with disgust as other wives behaved inappropriately at various functions where the champagne flowed freely; if a wife of his ever acted in such a way he would not tolerate it. But he could always rely on Zena to make him proud and he was proud that by and large he had rewarded her with his fidelity. Those few incidents on the boating holidays had remained undiscovered and he had ignored the many opportunities to have affairs at work as he was far too sensible to jeopardise either his career or his marriage.

Chapter 2

"Whatever life may be, and whatever horror men have made of it, the world is a lovely place, a magic place, something to marvel over. The world is an amazing place." D.H. Lawrence (The Lost Girl)

Jessica took a last lingering look at her classroom. The boards had been cleared and everything was neatly tidied away for her replacement. Now the time had come to leave she was actually quite sorry. She could clearly recall the day when this had first become her classroom, her very own space in which to organise and create the perfect learning environment. After all those months of training, the numerous job interviews and the endless waiting, the excitement had lit up her entire being. But the reality had not turned out to be anything as wonderful as her expectations and now she was desperate to flee and forget.

"Good luck to him," she muttered. " I hope he makes a better job of it than I did. Perhaps Ricky Smith will respond better to a male teacher. He needs a good role model in his life. I did my best but it was just not enough." Jessica felt bad about leaving at Easter. She would have liked to see the year out but it was so difficult and her health was suffering. She had successfully completed her first year and qualified as a teacher, but wondered how on earth they could have passed her and let her loose on another set of kids this year. True, last year's class had been particularly difficult and everybody reassured her she was not the first to have experienced problems with this cohort of children. But if only she could have done more to make them enjoy coming to school, that would have been a good start. As it was, most of the kids complained that the lessons were boring and their attendance was abysmal. She had survived the first year, hanging on to the thought that the following September she could make a fresh start with a new group of children. But the fresh start had not turned out as she hoped; having failed to establish a decent relationship with Ricky, the others had followed his lead and by the beginning of November she was in no doubt that it was going to be another unbearable year. Since other teachers told her how much they had enjoyed teaching Ricky there could be no other explanation other than that the fault must be hers. She just wasn't cut out to be a teacher. The additional complication of Steve had finally decided the matter and now she could not wait to put the whole sorry business behind her.

Just one week later, Jessica was ready to set off along the cut on Ragamuffin, a thirty-foot semi-traditional narrow boat that was old but in good working order. The previous owner had looked after her well; she had been regularly serviced and had her hull blacked every two years so Jessica felt confident that she would not have any unexpected major expenses and this was borne out by the surveyor's report. And if things got desperate she knew that she could always do some supply teaching. Jessica had been on a couple of boating holidays with Auntie Joan when she was a teenager. Having made her decision to spend her inheritance on a narrow boat she wasted no time. Handing in her notice on the last day of the Autumn Term, she knew there would be no going back. She had spent much of the Christmas holiday on the Internet, carefully researching the many pitfalls of buying a second-hand boat and was lucky enough to find Ragamuffin after only a few weeks of searching. The boat was just four years old and the engine had only done seven hundred hours. Her parents had agreed to store her belongings and one rainy day in early April, she went to collect her boat. She was driven there by her father, a sweet, gentle man by the name of Bob. "Aye, it's a lovely boat, Jessica," he said. "You've done well in finding this one. But please be careful - don't do anything silly. You must remember that cruising on your own is very different from being with a group of people. There'll be nobody to rescue you if you fall in."

"I'll be careful Dad, I promise."

"And if you're tinkering with the engine, make sure the key is out of the ignition."

"Yes Dad. I'm not stupid." Jessica retorted. She hoped that she would not have to do too much tinkering with the engine, even though she had bought herself a basic guide to engine maintenance just in case. When she was working out her budget for purchasing and maintaining the boat, she had wisely set aside a sum of money for repairs and servicing and she intended to leave most jobs to the experts.

"And phone us. As often as you can," Bob persisted.

"Yes Dad. But don't worry if you don't hear from me every week - I may not be able to get a signal."

"Well, just do best you can." Jessica was desperate for her father to leave so her adventures could begin but that did not stop the tears stinging her eyes as she watched him drive away. Before he left he had told her that if there was a chance of her getting into debt she must let him know; he had enough money in investments to be able to help her out if it came to it. But she wanted to prove that she could do it on her own and asking him for help would definitely be a last resort. Still, it was a good safety net to have, she thought.

As she set off on her first day's cruising, Jessica had absolutely no idea where she was heading. Barbara, finding it impossible to believe that it really was her daughter's intention to go just where the fancy took her, had thoughtfully bought a set of guide books that covered the entire waterway system of England and Wales. On her first evening, she opened Book 1, "London, Grand Union, Oxford and Lee", and started to make plans for where she might travel. Teaching in London had made her long for open stretches of countryside and these would be plentiful on the Oxford Canal. After a few weeks of cruising alone she may like some company and she could go and visit her old friend Karen, who now lived in Oxford. After that, who knows? She could head off west along the Kennet and Avon, she could continue along the Thames towards London or she could simply turn round and go back the way she had come. As a teacher, Jessica had become adept at juggling her time and this new absence of deadlines came as an unexpected treat. Out of habit she started to write a detailed journey plan, adding together the number of locks to the number of miles and dividing by three to work out how many hours she needed to cruise in a day to reach Oxford by a certain date. She chuckled with delight when she realised what she was doing. "You are not planning lessons now, you stupid girl," she scolded herself. "All you have to do is phone Karen and Jack when you get nearer to Oxford and arrange a date and time to see them."

On her second day of cruising, Jessica became an avid bird watcher. It started with a red kite, soaring above the trees beside the canal. To her delight, it swooped over the front of Ragamuffin, before climbing away out of view. She had never

21

seen a red kite so close before, yet she recognised it from its distinctive colouring and markings on the underside of its wings. After that, she scoured the hedges along the banks in search of kingfishers but every time she thought she spotted one, on closer inspection she could see it was only a great tit or a blue tit. She watched wagtails strutting along the towpath and wrens in the low branches of the hedges. Every so often she would spot a bullfinch flitting from branch to branch. There were also numerous pigeons, crows and magpies along the way, but these did not arouse the same level of excitement. She observed countless herons sitting on the bank and taking off with their majestic wings whenever the boat approached them, only to land a little way further ahead until the boat caught up again. She could not believe that a bird that looked so big when in flight could turn into something so slender when it was standing upright and marvelled at the ease with which it folded away those magnificent wings. Towards the end of the day she saw a mother mallard with her five baby chicks so tiny that they must be only a few days old. Over the next few days Jessica spotted many more baby ducklings with their mothers and wondered why the drakes were nowhere to be seen. She amused herself with the notion that they were all off on a lads' holiday; they had played their part and now it was up to the mothers to do the work. Swans, on the other hand, stayed as a pair for life and looked after their cygnets as a doting couple.

As well as baby ducklings on the canal, Jessica saw fields full of new lambs and tiny calves. As she steered Ragamuffin through the open countryside, she allowed her mind to wander. All these signs of new life were very appropriate, she thought, hoping her journey into the unknown would allow her to be reborn as a better and happier person. Her relationship with Steve had been so exciting to begin with; it was as if she had never been properly alive before she met him. Being with him had made anything seem possible. But the terrible guilt was a price too high. With every day that the affair had gone on she had learnt to hate - she hated his wife, she hated him and most of all she hated herself.

Jessica became quite skilled at taking Ragamuffin through the locks single-handedly. She had at first found the slimy green walls a little daunting as she precariously climbed the ladder to get herself out of an empty lock. But after doing this a few times she had grown in both confidence and agility. However, as she was entering the first of the three Hillmorton Locks near Rugby, she was followed into the lock by a baby duckling that was brave enough to swim away from its mother. She had closed the lock gate behind her and was about to go to the far end of the lock to lift the paddles when she heard the frantic squeaking. Looking down into the water below, she could see the tiny furry thing paddling uselessly around the space between the boat and the lock gate. The mother duck was still with the other chicks on the other side of the heavy lock gate, calling to her offspring but there was no way for her to get through. Jessica opened the gate to let the duckling escape but the silly bird just swam along the narrow gap beside the boat to the front of the lock. There was nothing Jessica could do but wait for it to find its way out again. While she was waiting, another boat arrived from the opposite direction, dropping off a couple of women at the bollards to get the lock ready. One of these women called out to Jessica, "What's the delay?" and Jessica explained to her that a baby duckling was trapped in front of the boat.

"Well, why can't we just fill up the lock and then it will be able to swim out at this end?" the second woman asked. Jessica explained that the duckling was so small that she was not sure how well it would cope with the strong currents. The pair agreed to wait and walked back to their boat to explain to their husbands what was going on. Jessica, meanwhile, walked to the open gate at the other end of the lock where the mother and the other babies were about to swim in.

"Oh no you don't," she giggled, quickly closing the gate to keep them out. She stayed by the gate, ready to open it again if the little duckling should find its way back. After about ten minutes the two women returned to the lock and a number of other boaters began to appear as a queue was developing from both directions. They all watched as the little duckling swam around in circles in front of the boat. It was in quite a quite a frenzy and did not appear to know how to get back to where it had come from. Finally after much discussion, it was agreed by everybody that they should fill the lock very slowly by just raising one paddle half way. The crowd watched the tiny bird being buffeted by the currents and disappearing from sight for a moment before reappearing behind Ragamuffin at the lock gate where it had first entered. Of course, the gate could not be opened now as the lock was about a quarter full. One of the boaters suggested they should re-empty the lock and open the gate to let it out. But impatience was brewing and some of the boaters insisted that they should continue filling the lock so they could all get on their way. Fortunately the duckling stayed behind Ragamuffin until the water level was high enough for one of the men to reach down and scoop it out with a large fishing net. It was then carried ceremoniously back to the bank where the anxious mother was waiting with the rest of her brood, whereupon a loud cheer and applause erupted from the waiting boaters. Jessica was soon able to take Ragamuffin out of the lock, leaving the gates open for the waiting boats to come in. She found the next two locks were already set for her to steer straight in; there was a great advantage in having a waiting queue of boats.

By the end of her first week, Jessica's body was aching from the unaccustomed exercise and she was ready for a rest. As she approached the junction where the Oxford Canal and the Grand Union came together at Braunston, she decided to take some time out and moor up for a few days. She had been to Braunston many years ago and had loved the excitement of so many different boats in one place. There were a number of chandleries where she could browse, although she knew she had to be careful not to spend too much money. But it would not hurt to look, she decided, and it would give her a better idea of what things might cost if she needed to replace any parts. As she approached Braunston late in the day, Jessica was concerned that she might not be able to find a suitable mooring before the junction where she had to turn right for Oxford. So she brought Ragamuffin into the first available space. It was quite a walk to the centre of the village from here but her decision was rewarded with a stunning view of Braunston and its imposing church steeple. The comforting sound of the sheep in the field alongside her was a much better alternative than the busy main London Road with its heavy lorries and speeding cars. The boat in the space behind her looked deserted but the one in front had a family aboard and Jessica felt reassured that this was a safe mooring spot. A young woman sitting on the back of the boat called out to Jessica as she was tying up the front rope. "Hi there. Had a good day's cruising?"

"Yes thanks. Although that wind was a bit of a killer today. You don't happen to know how far it is to the shops, do you?"

"It's about fifteen minutes. If you walk back to that bridge there, you will find a footpath that takes you across the fields to the village centre. Just head for the church and then carry on along the High Street. There is a small supermarket and a fab butcher opposite. Or if you want a proper path, just carry on along the towpath until you reach the marina, cross the footbridge and follow the path up the hill," the woman advised her kindly.

"Thanks a lot. That's really helpful. Enjoy the rest of your day."

Before setting off to the shops, Jessica sat on the stern of the boat lost in wonder at the world around her. The lambs in the adjacent field were very young, their brand new whiteness contrasting starkly with the dirty cream of their mothers' fleeces. She could see new leaves sprouting in the hedgerows and the bright sunshine of a forsythia bush further along the towpath. Jessica loved all shades of yellow but especially the bright springtime colours brought by aconites and daffodils, heralding the approach of summer. She was eagerly anticipating the arrival of oilseed rape crops that any day now would turn field after field into a blaze of colour, typifying the excitement of long summer days. After that would come the golden hue of cornfields, a more mellow shade of yellow that prophesied the end of summer and the drabness of the winter ahead. Jessica wondered where she would be by the time the yellows ended; would she still be travelling around the country on her boat or would she have managed to find something new to do with her life?

The following morning, Jessica lay in her cosy bed in her tiny cabin, thoroughly enjoying her idleness. "Why do I feel guilty?" she asked herself. "I can stay in bed all day if I want to. I have nobody to please but myself." She had actually woken quite early and for the first time in as long as she could remember, had taken the time to listen to the sounds around her. The dawn chorus was sensational with such an abundance and variety of song-birds that she could not identify them all. Full of her own happiness and sense of well-being, she snuggled down under the duvet and drifted back to sleep. She was awoken much later by a boat going past rather too quickly and hauled herself to the galley to fetch some breakfast which she took back to bed with her.

"Oh my God, I haven't done this in years. What have I been missing out on?" she chuckled to herself. Resting back on her pillows, Jessica began to reflect on the difference in her lifestyle since she had left teaching. It wasn't just having the time to lie about in bed all morning that was making her feel so fulfilled and relaxed, she thought. In school nobody had time to stop and chat but she had already discovered that on the canals most people were only to happy to lend a helping hand to other boaters and to share useful information about local amenities. She remembered the patience that had been shown while they were rescuing the baby duckling. There was a proper sense of community, with real values of the sort she had tried so unsuccessfully to foster in her pupils. "Perhaps they should close the schools and send all children to live on the canals for a year," she thought. "I have already learnt so much and I've only been living this life for a few days." It was such a contrast to school, where a simple request to pick up a pencil from the floor would bring the inevitable reply, "It wasn't me who dropped it, so why should I pick it up?" Jessica knew she had made the right decision. "Thanks Auntie Joan," she murmured aloud.

By the third day of cruising in The Narrow Escape, Rob had firmly established that the stern deck was his domain and his alone. He was greatly relieved that Zena had chosen to sit at the front while he steered through Braunston Tunnel as he had set himself the challenge of getting through without touching the sides. The previous afternoon, he had successfully negotiated the 1528 yards of the Crick Tunnel without incident despite having Zena on the back, getting in the way and distracting him by recounting what she had read in the guide book about the building of the tunnel. She had explained how, when the tunnel was built in 1814, its route had to be changed because of quicksand. While these facts were interesting enough, Rob was not in the mood for listening to her non-stop chatter. On reaching an open stretch of water he had tried his best to teach her how to steer but she was absolutely useless, driving him mad with her constant conversation with herself. "I need to go left so I've got to move this to the right."

"Do you need to keep saying that?" he had hissed and she had gone very quiet. But once her chatter stopped so did her ability to steer the boat and they would have crashed into the bank countless times if had Rob not grabbed the tiller at the last moment. In the end they had agreed that perhaps she was not made for steering and as she had mastered the locks so quickly it made sense for each of them to do what they were good at.

Zena was equally happy on the front of the boat. It was much quieter away from the engine where she could savour the solitude. She admired the craftsmanship of the hedgelayers who had knocked stakes into the ground between the bushes; between these stakes they had threaded the lower branches of the bushes, creating an impenetrable structure rather like a woven fence. The bank was studded with yellow flowers which Zena guessed were celandines. The branches of the trees were still bare, their lower trunks sheathed in ivy, reminding Zena of some green leg-warmers from the dressing-up box she had when she was a little girl. She used to put them on with some high-heeled shoes of her mother's. They were far too big for her of course and she must have looked ridiculous but at the time she thought she was a proper grown-up. She also loved to play with her big sister's make-up and was forever getting into trouble over it. As they approached Braunston Tunnel, having obediently checked the tunnel light was working and switched on all the lights below decks, Zena was free from further responsibility until they arrived at the other end. She settled herself comfortably on the soft cushions to make the most of the experience. As they passed through a steep-sided cutting she could see the tunnel mouth ahead. There was a boat coming the other way, its single headlight conjuring up in her imagination a picture of Cyclops, the one-eyed giant. As they entered the tunnel, Rob was forced to move further over to the right to give way to Cyclops, which caused him to scrape his precious boat against the rough brickwork of the tunnel wall.

"Fuck!" Zena could not suppress a quiet snigger and was grateful that Rob could not see her inane grin.

While the rough brickwork was making its mark on the pristine paintwork of The Narrow Escape, a group of lads were steering their hire boat out of the tunnel at the far end. They were in high spirits and fully enjoying their first holiday afloat. Having noticed that there was a boat following them, they decided to wait and save water by travelling as a pair through the flight of double locks down to Braunston. These lads were full of energy and competition and when the good-looking blonde from The Narrow Escape appeared on the scene they were keen to impress her. Although Zena was older than any of these youths, she could tell from the looks they exchanged between themselves that they thought she was hot. One of the group, a bronzed athlete called Nick, sat on the lock gate beside Zena and began to chat to her. "Have you come far today?"

"No we just set off from Welton this morning. How about you?" asked Zena, jumping off the lock gate to face her companion.

"We had an early start and have done the Long Buckby flight already. Unfortunately there were no other boats around so we had to go through all the locks on our own."

"That sounds like hard work. You must be exhausted," she cooed as she lifted her windlass to open the paddles.

"I'm a bit tired but there are enough of us to share the work. Must be much harder for you, having to do it all alone," he sympathised.

"Yes, I must admit I was very pleased to see all of you here for this flight. Thanks for waiting." Zena was struggling to turn the windlass so her athletic companion quickly came to her assistance. As he stood next to her, Zena could not help noticing what good shape he was in and she blushed as his body brushed against her.

"Thanks."

"My pleasure." He flashed her a meaningful smile. Meanwhile, one of Nick's friends who was steering their boat struck up a conversation with Rob as they waited side by side in the lock. By the time the lock was empty he had heard every detail of the building of The Narrow Escape and how vigilant Rob had been in keeping the boatyard on their toes throughout the process. As they slid into place in the second lock, the smug look was wiped off Rob's face as he witnessed his wife giggling flirtatiously with the boys. She appeared to be struggling to close the gates behind the boats and two of the group had raced across to help her. They were all laughing as they heaved the heavy gate together and the way Zena was looking at her helpers suggested to Rob that she was enjoying the experience rather too much. The boat descending in the lock caused Zena to disappear from Rob's view and he waited impatiently for the gates to be opened. This seemed a frustratingly slow lock to empty but when he was finally able to steer The Narrow Escape out into the open pound, Rob could see that once again Zena was being helped to close the lock gate behind him. This time she was with a different guy who had removed his shirt to reveal his muscular torso. When he and Zena set off together along the towpath to set up the third lock, Rob was further infuriated by his wife's animated expression and her new companion's attentiveness. Stuck on the boat there was nothing he could do but watch, letting his imagination fill in the supposed details of their conversation. As they finished the last lock and Zena ran down to join her husband she called out to her young helpers, "Enjoy the rest of your holiday. Hope we might see you again."

Nick and his friends guffawed loudly as they watched Zena trying to leap back aboard The Narrow Escape. For a moment it looked as if she was going to fall in. Rob was most unhelpful, leaving a formidable distance for Zena to jump and then complaining that she had taken too long. The lads finished closing the gates and bounded nimbly aboard their boat. The Narrow Escape was at the water point when they cruised past. "Thanks again. Have a good journey," Nick called amiably to Rob and Zena. But as they moved out of earshot of The Narrow Escape, the lads could not resist laughing about its pompous owner.

"Bow thrusters AND stern thrusters!"

"But the best thing of all was that the batteries for both sets of thrusters were utterly dead by the time they went through the last lock and he says they will take several hours to charge up again," his companion howled.

"Look at them now, trying to moor up. His wife can't pull the boat into the side with the rope. She's going in the water any moment now.

Chapter 3

"But having more freedom she only became more profoundly aware of the big want. She wanted so many things. She wanted to read great, beautiful books, and be rich with them; she wanted to see beautiful things, and have the joy of them for ever; she wanted to know big, free people; and there remained always the want she could put no name to. It was so difficult. There were so many things, so much to meet and surpass. And one never knew where one was going." D.H. Lawrence (The Rainbow)

Zena's struggle to pull the boat into the side of the canal was not helped by the fact that Rob had left the engine in reverse gear whilst he was shouting orders at her. Holding on with all her strength, she could not halt the boat as it moved relentlessly away from the bank. Just as she was losing her footing, she was startled by the slim brown arms reaching round her to grab the end of the rope. As the boat slowly moved into the side, she turned to look at the girl who had rescued her. She was dressed in dark jeans and a baggy grey sweater and was surprisingly strong for one so tiny. She wasn't pretty in the way portrayed by women's magazines but had a natural healthy glow that needed no make-up or accessories. "Hello there. Looked like you were going to fall in for a moment," laughed the girl.

"Yes, it was a bit close. Thanks for your help." The two of them made small talk until Rob interrupted their conversation. The enticing aroma of bacon wafting through the air from the neighbouring cafe boat had reminded him what he had heard from a fellow boater - you could get the most amazing sausage sandwiches at this cafe, cooked while you were waiting for the water tank to fill and then wrapped in foil to be taken away.

"Can you get me a sausage sandwich while I fill up with water?" he called to Zena. "And after that you can help me move the boat to that mooring spot just along there." Although he had previously planned to get further along on their journey to Stratford, Rob now wanted to spend the rest of the day in Braunston to touch up the scratched paintwork.

"If we're stopping, it would be a good idea to get some fresh milk and bread," Zena called back.

"Do you know how to find the shops?" asked Jessica.

"Er, no. I presume the village is that way?"

"I'm going to the shops myself. If you like, I'll wait for you and we can go together," Jessica suggested, as she took the forward rope from Zena and deftly tied it on to the rusty iron mooring ring.

"Yes, that would be good, if you've got the time. I don't want to hold you up."

"I've got all the time in the world," replied Jessica, still revelling in the unfamiliar experience of no schedule to rule her life.

After Jessica and Zena had helped Rob to secure the boat in its chosen mooring place and left him with his sausage sandwich, they made their way to the shops. They walked slowly, pausing often to admire the view around them. The village was on a hill overlooking the canal, with green fields stretching down to the water's edge and a marina full of boats on the opposite bank. Their conversation flowed easily and quickly and the two girls had learnt much about each other by the time they reached the top of the hill. Zena was full of admiration for Jessica's self sufficiency and the bravery of her decision to go travelling on a boat alone.

"That was only because I had no choice. I had made a mess of my life and needed a new start."

"I know only too well what that feels like," Zena said. "And I wish I had been as brave as you in taking control of my life instead of just letting things happen."

"How do you mean?" Zena explained that she had never had a career, and felt she had been something of a disappointment as a wife and mother. It had been Rob, with some encouragement from her mum and dad, who had decided they should marry when she was only eighteen. And it had been Rob who had announced that they should start a family straight away. Their sons had been sent off to boarding school because that was what Rob had said would happen. She told Jessica how her two boys evidently regarded her with the same contempt as their father and when they came home in the holidays it was as if they were strangers to her. They obviously adored Rob and were elated when they heard his key in the front door each evening. Whatever activities she arranged to fill the day for them could not make up for the fact that Daddy was at work.

"But you are their mother. Of course they love you," Jessica protested. "They're just boys, and boys don't go in for displays of affection. It's natural for them to idolise their father but that doesn't mean they feel nothing for you." So engrossed in discussion were the two girls that they failed to notice the grey clouds overhead and their conversation was brought to a sudden halt when the hailstones began to fall.

"Let's have a drink while the storm passes," shouted Jessica and they ran to the pub on the High Street.

"I'm hungry," said Zena. "Fancy some lunch?"

"Er, no, I'm OK. I'll get myself something at the shop. But you can have something."

"Don't be silly, I can't eat on my own. Let me treat you - Rob can afford it! And speaking of Rob, I'd better let him know I won't be home straight away." Reaching into her bag for her phone, Zena realised that she had left it on the boat. Rob was forever having a go at her for not carrying the phone with her all the time.

"What's the point of me spending all that money getting you the best phone on the market when you always leave it in the house when you go out?" he had shouted at her. At least she hadn't left her purse behind so she ordered sandwiches and chunky chips and a large glass of wine for each of them.

Once they were settled comfortably in the leather sofa beside the fire, Zena resumed the conversation. "So, do you think you will ever go back to teaching?"

"I don't know. At the moment I feel so physically sick whenever I think about going back. But the money won't last for ever so I will have to decide what I am going to do, if it's not teaching. I have never really thought about other career options, as I wanted to be a teacher from about the age of eight."

"I always wanted to be a nurse," confessed Zena.

"So what stopped you?"

"I don't know. I've probably got the qualifications I need to do a nursing degree, but Rob says I don't need to work and he wouldn't like me working shifts. He has a lot of pressure in his job and needs me to be there for him at the end of the day."

"And what do you need?"

"I don't know," replied Zena, jolted by the sudden realisation that she had never been asked that question before.

By the time the girls had eaten a leisurely lunch and completed their shopping, it was already late in the afternoon. Zena remembered that Rob would be waiting for her and she began to hurry down the hill.

"Hey, wait for me," called Jessica.

"I need to get back. Rob will be worried," Zena fretted.

"Oh let him worry, it will do him good. This view is too good to hurry." So Zena let herself be persuaded to sit on a bench and take in the spectacular view of the Braunston marina and the wooded hills beyond. It was a stunning sight and they sat in silence taking it all in until the two horses in the field next to the footpath cantered over to join them. As Jessica and Zena stood close together, stroking the horses' nuzzles, Jessica felt a surge of protectiveness towards this vulnerable girl. Zena sighed, "I need to get back. He'll be wanting his newspaper."

"Here, take my phone number before you go." Jessica scribbled the number on the back of Zena's hand.

When they arrived back at The Narrow Escape, Rob was standing on the front deck giving instructions on his mobile phone. "Well, what's Jenni got on at the moment? Take her off whatever she's doing and put her on this case. It's right up her street. Call me back if there's a problem with that." He rang off, shoving the phone angrily into his pocket.

"Bloody cretins," he muttered. Zena gave Jessica a brief hug before climbing aboard to join her husband.

"I'll come and find Ragamuffin to say goodbye before we leave tomorrow," she promised. Jessica told her she would like that and continued slowly along the towpath, the sound of Rob's angry voice making her anxious for Zena.

"Where on earth have you been? Didn't you know I would be worried about you? Why didn't you take your phone?"

"I'm sorry. We stopped for lunch at the pub until the storm passed. And then the shops were really busy. I've got some lovely fillet from the butcher."

"Did you get me a newspaper?"

"Yes, of course. Is your painting finished?"

"Only just, I had to wait for the rain to pass," Rob grumbled.

"Well done. Looks like it will be a lovely sunny evening and so your paint will be dry by the morning." Zena went down below to put the kettle on and stow away her groceries. She quickly stored Jessica's number on her phone before scrubbing the ink off her hand.

"You were gone so long I thought you must have been with Lover Boy," Rob said as she handed him his cup of tea.

"Who?"

"Lover Boy. That guy from the locks. Don't think I didn't notice you flirting with him. And he was definitely coming on to you."

"Don't be silly," replied Zena. "He was just a very kind and helpful boy."

"Oh yeah. Pull the other one. Don't you realise how much you humiliated me by acting like such a tart?" As Rob's face looked particularly ugly as he sat sulking behind his newspaper, Zena decided there was no point in defending herself or discussing it further. They spoke no more for the rest of the afternoon, and that evening Rob read his newspaper in silence while Zena cooked dinner. She could tell from Rob's body language that he was in a foul mood but did not know if it was to do with something at work or if it was her fault. Was he still angry about her going out without her phone or did he really believe she had been flirting with that guy at the locks? She made an extra effort with dinner;

Rob's steak was cooked exactly as he liked it, served with a pepper sauce and a selection of vegetables. As they ate the meal together, Zena was in a world of her own. She could still hear Jessica's voice in her head, asking her, "And what do you need?" The question had been such a shock, as she thought she had everything a girl could possibly need. But there was a want inside her of which she had previously been unaware. Now that she knew of its existence, the want would not go away. She realised that what she wanted most was to see her two sons more often. Term time seemed to last for ever and holidays passed all too quickly. She needed to hug her boys and to kiss them goodnight at bedtime. Zena knew she would never have persuaded Rob to change his mind about sending them to boarding school but was angry with herself for not trying harder to reach a compromise about weekly boarding, where they could have had the weekends at home. Rob had been so adamant that when he was at boarding school, it was the weekends that were the best part. He had told Zena that she had no right to deny the boys all the exciting sporting and musical activities that happened over the weekend just because she was too selfish to live without them. As usual, Zena had given in but she now blamed herself for not putting up more of a fight. Her boys were growing up as strangers and she was letting it happen. Rob had been equally firm on the matter of weekend visiting and would not even allow occasional phone calls as he believed that contact with home would create homesickness and weaken the boys' characters.

After dinner, when Rob's mood appeared to have softened a little, Zena tackled the issue again. "Rob, please could you reconsider letting me see the boys more often," she pleaded.

"No, it's fine as it is."

"But it's not fine. I'm not happy and I don't think the boys are either."

"They seem perfectly OK to me," he disputed.

"And how would you know? You hardly ever speak to them. Lots of parents go to the school to watch their boys play rugby or football, or to attend concerts and things like that. Why can't we?" Zena's voice reminded Rob of a petulant teenager, wheedling to get her own way. It made him want to smack her.

"Because it would unsettle them. My parents never came to see me and it toughened me up. You are just going to turn them into 'Mummy's boys' if you have your way," he replied angrily.

"Could we ask them what they feel? See what they would like?"

"Of course they would say they want us to go and see them more often. But they are too young to know what's best for them." Buoyed up from her conversation with Jessica, Zena was uncharacteristically outspoken.

"And you are the only one who knows what's best? Doesn't my opinion count for anything?"

"I don't want to hear any more of your whining. That's enough now. I have made up my mind that it is best for the boys to leave things as they are so that's the end of the matter." He took the bottle of whisky out of the cupboard and settled himself down to a DVD. Realising that she was not going to win the argument, Zena took herself off to the front cabin to read a magazine. A few times she picked up her phone to call Jessica, only to change her mind again. "You can't call her yet," she scolded herself. "The poor girl had to listen to you all afternoon. What on earth have you got to say that won't wait another day or two?" Zena was excited about her new friend. She realised that although she and Rob had plenty of acquaintances, she didn't have any real friends of her own. All her schoolmates had lost touch when they went off to university, finding their new lives far more exciting than Zena's pregnancies and babies. Her old friends had been replaced with the wives of Rob's colleagues so she was seldom short of company but she never had the sort of conversation with them that she had enjoyed today. Jessica had been so easy to talk to and had shown a genuine interest in hearing what she had to say. Zena resolved to keep in touch with her. It would be exciting to find out where her travels would take her and to hear about her adventures. She hoped that Jessica would manage to sort out her future career, whether it was a return to teaching or something else. She wondered about boyfriends; Jessica hadn't mentioned any so Zena guessed she did not have that special somebody in her life. Zena could not imagine anybody as self-sufficient as Jessica ever feeling lonely but she promised herself that if Jessica should ever need it she would provide a good listening ear for her.

When Rob came into the bedroom and started to remove her nightdress, Zena resented the interruption to her thoughts. "Why does he always assume this is OK?" she thought, wanting to tell him that she was not in the mood tonight. However, Zena said nothing, knowing from years of keeping her husband happy that it would soon be over if she put on a convincing enough performance to satisfy his ego.

Back on Ragamuffin, Jessica was restless. During the last week she had been happier than she had been for a long time, much happier than she deserved, she thought. But still she wanted more; there was a cavernous chasm of emptiness within her. Listening to Zena talking about her husband and two sons had made Jessica start to consider the state of Steve's marriage. Why had he chosen to stay with a wife who obviously made him so unhappy? Was it just because of the children? How different her life would have been if Steve had left Ali as he had promised. If only he was to phone her now. She imagined what it would be like to hear him utter those longed-for words that he had finally ended his marriage. But there was nothing she could do but continue to wait. It was up to him now. But being patient was so difficult and with more time on her hands she was finding the waiting and the wishing were becoming intolerable. Realising that there was no point in dwelling further on this thought, she turned her attention to her new friend. Although she had been loyal to her husband and said nothing bad about him, it was obvious to Jessica that he did not treat her well. Jessica wondered how such an intelligent girl could have allowed herself to become so downtrodden. Having noticed Zena's reaction to her question about what it was that she needed, Jessica could tell that she was unaccustomed to thinking of her own wants and needs - it was all about Rob and the boys. She hoped Zena would ring her; she would love to help her to develop more self-confidence and assertiveness.

Jessica filled her evening with jobs on the boat and watching TV before going early to bed. After a couple of hours of tossing and turning, it was clear that she was not going to get to sleep so she pulled on her clothes and went for a walk. As she left the boat, the screech of a nearby owl filled Jessica with joy at the beauty of her surroundings. It was a cloudless night with a bright full moon high in the sky and Jessica studied its reflection in the centre of the canal. With the branches also reflecting in the water, it looked as if the moon were a white ball balanced between the fingertips of a pair of hands.

"Very D.H. Lawrence," she thought, "I really must read "The Rainbow" again." The air was cold and she was glad of her warm coat; having forgotten to bring her gloves, she shoved her hands into her pockets. Unsurprisingly at this time of night there was nobody around; while one or two of the boats she walked past still had lights in the cabin windows, most were in darkness. Pausing on the towpath to look at the moonlit scene around her, she heard another cry of an owl and a single car speeding along the nearby road. Other than that the silence was absolute. The Narrow Escape was moored about ten minutes' walk away and Jessica was looking out for it. When she got there, she could see a light in the forward cabin and paused beside the boat to listen. She wondered if Rob had given Zena a hard time for staying out for so long and not having taken her phone with her. She could hear nothing inside but guessed that any argument they had had would be over by now. Jessica continued along the towpath, past the deserted cafe boat and over the cast iron footbridge beside the marina. The jetty lights and their watery reflections made a pretty sight. She wandered further on until she reached the brick footbridge over the canal where she and Zena had crossed earlier. She stood for a while on the bridge, gazing down into the still water, watching the moon's reflection sway gently in the ripples. By now, Jessica was shivering and she remembered her cosy bed waiting for her on Ragamuffin. She briskly retraced her steps, noticing The Narrow Escape was now in complete darkness. "Sleep well my friend,"

44

she whispered and headed for home. Almost immediately she noticed the sound of footsteps on the towpath behind her. Looking back over her hunched shoulder, she could see the silhouette of a figure on the towpath about thirty metres behind her. She quickened her pace, remembering too late the promise she had made her father that she would be careful. "Perhaps this wasn't such a clever idea," she thought, reaching in her pocket to find the key to Ragamuffin. She wondered for a moment if she should knock on one of the other boats to ask for help but decided against it when she saw that her increased speed had put a greater distance between her and the figure behind.

"False alarm, thank goodness." She heaved an audible sigh of relief. But her heart was still pounding as she climbed aboard Ragamuffin and fumbled with the key. She bolted the door firmly and without turning on the lights she looked out of the window to observe the man who had been following her. She could now see there was a small dog running ahead of him and she laughed at herself for being scared of a harmless man walking his dog. Undressing quickly, Jessica scrambled back into bed and was soon feeling safe and snug in her cosy nest. But sleep pulled her into a world of terrifying nightmares that further troubled her anxious mind.

Chapter 4

"A man falling into dark waters seeks a momentary footing even on sliding stones."George Eliot (Silas Marner)

Early in the morning, Rob set the The Narrow Escape free from its moorings and steered slowly towards the junction with the Oxford Canal. He turned left towards Napton; had he not been so distracted he would have admired the impressive white-painted iron bridge that spanned both sides of the little island at the junction. Zena was still in bed. He didn't want to wake her - what could he say? "If she had not flirted so outrageously at the locks yesterday, none of it would have happened. She humiliated me. She disappeared for hours after picking up that bloke at the locks, leaving her phone behind on purpose so she could see him. Did she really think I wouldn't notice where she had tried to clean a phone number off her hand? She must think I'm stupid. And then there was all that nonsense about visiting the boys at school. She was so argumentative. Why couldn't she just have left it alone?" But Rob knew that whatever Zena had done it did not excuse the way he had treated her in bed. He blamed the film he had been watching and the half bottle of whisky he had drunk. His uncharacteristic loss of control had caught him by surprise and it worried him that he had found Zena's resistance so much more exciting than than her usual acquiescence. "She was asking for it though. I had to show her who is the boss."

Zena had suffered throughout the night. She had never seen such fury in Rob's eyes and it was this image that kept her awake even after the pain had subsided. She kept asking herself what had provoked such rage and could think of nothing she had done to justify him being so cruel to her. "Was he really jealous because he thought I was flirting with that guy at the lock or was it because I went out for lunch without my phone?" she wondered. "But that's nonsense. It must have been because I argued with him about seeing the boys. I don't know what else I can do to change his mind. He just won't listen to me." Feeling disgusted and betrayed, Zena had wanted to get away from Rob. Lying in bed next to him was horrible. She knew that all she had to do was to find a boat called Ragamuffin and she could hide there safely. But getting out of bed would involve climbing over the sleeping body of her husband and if she woke him she risked a repeat episode of his brutality. "Perhaps it was my fault. It was my punishment for being so argumentative. Maybe now he has got it out of his system, it will be all right. I should just see how he is in the morning and phone Jessica for help if I need it," she decided.

The dawn chorus had begun by the time Zena had drifted off to sleep. When she finally woke, Rob was not in bed and it felt like the boat was moving. She could certainly feel the gentle vibrations of the engine. Sitting up quickly and pulling back the curtain to reveal the open countryside passing by, Zena felt helpless. Yesterday she had met a friend who could help her, and she was being taken away from her too soon. Philosophical as ever, Zena dismissed her disappointment and searched for positive solutions. "Perhaps this is for the best. This is fate telling me Jessica is too dangerous an influence. I must forget all about what I need and I must work hard on rebuilding the trust between Rob and me. How stupid of me to let somebody I hardly know make me risk everything. Twelve years of marriage should count for more than that. Until last night, Rob has always treated me well. I owe him the chance to put things right. I must make it work." So

Zena showered, dressed, put on her make-up, combed her hair and examined herself critically in the mirror before going to ask Rob what he would like for breakfast.

Rob was relieved that Zena appeared to have forgotten or at least forgiven his unforgivable behaviour from the night before. She was acting as if nothing had happened, cooking him breakfast and smiling sweetly as she delivered it to him at the back of the boat. He vowed that he would make it up to her and that nothing like that would ever happen again. He could not understand why he had acted so badly - that was the behaviour of a working class lout, not somebody of his status. He had been brought up to be a gentleman. Life had been kind to Rob; as a child he was used to having his own way both at school and at home. He enjoyed boarding school, being both academically gifted and good at sport, and had been a natural leader. He had never had to really fight for anything. At home in the holidays his mother had thoroughly spoilt him to make up for all the time he was away and his younger sister adored him to the extent that she would dedicate herself to waiting upon him like a little servant girl whenever he was home.

The sun was shining when they reached Calcutt and Rob was relieved to see that Zena was smiling as she jumped off to set up the locks. Although it was still quite early, there was a queue of boats waiting to go through the locks and he watched Zena chatting to other boaters as they waited. It was gratifying that she returned to The Narrow Escape after a few minutes to check there was nothing that he needed. Rob noticed too how Zena avoided all the men at the locks, making a point of talking only to female boaters. He thought how good she looked standing next to other women and enjoyed the envious glances of their menfolk when they saw Zena. They were even more covetous when they set eyes on The Narrow Escape.

"I've got the best-looking girl and the most expensive boat; what more could a man want?" he thought. He decided it was time he bought Zena a spectacular gift to tell her how sorry he was and also to show her how proud of her he felt.

Zena was well aware that Rob was scrutinising her at the Calcutt locks and determined to give him no excuse for criticising her behaviour. She was cold to the point of being rude to any guys that spoke to her and deliberately struck up conversation with the women. One of these noticed the bruise on Zena's wrist. "Oh that looks nasty," she said.

"Yes, I let the windlass slip when I was winding down a paddle," Zena replied rather too quickly. When she noticed the woman glancing at the matching bruise on her other wrist, she realised how implausible was her explanation. Fortunately her companion didn't ask any more questions but her contemptuous stare at Rob made it clear that she had guessed the source of Zena's injuries. Zena was relieved that this woman was on a boat going in the opposite direction; she seemed to be the sort of person who might not be able to resist saying something through the flight of eight locks at Stockton. Zena wanted the events of the previous night to be forgotten; she did not need another woman fighting her corner. After all, it was Jessica's influence that had made her stand up to Rob and she had seen where that had got her. Quiet submission was the best way to an easy life, she concluded.

Jessica woke to the sound of boats on the move. It was later than her usual waking time but she did not feel refreshed. Her body ached and she was troubled by a mixture of memories from her night-time walk and half-remembered images from her dreams. She had dreamt that the man who had been following her along the towpath was Steve and that they had been fighting. She had given him a hard shove and he had fallen into the canal. While she was deciding whether or not to rescue him, the dream had come to an abrupt end. "Well, Auntie Joan, you told me to follow my dreams. Obviously then, I need to give Steve the push!" Amused at the thought and empowered by her physical supremacy during their imaginary fight, Jessica made up her mind that, whatever he may do or say to try to change her mind, Steve belonged in the past. To help her forget him she decided that the best medicine would be a quick fling with somebody else and as soon as possible. Something purely physical to stave off her carnal cravings. "It's time to leave Braunston and head off towards Oxford and my new life," she announced. Pulling back the curtain, she marvelled at how the sunshine lit up the feathers of a pair of swans just outside her window. Their radiance was exquisite. Beyond them, wavering reflections of elders on the opposite bank looked to Jessica like inquisitive fingers reaching down into the water. "A good day for cruising. Time to get up and head off," she thought as she heaved her tired body out of bed. As she breakfasted on porridge and toast, she looked at the guide-book and contemplated the next part of her journey. She needed to turn right at the junction and head towards Napton. After that she would come to another junction, where she needed to go straight on instead of turning right towards Warwick.

While Jessica was untying Ragamuffin she had a brief conversation with the guy on the boat behind her who looked like he was also preparing to set off. Jessica admired his boat, a beautifully painted working boat with a tiny cabin on the back, by the name of Bordesley. He was obviously an enthusiast. "You planning on going far?" he asked Jessica.

"Not sure yet. Depends on the weather," she replied. "How about you?"

"Oh, just as far as the marina at Calcutt. The boat needs blacking."

"Well, have a good journey. I don't think I'm going past Calcutt, but perhaps I'll see you around sometime."

Jessica steered Ragamuffin under the first arch of the white-painted bridge at Braunston Turn where The Narrow Escape had travelled earlier that morning. Unlike Rob, she marvelled at the amazing engineering of the bridge. She thought too of the hard labour of the men who had built the embankment to create this straight stretch of canal. She loved the name of this embankment - Braunston Puddle Banks - but guessed the reality of its building was less romantic than its name. She tried to imagine the gangs of labourers moving this mountain of heavy earth without the help of modern machinery. They would have worked in all weathers, from days when it was unbearably hot to times when the rain, sleet or snow poured down all day. She thought about how heavy their wet clothes and mud-covered boots must have been. "Thanks old mates," she said. "You'll be pleased to know your efforts are still being appreciated." As Braunston disappeared behind her, Jessica started to look out for Napton Hill. She knew from her guide-book that the canal would follow the contour lines around this hill before ascending the set of locks to Marston Doles where she hoped to arrive by the end of the day. But before she had gone more than three miles from Braunston, Jessica noticed the red warning light on her control panel. She looked quickly at the temperature gauge, which was reading a hundred degrees and decided to stop. Steering the boat to a convenient mooring spot, she switched off the ignition immediately. As she was tying the mooring ropes she cursed under her breath. She recalled what she had read in her book about engine maintenance. "I bet it's the alternator belt. Why oh why didn't I buy a spare while I was in Braunston? How stupid of me." As Jessica lifted the deck board, she felt the heat coming off the overheated engine and smelt the worrying stench of burning. "Now what am I going to do? I suppose I'll just have to walk back to Braunston to buy a new one." Jessica knew that she could always telephone a boatyard for help but dreaded to think how much that would cost. However, luck was with her; just as she was locking up the boat and setting off on the walk back to Braunston, along came an old working boat called Bordesley.

"Hello again. Everything all right?" called the man whom she had met earlier.

"No, I've broken down. Alternator belt, I think." The owner of Bordesley pulled in to moor just in front of Jessica. She held the mooring ropes for him while he hammered in a couple of mooring pegs.

"This is very kind of you but I don't want to make you late. I can walk back to Braunston and buy a new alternator belt."

"Don't you have a spare?" The guy was obviously unimpressed by her stupidity. Jessica felt embarrassed.

"Well, let's have a look anyway. It may be that I can't help, but it won't hurt to try. I'm Andy, by the way." It turned out that the alternator belt did indeed need replacing and although Andy carried spares, they were not the right size for Jessica's boat.

"Well, the boatyard at Calcutt stocks belts. I can tow you there."

"Well, yes please then. Thank you so much." As Ragamuffin was towed along by Bordesley, Jessica stood at the tiller trying to steer as best she could, although without the engine running this was not easy, especially on this particular stretch of canal where the bends were so numerous and nasty. She thought about Andy and her helpless state reminded her of damsels in distress.

"What a kind guy. He could have just cruised past; he's a real knight in shining armour. Of all the boats to come past at the right time, I was so lucky that it was him." Without the engine running, it was eerily quiet on the back of Ragamuffin and a sense of peace descended. She watched as Andy steered them both through a tight bridge, cleverly avoiding the boat that was moored just beyond. She thought again about her plan to have a quick fling to take her mind off Steve. If she was serious about it, then there was no time like the present. "I wonder if he's married? Could he be my new Mr Right? Auntie Joan would have liked him. I don't know if I fancy him enough, but maybe I could in time....." Jessica began to imagine herself in Andy's arms and wondered how good he was at foreplay. Her fantasy was soon interrupted by a shout from the boat in front. Bordesley had gone aground. There was nothing Jessica could do but wait while Andy used the pole to push his boat out of the shallow water. She watched him climb nimbly on to the roof of the cabin, admiring his strength and agility. "Mmm, yes, he is rather gorgeous," she realised and allowed her mind to wander back to her interrupted fantasy.

Bordesley was soon afloat again and the rest of the journey to the boatyard was uneventful. They moored above the top lock and Jessica walked down to the boatyard. Andy waited while she bought the right alternator belt and then he stayed to help her fit it. "I won't do it for you," he said. "Best if you learn how to do it yourself. But if you need a hand, I'll show you." The repair took Jessica about half an hour to complete and she guessed it would have taken Andy half the time. She was grateful for his patience and at the same time pleased that she managed to do the job without his help. When she had finished she asked Andy if she could pay him for his trouble.

"No, not at all. It's what we do on the canals - we all help each other."

"Well, take these at least," said Jessica, handing him a couple of cans of beer.

"No, honestly, there's no need," he insisted and Jessica was worried she may have offended him. But she wanted to enjoy his company for a bit longer, curious to discover what it would be like to play the damsel to this knight in shining armour. She was trying to think up another delaying tactic when Andy said,

"I need to be off now anyway. I need to go through this lock and down to the boatyard. I hope you don't have any more trouble."

"Well, thanks again. Would you stay and have a cup of tea or coffee with me before you go?"

"No, honestly, I must go. My wife will be waiting for me in the car park."

"Oh. Er, well, tell her I'm sorry to have made you late."

"Don't worry, she's used to it. She'll understand," he laughed.

Rob and Zena were fortunate to meet up with another boat, an immaculate seventy-footer by the name of Diamond Blue, at the top of Stockton Locks. Rob was keen to talk to the guy at the helm of this boat to find out if he owned it. It was certainly bigger than The Narrow Escape but he was sure it could not be fitted out to the same high specification. He soon learned that the helmsman, a chap called Rhys, was not actually the boat's only owner, but was one of a group of six who had the boat on a time-share basis. His superiority once again restored, Rob was eager to find out how the time-share worked.

"Oh, that wouldn't do for me at all," he said, when Rhys had finished explaining. "I am needed so often at work that I never know in advance when I will be able to get away. Owning our own boat means that we can go away whenever we have the opportunity."

"But doesn't that mean you are only able to make short trips close to your marina?"

"Well in theory yes. But there are ways round that if you're clever. You buy temporary moorings where you can leave the boat safely and use a taxi to get back to your car. That's what we're doing now, in fact. We're going to Stratford but there won't be time to get back to our moorings on the Grand Union so we've paid for a month at the boatyard there."

"Sounds expensive."

"Yes it is. But then, so was the boat." Rob went on to tell his new companion about all the extras that had been installed on The Narrow Escape. Rhys was suitably impressed, telling Rob that he had inspired him to get his own boat one day and he would greatly appreciate his advice when it came to designing it.

While the boats moved down the flight, Zena got to know Rhys's wife quite well. She was a buxom brunette called Rachel and remarkably strong and agile. Zena found her the ideal companion as she was not only quick to open paddles and lock gates but also loved the sound of her own voice. Free from the effort of making conversation, Zena was able to daydream. Recalling the question that Jessica had asked, she wondered again what it was that she needed and once again her thoughts turned to her boys. She only needed them; nothing else was important to her. When they stopped for lunch, Rob told Zena that he and Rhys had arranged to meet up for a meal in Warwick the following evening so they could journey together again. Diamond Blue would be stopping for the night at the bottom of the Stockton locks but Rob was keen to press on and get closer to Leamington Spa before they moored as he wanted to have time to look around the shops the following morning. Zena thought that was odd as Rob hated shopping but she did not risk annoying him by asking questions.

Zena had lost count of the number of paddles she had raised and lowered since they left Braunston and was exhausted by the time they moored up for the night at Fosse Locks. After putting a casserole into the oven for later, she sat on the front deck contemplating the beauty of her surroundings. The bare silhouettes of trees on the horizon were bathed in the golden sun of the early evening. Serenaded by a blackbird in the tree above her head, she idly observed the cattle in the field opposite. The calves, about fifteen in all, were playing bucking broncos while the cows looked on sedately. She loved the tiredness of her body; there was something sublimely satisfying at the end of a hard day's physical exertion. Pleased that Rob had designed a boat that had room for a bath, even if it was such a tiny one, she climbed into the hot bubbles as darkness fell. She sat in the hot water, considering the events of the last twenty-four hours. Working the locks had been just the therapy she needed, making the events of the night before seem like a bad dream, something that happened a long time ago. It had been such a joy to meet new people along the journey, most of whom were friendly and chatty. Rachel and Rhys seemed especially good company and it would be useful to have their help through the notoriously arduous Hatton Flight. As she was scrubbing at her scalp, Rob called through the bathroom door, "Would you like a glass of wine?"

"Yes please."

"Would you like it in there?"

"No, please could you put it in the bedroom. I'll be there in a minute." Zena decided she liked this conciliatory attitude of Rob's; without a word being spoken, they both knew that he was sorry and was trying to make amends. She felt optimistic that they could put behind them the events of the previous night and move on. Braunston seemed so far away now. Remembering Jessica, she toyed with the idea of phoning her as she felt bad that she had left without saying goodbye. "Best not to upset the apple cart," she decided. "She will only make trouble between me and Rob again. It was her fault that I was so argumentative last night." Wrapping herself in her fluffy bath sheet, she strode into the bedroom and deleted Jessica's number from her phone.

Over dinner in Warwick the following evening, Rob discovered that Rhys's wife, Rachel, remembered him from one of his earlier boating holidays. He could not recall having met her before but it would appear from the way she was teasing him that something had definitely happened between them. He wondered how he could shut her up before Zena and Rhys worked out what was going on. It was a huge relief when she whispered to him, "It's OK, your secret's safe. I'm not going to tell." But when Zena proudly showed off the brand new necklace that Rob had given her that afternoon, Rachel looked decidedly jealous and winked brazenly at him while she said mischievously, "And what do I need to do to get a piece of jewellery like that, Rob?" Zena did not appear to mind the comment and thanked Rob again for such a beautiful present. He was pleased with his choice, noticing each time Zena moved her head how the tiny diamonds shimmered in the eighteen carat white gold chain. During the conversation after dinner it turned out that Rhys was something of a cook. He and Zena began to share their favourite recipes and were talking so animatedly that Rachel moved seats in order to talk with Rob. Having bought Zena the necklace, Rob felt absolved of his previous sins and he forgot his vows to be a better husband as Rachel's hand moved along his thigh. The other pair were too engrossed in their conversation to notice Rob surreptitiously stroking the back of Rachel's neck.

Chapter 5

"The wood was silent, still and secret in the evening drizzle of rain, full of the mystery of eggs and half-open buds, half unsheathed flowers. In the dimness of it all trees glistened naked and dark as if they had unclothed themselves, and the green things on earth seemed to hum with greenness." D.H. Lawrence (Lady Chatterley's Lover)

With her new alternator belt fitted, Jessica continued her journey round the village of Napton and deliberated whether it was too late to start the flight of locks as she had originally intended. Seeing rain clouds ahead, she decided to call it a day and moored near the bottom of the locks. Her guide-book informed her that there was a waste disposal bin near the first lock so she walked along the towpath with her accumulated bags of rubbish. The yellow medley of forsythia bushes, daffodils and celandines brought sunshine into her heart. When she arrived at the water point she came across a man and woman who were having quite an altercation. "There's a good pub here where we could eat," the woman argued. "If we don't stop here, we will have to moor in the middle of nowhere. And it looks like it is going to rain."

"Yes I know, but there could well be a queue at Claydon which will hold us up. We have to get the boat to Banbury by Saturday morning."

"If you had got up earlier this morning, we could have reached Fenny Compton where there is another pub. Now I'll have to cook dinner again and I'm supposed to be on holiday."

"Well I'll cook dinner then," her husband snapped. As Jessica walked away from this scene, she reflected on her new freedom. Being alone had its drawbacks but when she watched couples arguing like that, she was relieved to be single. It was so good not having to stick to a timetable. She could go wherever she pleased and stop when it suited her. Her decision to leave teaching had been a good one, her decision to leave Steve an even better one, she thought. When she reached Ragamuffin, she rested on the front deck and enjoyed her surroundings. It was bliss to sit and listen to the various songs of the many birds that were hiding in the trees and hedgerow beside the boat. A female blackbird was busy building a nest in the tree beside her, flying back with mouthfuls of grass and twigs every few minutes and eying up Jessica suspiciously before entering her nesting site, as if to say, "Are you still here? Me? I'm not doing anything. Don't bother looking up here for a nest." In the distance she could hear the occasional neighing of a horse. She watched the mallards busily pecking at the foliage along the bank and admired the dark beauty of the rapidly approaching rain clouds. When the first drops of rain began to fall, instead of hurrying down below for shelter, she took the time to watch how each raindrop created circles of ripples on the surface of the canal, gently spreading out until they hit the bank and were gone. She saw droplets of water forming on the tiller, growing steadily bigger and more pendulous until the point where they could no longer hold on and they dropped with a soft splash on to the decking beside her feet. After sitting there for several minutes Jessica grew cold so she tore herself away from the miracles of nature to seek warmth and comfort in her cosy cabin. She stood and watched through the window as the rain continued to batter the surface of the canal, working it up into a frenzy of light and movement. Air bubbles were appearing on the surface of the water, their lives ending almost as soon as they had begun. She stood mesmerised by the beauty of it all until the rain eased and it was then that she realised how hungry she was. Having shopped at Braunston, Jessica had plenty of food on board but decided that she would treat herself to a meal out to celebrate her escape from her old life. She knew that she had to be careful with her money but at the same time she was aware that she needed to meet people and the best way to do that was in a pub.

The pub was beautifully positioned alongside the canal and Jessica considered eating at one of the tables outside but chose instead the more sociable atmosphere of the crowded bar. Sitting herself on one of the bar stools, she ordered herself a lager and asked to see the menu. To her relief, there was a large selection of meals at reasonable prices and she eagerly ordered a meat pie with chips. While she was waiting for her meal to arrive, Jessica chatted to the landlord who enquired if she was on a boating holiday. "Yes, well sort of. I live on the boat and I am not working at the moment so it's quite an extended holiday."

"You lucky thing. I would love to do that if I could afford it." Jessica explained about her inheritance and how she thought her aunt would have approved of the way she was using it. The landlord was keen to hear about her boat and where she had travelled so far.

"I'll have to go back to work sometime though. It wasn't that much money!"

"Well, we need to take on more staff here during the summer months, if you think you'd like that?"

"Oh really? I'm not sure yet what I want to do or where I'll be this summer."

"Take the number anyway and give us a ring if you're interested," he said, handing Jessica a card with all the contact details printed on it.

"Yes, I will certainly think about it," she replied.

When her meal arrived Jessica looked for a table where she could sit. There was a sizeable group of people occupying two tables and they made room for her to join them. They were a lively bunch - two families who had met up coming through the Claydon and Napton locks. Although they had only known each other for a couple of days they already got on so well that they were like old friends, joking and teasing each other. They went out of their way to make Jessica feel welcome. When they left, they asked her the name of her boat so they could look out for her in future. When they had gone, Jessica decided it was time for her to leave too and went to settle her bill at the bar. The landlord spoke warmly to her as she gave him the money. "Don't forget, give us a call if you want a job. I couldn't help noticing how easily you chatted to those customers who were complete strangers to you. You would be a natural barmaid."

"Thanks. I'll think about it," Jessica replied. On her way out of the pub, she discovered a box of second-hand books. She did not have a book to swap but decided it would be all right if she took one. All over the canal network were book swap boxes like this and she reasoned that she could return the book to a different box when she had finished with it. Amongst a lot of trashy romantic novels and spy stories in the box she was delighted to find two old favourites: "The Rainbow" by D.H. Lawrence and George Eliot's "The Mill on the Floss". She took both.

When Jessica returned to Ragamuffin, she was suddenly overwhelmed by a tremendous sense of isolation. It had been great fun talking to those people and there was even the possibility of a job if she wanted it, but having been with such a lively crowd, her solitary state seemed even more pronounced. She phoned her parents and it was comforting to hear familiar voices. Although Jessica tried to sound cheerful her dad must have sensed her loneliness. "Don't forget love, if you want to come home for a bit, I'll come and pick you up. Your mum and I would love to see you."

"Thanks, dad. I'm fine, honestly. I've met some amazing people and I'm going to stop off at Oxford to see Karen and Jack."

"OK then, but don't forget, there is always a bed made up for you here whenever you want it."

In bed that night Jessica slid her hands gently and slowly along the inside of her thighs. A little erotic fantasy would make her feel much better, she thought. She created for herself a mental image of Andy standing on the roof of his boat and recalled the way his muscles had flexed while he was pushing on the pole. "Gives a whole new meaning to pole dancing," she thought. Then she visualised the handsome face of the pub landlord. He did have the most extraordinarily kissable lips and gleaming white teeth. He was a bit too old for her but with age comes experience and she guessed he would be a considerate lover. But however hard she tried, she could not keep images of Steve from working their way into her fantasies. "How is he coping?" she wondered. "And is he missing me?" She gave up on her fantasies and started to read "The Rainbow" which helped clear her mind until she came across a passage that took her straight back to Steve. "*And then, in the darkness, he bent to her mouth, softly, and touched her mouth with his mouth. She was afraid, she lay still on his arm, feeling his lips on her lips. She kept still, helpless. Then his mouth drew near, pressing open her mouth, a hot, drenching surge rose within her, she opened her lips to him, in pained, poignant eddies she drew him nearer, she let him come farther, his lips came and surging, surging, soft, oh soft, yet oh, like the powerful surge of water, irresistible, till with a little blind cry, she broke away.*" That passage was too unbearably reminiscent of that first time with Steve. She had known it was wrong and she had tried to stop but Steve as always had been too persuasive for her. He was like a drug; just one moment of stupid weakness and it seemed she would be forever hooked. She tried to recall one instance when she had said no to Steve and it dawned on her that she had never refused him anything. She had loved him so much that any idea of his was worth pursuing, any wish that he might have was always her pleasure to fulfil. It was as though he had bewitched her, subservience having always been alien to her before she met him.

The following morning brought heavy rain and Jessica found the Napton flight very hard work indeed. Cruising alone meant that at every lock she had to tie up the boat, set the paddles, open the gates, return to the boat and bring it to the lock, stepping off just at the right moment to pull the boat into position with the rope. When she had finished, she had to climb back on the boat and steer it to the bollards, tie up again and go back to close the gate behind her. Once or twice she met another boat going in the opposite direction and the crew from that boat would help her but most of the nine locks she did by herself. She was ravenous by the time she reached Marston Doles, where she stopped long enough for a sandwich and a drink. She was quickly back on the tiller again for, despite the rain, she wanted to keep on the move. Hard work was the best cure for self-pity, she reasoned. The next ten miles were lock-free and as the canal meandered around the hills, steering the boat was more demanding than usual. Jessica had a few near-misses when boats appeared around blind corners and each time she laughed with the person steering the other boat. She did actually collide with one boat but as neither was going fast, no harm was done. "Oops, sorry, didn't see you there," she called.

"No problem. Think I was too far over your side anyway," came the gallant reply. With the gradual dispersal of the clouds, Jessica found her mood steadily lifting and she marvelled at the spectacular panorama. "I can see for miles and miles," she gasped as the sun came out and transformed the grey landscape to a tapestry of green. The canal was high up above a valley, and for mile upon mile were emerald patches dotted with the creamy pattern of sheep and lambs. Beside the canal was a muddy field of cows, laboriously lumbering towards the farm buildings. From the insistent sound of their mooing, Jessica guessed it must be milking time. A little later she came across a calf that had got itself stuck in the mud at the edge of the canal. The more it thrashed about, the more entrenched it became. Its mother stood anxiously at the water's edge mooing miserably. Another boater had stopped in front of her and he was trying to shoo the calf back to the far side. This was only causing the poor creature to become more frightened and Jessica could see its eyes were wide with fear. She put her engine into reverse and tied up on the towpath opposite. She then found the number of the Canal and River Trust and called for advice. A lovely lady answered and asked her for specific information about the location. She promised to get one of their workers from Napton or Claydon to contact the farmer directly and said the best thing that Jessica and the other boater could do was to leave it to them and to continue with their journeys. Jessica shouted this information to the man on the boat in front of her and he agreed to move on. Jessica was soon on her way again and enjoying the scenery once more. In the distance she could just make out the church tower and steeple of a couple of villages. When she passed by the pub at Fenny Compton, she was surprised at just how many boats were moored there. Shortly afterwards, she went through a very long straight stretch of canal which was described in the guide-book as Fenny Compton Tunnel, although in reality it was not a tunnel but a narrow cutting. She was relieved to reach the end of this stretch without meeting any boats coming in the opposite direction.

By the time Jessica tied up at Claydon Top Lock in the late afternoon, she was feeling both elated and exhausted. She sank on to her seat on the front deck and settled down to enjoy her book. Another couple of boats arrived later and moored behind her. Jessica asked the people aboard about the calf that was stuck in the mud. Since none of them had seen it and did not know what she was talking about, Jessica guessed that either the calf had managed to free itself once it had been left in peace or else the farmer had come along and rescued it. It did not matter that she would never know exactly how it had got free, she was just relieved that the poor thing was all right.

The next day Jessica queued in the pouring rain with a line of other boats for her turn at the Claydon Locks. She could not understand the delay as the Easter rush was over. She spoke to the man from the Canal and River Trust who was directing proceedings at the lock and he told her it was due to a water shortage. They were closing the locks at two each afternoon and not opening them again until ten the following morning. That would ensure there was a queue on each side of the lock so as one boat went up another went down, thus avoiding unnecessary emptying and refilling of the locks. Jessica laughed with some of the other boaters in the queue about this supposed water shortage as they stood huddled under their umbrellas. "After all this rain, how can there possibly be a drought?" one woman asked.

"He says it's because we have had such a dry winter the reservoirs are still half empty."

"More like they don't want to spend money on electricity to pump the water back up to the top," suggested one angry boater.

"Well, that's boating," said a more philosophical member of the group. "I always say that if you're in a hurry, you should catch a train."

"Well, there could be worse places to hang about," said Jessica, gazing around her at the picturesque scene. All around her were innumerable shades of green, brought alive by the wetness. Even in the rain it beat the inner-city classroom where she would otherwise have been. "Anybody want a cuppa while we wait?"

Despite the delay and the awful weather Jessica was in good spirits when she reached Cropredy by lunchtime. The queues had actually been a great help to her; the presence of so many boats queuing each side of the locks meant there was no shortage of people on hand to operate the paddles and gates, enabling Jessica to hold Ragamuffin's centre rope or even stay on deck while other people did the hard work. As she arrived in Cropredy the sun was shining once more and Jessica was amazed to see a group of gondolas, each one steered rather haphazardly by the person working an oar at the bow. Jessica was anxious to avoid colliding with one of them and was thankful that they kept close to the bank until she was safely past. She stopped for a short time to buy some fresh bread and milk before taking a stroll around the pretty village, after which she set off down the remaining locks to Banbury. There were now fewer boats around so Jessica had to operate most of the locks single-handed. But as these locks were spaced out every half mile or so she had time to recover between each one.

Rob was thinking about Rachel as he steered along the Stratford Canal. They had parted company after the Hatton Flight but Rachel and Rhys would also be heading down to Stratford after they had collected some friends at Kingswood. He wondered if their paths would cross and he hoped not. While it was gratifying to know that women still found him irresistible he suspected that Rachel might be more trouble than she was worth. He also had other plans for when they arrived in Stratford. He had already arranged for one of his clients, David McGovern and his wife Katrina to join them for dinner on the boat, after which they were all going to the theatre together. Rob was keen to show off The Narrow Escape to David. He owned a yacht on the River Thames and Rob guessed he would be certain to appreciate the quality of the fittings and many accessories on board The Narrow Escape. They planned to moor in the Stratford Basin, right next to the theatre, so they could come back to the boat for drinks in the interval. He visualised them all, sitting on the front deck, drinks in hand, while passers-by admired their style.

Before they reached Stratford they dropped down through a flight of eleven single locks with very stiff paddles. All the boats that day seemed to be heading towards Stratford and The Narrow Escape was following closely behind the boat in front. For the first part of the flight, Zena had to wait for that boat to leave before she could re-fill and empty each lock. It was hard work - much harder than the Hatton Flight the previous day when she and Rachel had worked together as such a good team. It was also quite monotonous with no company. She could see the woman from the boat in front and each time The Narrow Escape caught up they waved to one another but they never had the opportunity to talk. Waiting alone for each lock to fill gave Zena time to appreciate the beauty of her surroundings. Resting on a bench beside the first lock, she spotted a robin with a beak crammed full of food darting into a tiny hole in the hedge. Almost immediately it was out again and off in search of more. When the lock was almost full and the sound of rushing water subsided, she could hear the cheeping of the baby birds impatiently calling for their next meal. She remembered how fretful Lawrence had always been when his next feed was due, that open crying mouth demanding milk from her with the same urgency as those little creatures who were now demanding insects. Zac had been a much more placid baby. She wondered if that was just because of his nature or whether it was because as a second child he had had to learn to be patient. Zena wondered if it was her fault that her eldest son was so demanding and so like his father. She hoped that she had not failed Lawrence by spoiling him as a baby. As she went further down the flight, Zena made a conscious effort to tear her thoughts away from her sons and her failure as a mother. She admired the unusual lock-keepers'cottages and their well-tended gardens, mostly decorated with grape hyacinths, tulips and daffodils. "These will be so pretty when there are more flowers in the summer," she thought. Noticing the iron bridges, made in two halves with a split in the middle through which the ropes of horse-drawn boats would have been passed, Zena tried to imagine herself back in the nineteenth century. Acknowledging that she would not have enjoyed that way of life at all, she was thankful for all the luxuries aboard The Narrow Escape.

About half way through the flight they met some boats coming in the opposite direction and Zena witnessed her first example of "canal rage" when the woman on the boat in front of The Narrow Escape had committed the apparently unforgivable mistake of stealing somebody else's lock. This woman had seen that the boat coming upstream was only just entering the lock below while her husband had already brought their boat out of the lock above and closed the gates. It would therefore take longer for the boat coming towards them to reach the empty lock so she filled it for her boat rather than waiting for the other boat to arrive first. Consequently she wasted a whole lock-full of water as well as keeping the other boat waiting. The man from the boat coming upstream was so incensed by this behaviour that he would not let the matter rest even though the woman apologised. By the time Zena arrived on the scene, the woman was in tears and her irate husband and the other man were having a shouting match. Zena tried to console the woman while Rob came off The Narrow Escape to negotiate a truce between the two men. At the following lock, Zena came across

71

another quarrel - this time it was a stroppy adolescent having an argument with his mother who was trying to stop him from lifting the paddle gear too fast. Lacking a proper understanding of how the paddles worked, he could not grasp the importance of what he was being told and he was shouting at his mother in a frustrated whining voice."Look, there's water coming out. There's still water coming out if I lift it only half way, so what's the point?" He threw his windlass on the ground in frustration and sat sulking on the balance beam. Zena felt sorry for both the boy and his mother and made herself a promise that before they set off she would explain properly to her boys how the locks worked.

They moored up in the centre of town quite early in the afternoon. Zena had already used Rob's iPad to locate the nearest supermarket and discovered there was one quite close to their mooring spot where she could stock up on the ingredients she needed to prepare a meal matching the status of their guests. As they left the boat to go shopping, Zena was surprised at how busy the town was; one moment they were on a tranquil canal, the next they were in the midst of a major tourist destination. The streets were so crowded that Zena was glad Rob had offered to help her to carry the shopping back to the boat. Afterwards, he disappeared for a walk along the River Avon while she made herself busy in the galley. This suited Zena fine; she could listen to the music of her choice on the radio while getting on with the cooking. Although the galley was not as easy to use as her kitchen at home, Zena was confident that she could produce a meal that would make Rob proud. She was so engrossed in her preparations for the evening dinner party that she was oblivious to what was happening outside and had no idea that it was raining until Rob arrived back on the boat with his oilskin coat glistening with wetness.

"Why didn't you bring in the cushions from the front deck?" he complained. "Stupid girl. They're soaking now. How can we sit outside for interval drinks on wet cushions?"

As Rob stormed off to use Zena's hair dryer on the cushions, his phone rang. "Hello, Rob?"

"Yes?"

"David McGovern here. I'm afraid we won't be joining you this evening. Katrina has the most dreadful migraine and she just has to go to bed. I'm sorry about the late notice but it's only come on this afternoon."

"Oh. Sorry to hear that. Give Katrina my best wishes and tell her I hope she will soon be better."

"Will do. Hope you haven't gone to too much trouble."

"Oh not to worry, it's just one of those things."

"Well, I hope you enjoy the theatre. I'll be in touch."

"OK. Perhaps another time?"

"Yes, we must meet up soon."

Rob's face was darker than the thunderclouds outside as he returned to the galley. "Is there a problem?" asked Zena.

"Yes, you could say that. His wife's got a headache."

"Never mind. We can still enjoy the meal and the theatre," soothed Zena, pouring him a large glass of wine.

Despite his disappointment, Rob had to admit that his wife's meal that evening was outstandingly good. The starter was hot and spicy prawns served with crusty bread that Zena had heated in the oven. This was followed by roast pork loin with stilton and a honey and port glaze. The vegetables accompanying this dish were cooked to absolute perfection. Then there were two desserts - mini coffee cupcakes and zabaglione trifles. Finally, Zena produced a cheeseboard with no less than seven different cheeses from which to choose. "David and Katrina don't know what they've missed," Rob said as he finished this feast. "Thank you love, that was amazing."

"I'm glad you enjoyed it. It's great cooking meals for a man who really appreciates it. But I think I'd better leave the washing up until we get back from the theatre," said Zena. "I don't want to make us late."

Rob found the play quite tedious as Shakespeare wasn't really to his taste and he wondered what had possessed him to buy tickets in the first place. He shifted uncomfortably in his seat, grateful when it was time for the interval. "You know what? I would rather go back and do the washing up than watch any more of this rubbish," he told Zena.

"Oh, I was enjoying it. But I could see you weren't comfortable. Come on, we'll go back to the boat."

"No you stay and see the rest of it. Give me a call when it finishes and I'll come back and collect you." Zena, reluctant to admit that she had forgotten to bring her phone with her, persuaded Rob that she would be quite all right walking back on her own. The boat was moored very close to the theatre and there would be enough people around for her to be in no danger.

On his return to the boat Rob spotted Diamond Blue moored on the other side of the basin. Seeing Rhys on deck, he strolled over to talk to him. Rhys introduced him to his friends and Rachel said they were all going out for a drink, if Rob and Zena would like to join them. Rob declined the invitation, explaining that Zena was at the theatre and he needed to wait on the boat for when she came back. When he returned to The Narrow Escape to make a start on the washing-up, he could not understand how Zena could possibly make such a mess preparing one meal. She seemed to have used every utensil in the galley. "Why can't she just wash up as she goes along?" he muttered. "Stupid girl has no idea." He decided have a drink while the first load of washing-up was draining. Just as he was drying his hands he heard a knock on the door and saw Rachel's head peeping round. Her red stiletto heels clicked as she stepped sexily down the steps, at the same time undoing the buttons on the raincoat she was wearing to reveal to Rob her nakedness beneath. "Hello, fancy a drink for old time's sake?" She waved a bottle of his favourite whisky at him.

"I thought you'd gone out with your friends."

"I got a headache and told them to go without me," she replied. "But strangely enough, it's nearly better now. I'm sure a little lie-down on your bed is all I need to make a full recovery.

Chapter 6

"All the day before she had been filled with the vision of a lonely future through which she must carry the burthen of regret, upheld only by clinging faith. And here, close within her reach, urging itself upon her even as a claim, was another future, in which hard endurance and effort were to be exchanged for easy, delicious leaning on another's loving strength!" George Eliot *(The Mill on the Floss)*

Jessica found a mooring spot on the northern outskirts of the town of Banbury. On the towpath side was a park; a large factory dominated the far side of the canal. Jessica wondered if it might be noisy but it was actually very quiet; she was more bothered by the constant hunger induced by the smell of baking bread. Catching sight of some children playing in the park, Jessica's mind returned to school. While she certainly did not miss the pressures of teaching, life was very strange without children. She could picture every one of her class and wondered how they were getting on with their new teacher. Part of her hoped her successor would have as little success as she had done so that everybody would know it was not after all her fault. However the better side of her character wished him well as she could not bear the thought of her children being unhappy. When she caught herself reminiscing fondly about Ricky, Jessica knew she was being ridiculous. "That little sod ruined every day of your life for two whole terms! You are beginning to lose it big time if you are missing him. Time for some company, I think." She found Karen's number and waited nervously for an answer, silently praying that they were not away for the weekend. "Hi Jessica! How lovely to hear from you. Where are you now?"

"Banbury."

"That's not far. Would you like us to come and collect you?" Karen offered eagerly.

"Well I was wondering what you were doing next week? I can get the boat to Oxford by Tuesday night. I was hoping to stay in Oxford for a few days and catch up with you when it suits you."

"Why don't I come and collect you now? You can stay with us overnight and we'll take you back tomorrow. And then we can meet up again next weekend when you bring the boat to Oxford. I can't wait to see it."

"But it's very short notice. Are you sure Jack won't mind me just turning up out of the blue?" Jessica hesitated.

"It's Saturday night and we've got nothing else planned so why not? Jack will be delighted to see you." The prospect of a long soak in a proper bath with all the comforts of soft carpets and fluffy towels was too much for Jessica to resist.

"Yes please, if you're sure that's all right. And could I be really cheeky and bring my dirty washing?"

"No problem. If you walk down to the bus station I'll pick you up there. Say in about an hour?"

"That will be great. Thanks Karen."

Having a meal cooked for her by her old friend was an exquisite treat for Jessica. It was nothing elaborate, a simple shepherds pie, but sitting down at a big table with two such lovely people was something she thought quite special. While Karen was cooking, Jessica had luxuriated in a hot bubble bath whilst her laundry was in the washing machine. It was bliss. Although she loved living on Ragamuffin, it was quite basic ("Just glorified camping" was how she described it to Karen) and after just a few weeks on the canal she certainly appreciated the comfort of a proper house.

Jessica had been at university in Sheffield with Karen and they had shared a house together. Jack had been at Sheffield too and he and Karen had got together in their final year while Jessica was training to be a teacher. They had kept in touch since then but Jessica had found precious little time to visit them. Jessica had no other college friends; in her first term at Sheffield she had started a serious relationship with a boy in his second year and she had adopted his crowd rather than making friends of her own. When they split up at the end of the year, his friends went with him. She had made acquaintances during her year of teacher training but they had all been too busy with their new careers to keep in touch. Meanwhile, Karen and Jack had both managed to find jobs in Oxford and had moved into this house together. Watching the two of them together now, Jessica thought she had never met such a well-matched couple and she envied them their settled lives. When she was with Steve she had imagined they would eventually enjoy the same domestic bliss. That looked very unlikely now.

After they had finished eating, Jack asked the question that had been hanging in the air since Jessica had arrived. "So, Jess, what's the plan? Take a gap year and then go back to teaching?"

"I'm not sure. I don't think I am cut out to be a teacher after all."

"But all your hard work getting qualified," interrupted Karen. "It's such a waste."

"Yes I know. And teaching was all I ever wanted to do. But it's so difficult. I'm fed up with having no time for a social life and it's constant attrition in the classroom," Jessica whined.

"But you did choose to work in one of the most deprived areas of the country," argued Jack. "If you got yourself a job here in Oxford it would be very different." Pushing back her chair, Karen moved round the table to where Jessica was sitting. She gave her a big hug.

"That would be really cool. You could be our lodger while you got yourself sorted with a house."

"Well maybe. Although I could still live on the boat if I worked in Oxford. But I need to give myself time to consider all the options. I may even try my hand at a different career."

"Such as what?" Karen asked.

"I have absolutely no idea. That's why I need time."

"Well, don't leave it too long. When you have had a rough experience, it's best to get "back in the saddle" as soon as possible they say," argued Jack, refilling Jessica's empty wine glass.

"Maybe, but I'm not ready yet," replied Jessica. "I think I got out just in time. Any longer and I would have had a breakdown, I'm sure. I still feel physically sick whenever I think about a classroom."

"You poor thing," said Karen gently. "It must have been awful."

"Yes but I'm so lucky. I've got the opportunity to travel around the canals for a year and not many people can do that. I intend to make the best of it."

"So where are you going next?" asked Jack. Jessica told them all about her plans to go down the River Thames to London. She invited Karen and Jack to visit her there, offering them her double bed for a couple of nights. When they learnt that this would mean Jessica would be sleeping on the living room floor, they gave her an old folding camp bed to keep on the boat. After dinner, as they all watched a film together, the sight of Karen and Jack snuggled up together on the sofa made Jessica feel singularly single. That night she dreamt about a new boyfriend, but the man in her dreams had no face.

After waking up quite late, Jessica walked with Karen to buy newspapers. On the way she told her how pleased she was to see the pair of them still so "loved up". Karen reassured her that she would be equally happy one day but Jessica said she was not so sure. She had found the man she would like to be with forever and he was married. Karen told her how pleased she and Jack had been when Jessica told her that she had ended the affair with Steve. They had seen the bad effect it was having on her. "But I still don't really think of us as having split up," Jessica confessed. "I'm just waiting for him to leave Ali. When he's free we could have a future together, I'm sure. I've left the school so now I don't need to teach his children any more, there would be nothing stopping us, when he leaves Ali."

"But there's too much history. How could you possibly face his children? They will still think of you as their teacher. Their teacher who they loved was the one who stole their daddy and made their mummy so unhappy." Jessica went quiet for a while, slowly accepting the truth of Karen's words. Her voice was hoarse when she finally spoke.

"You're right, of course. It's all such a mess. I know I am being stupid. But I love him."

"Then you need to find somebody else to love."

"You're right of course. Believe it or not, I have been looking."

On their return to the house they discovered that Jack had been busy in the kitchen cooking bacon, sausages, mushrooms, tomatoes, eggs and fried bread. Jessica tucked in hungrily. "That was the best breakfast I've ever had," she told him as she finished eating. "Thanks Jack, you've really spoilt me."

"Karen and I couldn't help noticing how much weight you'd lost," he said. "Thought we should fatten you up."

"You should have seen me a couple of months ago," replied Jessica. "I've put on half a stone since I stopped working." They spent the rest of the morning reading the papers and chatting casually together. Karen drove Jessica back to Banbury in the afternoon and walked with her to the boat.

"This is Ragamuffin," announced Jessica proudly as they arrived.

"She's so sweet! Can I have a look inside?" Jessica was proud to show her friend round her little boat. Entering from the front there was a small lounge, with a multi-fuel burning stove, portable TV set, a tiny sofa and a folding table with two stools. In the adjoining galley area, the gas stove, fridge and sink provided all that Jessica needed. Cupboard space was limited but well-organised and the shelves were stacked with provisions. "I thought you said it was like camping," Karen laughed. "This is much better than I expected."

"Yes it is rather good," admitted Jessica. "But you should see some of the boats, with washing machines and everything!"

"So what do you do about laundry?" Karen asked.

"I find good friends like you," replied Jessica, indicating the bags of clean clothes and bedding they had brought back with them. "Or I can visit launderettes. A lot of the small stuff I do by hand, and hang it at the front of the boat."

"So you show your knickers to the world!" laughed Jessica.

"You could say that. Not that anybody is interested in my knickers."

"We'll have to see what we can do about that," replied Karen. She went on to tell Jessica that if she really meant what she had said about finding somebody to replace Steve, she knew just the person. A friend of hers was single and she intended to invite him for dinner at the weekend so Jessica could meet him. Jessica warned her against expecting too much.

"I can't promise it will come to anything. As you know, I'm still very mixed-up about Steve."

"No harm in trying though. It would do you good to get laid." Jessica admitted to herself that she was lonely and this would be the ideal opportunity to rid herself of Steve altogether. It would be so wonderful if she could find somebody to make her as happy as Jack and Karen so obviously were. They walked through the small bathroom into the cabin at the rear of the boat where there was a double bed, wardrobe and chest of drawers. From there a door led out on to the stern deck. "Well, I think it's lovely," said Karen. "I'm really looking forward to coming to visit you."

"Any time," said Jessica. "I'll be on the Thames for three weeks when I leave Oxford and then I'll be heading up the Grand Union. Although I know you poor working folk can only do weekends!"

"OK, don't rub it in," Karen replied.

After Karen had returned to her car Jessica decided to explore Banbury. She found a good shopping centre right beside the canal but unfortunately the shops were all closing for the afternoon. She resolved to come back in the morning and in the meantime she took herself for a stroll around the rest of the town. She thought the famous Banbury Cross was a little disappointing; her childhood memories of the nursery rhyme had led her to believe it must be something quite unique. But at least she had seen it. The following day she visited the shops in Banbury and hunted down some great bargains for her summer wardrobe. She was used to shopping for smart clothes for work and had to remind herself that summer skirts and dresses would now be of no use to her. Instead she chose cheap tee shirts, shorts and lightweight trousers, all in dark colours that would hide the dirt. "All I need now is some good weather to match," she thought, looking at the grey sky. "Perhaps the sun will be shining by the time I reach Oxford."

It took until the following Friday morning for Jessica to travel to Oxford from Banbury, a distance that had seemed so much shorter by car. She found the journey immensely satisfying; the pretty Cherwell valley offered an idyllic landscape and the locks were few and far between. At one point the canal and the river joined together and after the recent heavy rain the water was quite fast-flowing so Jessica checked the level indication board to make sure it was safe to go on. The water level was on yellow so Jessica took Ragamuffin on to the river and they were carried briskly along on the current. Jessica found this a pleasant change from the slow pace of the canal and was full of eager anticipation at the prospect of her journey along the River Thames.

She found moorings about half a mile from the end of the Oxford Canal and from there she walked into the city. She was amazed at how busy everything was; with so much traffic on the road and so many tourists crowding the streets she was glad when it was time to start heading back to the boat. But even on the towpath she was caught up in the rush hour of cyclists and walkers on their way home from work. Jessica was taken aback by the hectic milieu; having adapted to the pace of canal life she hated to watch people pushing past one another without giving way. She smiled and spoke to a few passers-by but they stared as if there was something wrong with her.

Karen and Jack lived a fair distance from the canal so they had arranged a meeting place where

Karen would pick her up by car that evening. Although she had seen them only the previous weekend, Jessica was looking forward to spending more time with her friends. She knew she was always welcome at their house and felt better about taking advantage of their hospitality now there was the possibility of them staying with her on the boat. Arriving at the agreed meeting place, a pub car park near a bridge over the canal, she was pleased to see Karen already waiting, standing beside her old car and watching out for her. The two friends gave each other a hug and Jessica handed Karen the wine and flowers that she had bought as a way of saying thank you. She threw her rucksack on to the back seat of the car. "Hi again. Had a good week?" she asked breezily.

"Not really. Work's been so busy. I'm glad it's Friday." Fridays had no particular significance for Jessica now but she could still remember that wonderful feeling of relief when the weekend finally arrived.

"Why don't you let me do the cooking this evening?" she suggested. "I've not been at work all week."

"Thanks but we've decided to get a takeaway tonight, if that's all right with you? But you can help me cook dinner tomorrow if you like. Michael will be joining us." Karen pulled rapidly out of the car park and into the stream of traffic, causing Jessica to hold her breath momentarily while she waited for the crunch. It did not come and Jessica remembered that, unlike boats, cars have brakes. "Michael. Is that the guy you were telling me about?"

"Yes and don't worry if you don't fancy him. Don't think you've got to get off with him or anything just because we've set this up. But I'm sure you'll like him, he's very easy to get along with."

"Does he know about me?" Jessica asked in alarm.

"Yes. Thought it was only fair to warn him that we'd arranged a blind date."

"No pressure then," said Jessica, pleased that Karen could not see her cheeks reddening. Her stomach was in knots.

The following evening, Jessica discovered that Michael was just as easy to get along with as Karen had promised, and once the initial awkwardness had passed they talked non-stop. Jessica had never known anybody with whom she felt so at ease from the moment they first met. He told her about his work as an electronics engineer working in renewable energy products, which he obviously enjoyed a great deal. Jessica loved his enthusiasm and hoped that one day she might find a career to excite her in the same way. She decided against talking about her disastrous teaching experience but instead told him all about Ragamuffin. "I'd love to see her," he said.

"Well I hope to travel down and moor up on the Thames on Tuesday. You're welcome to come for a quick boat trip then, if you're free," Jessica suggested quickly.

"As it happens, I've got some holiday owing to me. I'd love to join you if you're serious."

"Oh yes, you can help me with the Isis lock, where the Oxford Canal meets the Thames. Then I can drop you off somewhere on the other side of

Oxford. It would be good to have another pair of hands and some company."

"If you could take me as far as Abingdon I can easily get a bus back to my flat in the centre of Oxford."

"That would be great. It would take us three or four hours, I should think. You'll probably have had enough of me by then."

"I doubt that very much," replied Michael, revealing delightful dimples in his cheeks as he smiled at Jessica. Karen was amused to see Jessica getting on so well with Michael and while they were clearing away the dishes she teased her.

"So you're going to seduce him in that cute cabin on Ragamuffin?" she joked.

"No it's nothing like that. He's nice and it would be good to have some company for a change," answered Jessica. At the moment, the thought of sleeping with anybody other than Steve still filled her with dread. It had been over two years since she had been in a relationship with anybody else. Michael was not particularly good looking but neither was he ugly. He was slightly taller than her, with curly brown hair, and very slightly overweight. She liked his smile and the sparkle in his eyes. He had good dress sense too, with jeans that were not too baggy, a checked shirt and leather jacket. She wasn't prepared to rush into anything but she knew that if she and Michael should be lucky enough to hit it off there was no hurry for her to leave Oxford. She could always take her boat back and moor on the Oxford Canal if her river licence ran out.

Sunday afternoon arrived all too quickly but Jessica felt excited as she said goodbye to Karen and Jack. "If I stick to my plans, I should be quite close to Richmond by the weekend after next," she informed them. "If you are free I'd love you to come. Or the following weekend, I should be in West London, heading towards Rickmansworth."

"If you stick to your plans..... Has that got anything to do with Michael by any chance?" teased Karen.

"Might have. I'll give you a call," replied Jessica, blushing slightly. "And thanks again for everything. It's been fabulous."

On Monday Jessica once again ventured into the crowded city. Her river licence for the Thames was not valid until the following day and it was a good opportunity to see Oxford. By lunchtime, after strolling around some of the old college buildings, the Ashmolean Museum and the Museum of Modern Art, she was exhausted. She walked down to sit in Christ Church Meadows where she soaked up some spectacular views of the city while resting in the sunshine. Watching the groups of students and pairs of lovers made her suddenly feel nostalgic for her days at university. "I'm only twenty-five, not much older than these kids around me, but I feel as though my life is rushing past. All of a sudden, one of these days, I'm going to wake up and it's already too late to live my life. I need to make up my mind what I'm going to do and it would be good to find somebody to do it with." She started to daydream about Michael. She had those first date jitters, hoping he would like her and that the relationship might develop into something beautiful. But she had grave doubts about her ability to love anybody else the way she loved Steve. If only she could experience a relationship like the one Karen and Jack had. They seemed to fit together so well, constantly touching and looking at one another the way couples do. She longed to meet somebody she could have introduced to her Auntie Joan as the boy she was going to marry. "Surely, that's not too much to ask," she said aloud. A lady walking past with a pushchair stopped to give her a strange look. She realised that she was crying.

"Are you all right?" the lady asked.

"Uh? Yes. Sorry, I was miles away."

"Anything I can do?" Jessica assured her that she was all right, just grieving for her favourite aunt who had died recently. Having recovered both her energy and her composure, Jessica walked down to the river where the rowing eights were in training and punts were all over the place. She watched as people on the tillers of the narrow boats anxiously revved their engines in reverse, trying to simultaneously stop and manoeuvre when punts or rowers cut in front of them. "I must remember to do this bit of the river very slowly tomorrow," she thought. "I don't think Michael would be too impressed if I ran over Oxford's best hopes for next year's Boat Race.

Chapter 7

"And woman is the same as horses: two wills act in opposition inside her. With one will she wants to subject herself utterly. With the other she wants to bolt, and pitch her rider to perdition." D.H. Lawrence (Women in Love.)

Jessica was up early tidying and cleaning the boat before Michael arrived. They had agreed that he would come at about nine and she wanted everything to be ready in good time so that she could be relaxed when she greeted him. "Thank goodness I did more laundry at Karen's this weekend. It wouldn't do to have wet underwear hanging around," she thought. Just after eight forty-five, when everything was in perfect order, Jessica filled the kettle and put it on the gas hob to boil.

"I bet the gas bottle chooses this moment to run out," she thought. But even if it had, it would not have mattered as Jessica knew how to change over from one bottle to the other. A loud knocking at the back of the boat announced Michael's arrival. He was early. Jessica went to the bow end to welcome him. She did not want him walking through her bedroom. "Hello, anyone aboard?" called Michael from the towpath. When he saw Jessica he walked towards the front of the boat.

"Sorry, I wasn't sure how long it would take me to find you," he said. "And it seemed a bit silly to walk up and down the towpath until nine o'clock."

"That's fine. Come aboard," As he came down the steps Michael handed Jessica a beautiful bunch of red roses.

"Oh, thank you," she said, realising that she didn't own a vase. "They're lovely. I'll just put them in here for now." Jessica grabbed a bucket from the cupboard in the bathroom and put the bucket into the shower cubicle, hoping he wouldn't think that she was treating his gift lightly.

"Tea or coffee?"

"Coffee please. White, one sugar."

Jessica steered Ragamuffin down to the end of the canal, with Michael standing beside her at the tiller. Having company made a pleasant change. They watched as a moorhen struggled to stay on a nest that bounced vigorously up and down in the boat's wash. They laughed simultaneously. "Would you like a go at steering?" Jessica enquired, offering Michael the tiller.

"Yes please later, when we haven't got all these moored boats. It's a bit crowded." It turned out that Michael had been on a narrow boat before and he was able to work the locks without any help from Jessica. He also steered superbly so Jessica made the most of the opportunity to take it easy and enjoy the views. They travelled quickly through Oxford despite having to negotiate all the small motor-boats and teams of rowers. Michael enthusiastically pointed out the names of the various boathouses along the way. All too soon they were at Abingdon. Michael helped Jessica to tie up Ragamuffin in an ideal mooring spot just before the bridge. "Can I get you some lunch before you leave?" Jessica asked hopefully. She liked Michael and was not ready to say goodbye yet.

"Why don't we go out to eat?" he suggested. "My treat of course." They found a good pub close to the river where they discovered they shared the same taste in red wine. After lunch they walked back to the boat very slowly as if they were trying to make the day last longer. Jessica, sure that Michael was no more ready to say goodbye than she was, felt it was up to her to say something. "Look, Michael, I don't need to travel any further today. Why don't you stay and have a meal with me tonight? It won't be anything posh like that lunch but I can offer you something simple."

"Yes please. I'd love to," he replied without hesitation.

The rest of the afternoon passed very quickly and they soon established that they had more in common than their taste in wine. When Michael looked at Jessica's tiny collection of CDs, he complimented her on her choice. "If I didn't have space for a massive collection, these are exactly what I would have chosen," he said and went on to scrutinise her small selection of books on the shelf. "I see you are D.H. Lawrence fan," he said. "It's so refreshing to find somebody who reads proper literature. Which is your favourite Lawrence novel?"

"Oh, I don't really have a favourite. What about you?"

"Sons and Lovers, I think. Did you see the film?"

"Yes. That scene in front of the fire was quite interesting," she laughed. While he was putting on a CD, Jessica hunted for a suitable container to replace the old bucket that held her roses and was pleased to find a plastic jug that would do the job. "Sorry, I didn't think about whether or not you'd have a vase," he said. "That was thoughtless of me."

"Don't worry. This will do fine. It's not very elegant but it's the roses we want to look at not the container. They're lovely, by the way."

"Lovely flowers for a lovely lady," he laughed. Jessica found a bottle of Shiraz that she had been saving for a special occasion and poured a large glass for each of them.

"Hey, are you trying to get me drunk?"

"You're not driving are you?" she replied. "I guessed you would be walking when you said you could catch a bus back to your flat."

"No I don't need to drive. And if I get too drunk to catch a bus, I suppose I could always stay the night?" He peered into her face as he spoke and Jessica could not help laughing at his cheeky grin.

"Yes you could do that," she replied, thinking of the spare camp bed that Karen and Jack had given her. Sitting facing one another on the two folding stools, they sipped their wine and talked about Oxford. "The boathouses were quite spectacular," said Jessica. "Although perhaps I wish there hadn't been quite so many of them. Those rowing boats were a bit of a nightmare."

"But we managed to miss all of them, didn't we? The city looked really good from the river, but you have missed what I think is the prettiest part - Port Meadow - which is upstream of where we came on to the Thames at Isis Lock. "

"Next time I come to Oxford, I will go that way then," Jessica declared.

"You haven't shown me around the rest of your boat yet."

"Oh sorry. There really isn't much else to see. There's the bathroom, and beyond that is the bedroom."

"Can I have a look?" urged Michael.

"Yes of course," replied Jessica. Michael followed her to the bedroom and before she knew what was happening his arms were around her.

"I don't know about you," he said, "but I fancy an early night." Jessica was taken by surprise.

"Slow down. I'm not ready for this yet," she said. But she let him kiss her and allowed him to pull her down on to the bed where they continued to kiss. Michael was not as good at kissing as Steve was but it felt good to have physical contact again. As his hands started to wander over her breasts, she stopped him. She could not get Steve out of her head. "Please, can we just kiss for now?" But Michael acted as if he hadn't heard her and his hands were all over her. She tried to push him off.

"I said no. I'm not ready. We hardly know each other." Michael looked at her in confusion.

"But you invited me to stay the night. I thought this was what you wanted."

"I meant you could sleep in the spare bed," Jessica clarified.

"Well, we're here now. We can just kiss if you want," he cajoled. By now, Jessica was trapped between Michael and the side of the boat. She felt his

94

breath on her neck and tried to move away. But he responded by whispering into her ear. "You're so beautiful." Jessica knew she had to put an end to it.

"Please, stop now. I don't want this," she shouted. With an enormous effort fuelled by fear she forced herself off the bed and across to the far side of the cabin.

"I'd like you to go now," she said forcefully.

"But we've only just started. Come back to bed."

"No, please leave." Jessica was scared, having been hit by the sudden realisation that she had placed herself in a vulnerable position, alone with a guy she scarcely knew. He could so easily rape her. Quickly unbolting the cabin doors, she stumbled out on to the stern deck. Her shirt was still undone but she needed to get outside where her screams for help could be heard if necessary. Michael, seeing that that her terror was very real, collected his coat and rucksack and climbed off the boat at the bow end. Not wishing to frighten her further, he made no attempt to walk past the rear of the boat but headed off across the parkland beside where they were moored. "I'm sorry, I didn't mean to scare you," he called. Jessica watched until he was out of sight then rushed inside, bolting all the doors securely before allowing herself to subside in a sobbing heap on the cabin floor.

"Oh Steve, where are you?" she cried in despair. "I don't want anybody else but you. This has gone on too long and I can't bear it any longer."

Zena accepted that she would never know the exact details of what had happened while she was at the theatre. She had come back to the boat to find Rob slumped in the armchair in his dressing gown, his wet clothes lying in the bath. She could not understand how falling into the canal could have resulted in a black eye. When he had refused to talk about it she had at first presumed that he had been in a fight and was too embarrassed to admit that he had come off the worst. Her persistent questions had caused him to fly into a rage so she had left him alone and finished the washing up. It was not until later that she noticed there were two whisky glasses on the coffee table and the double bed had not been made up as she always left it. The following morning when she noticed Diamond Blue moored up nearby it was easy to guess that Rachel was involved. The way those two had been carrying on in Warwick it was pretty obvious. It was not the first time he had been unfaithful to her; she remembered the first time being when Lawrence and Zac were very young. It had upset her back then but now she was surprised to admit that she did not even care whether Rob and Rachel had actually done the dreadful deed before being caught by Rhys. She was more hurt that he should take her for such a fool.

Although her experience of being betrayed by Rob was very far from ideal, it had at least offered something different from her usual mundane existence. For the first time in years she had felt real emotion, proper anger that reminded her she was still alive. A few days back at home however, and the trip to Stratford seemed no more than a bad dream. Her life resumed its dull sameness; the highlight of her day was when Rob came home and she would set a mouth-watering dinner on the table in front of him. She watched cookery shows on TV and searched the Internet for new recipes to try. Rob was full of praise for her cooking and was always proud to bring colleagues and clients home for a meal. He was unaware that it was not for him that she did it but for herself, her only satisfaction in life coming from the creation of culinary masterpieces. She continued to work hard in the gym every day, followed by a few lengths of the swimming pool. She maintained her regular routine of visits to the hairdresser, having her nails manicured, her eyebrows treated and her body waxed. Sometimes she went shopping for clothes, shoes or handbags and on these occasions she would arrange to meet up with an acquaintance for coffee or lunch and they would fill the time with idle gossip. She had a beautiful house, which was cleaned for her twice a week and a luxury car that was a real pleasure to drive so there was nothing more she could possibly need. Except a purpose. She knew that there had to be more meaning to her dreary existence than entertaining Rob and his guests, making herself look good and performing her marital duties when required.

Zena's daydreams often included Jessica; imagining her travelling to different places and meeting new people filled Zena with envy. She wished she had not been so foolish as to delete Jessica's number in that moment of panic. It would have been interesting to know where she was and what she was up to; the opportunity to live vicariously through Jessica's experiences might have brightened up her own meaningless existence. Zena had still not forgotten Jessica's question. Accepting that Rob was not going to change his mind about letting her see Lawrence and Zac more often she knew that particular need would remain unsatisfied. But there was another need and she calculated that was a battle that she stood some chance of winning. So when Rob was in a particularly good mood one evening she tentatively brought up the idea of going out to work. "Oh, not that nonsense again. You already have a job, which is to be a good wife to me so that I can continue to be successful and look after you in the style to which you have become accustomed," he declared in his usual pompous manner. "And you do it very well."

"I'm not talking about a career like nursing or anything," she argued. "I understand that I can't take on anything that would upset the way things are but I'm just so bored. If I could find myself a little part-time job during the day that I could fit around looking after you, it would make me more fulfilled."

"And what about your other job, as a mother? When the boys are home from school, you need to be here for them," he countered.

"I realise that Rob, I'm not stupid. I will have to take on something temporary or in term-time only so I could still be here for the boys."

In the end, after much reasoning from Zena, Rob agreed that she could investigate the job market and they would discuss it further if and when she found something suitable. Rob believed that in the unlikely event that the sort of job Zena was describing did actually exist, no employer would take on somebody of Zena's age who had never worked since leaving school. He was right of course. Once Zena started to explore the job-market it became apparent that she was not very employable. In each potential advertisement she looked at the requirements for the ideal candidate and found that she was lacking. She offered her services as a volunteer in the local Oxfam shop only to be told that they had no vacancies at present but would keep her name on file for future reference. This was a bitter blow but Zena was determined not to give up, and one day in early May it looked as though she had finally found the solution. A nearby comprehensive school was looking for midday supervisors to start immediately. She eagerly phoned the school for more information and they asked her to come in for a chat. She went along to the school without telling Rob. It was all looking very positive until she asked about term-time dates and discovered they were slightly different from those of the boys' school. Zena's face fell as she realised it was not going to work out after all. "But there is another possibility," said the deputy headteacher, Miss Webb. "We are always in need of relief supervisors to cover at short notice when one of the permanent members of staff is sick. Would that interest you?"

"Oh yes," said Zena. "As long as the boys were not at home, I would love that."

"It would be a good start," said Miss Webb. "It would get you back into the job market at least. And it would help us out." So Zena took the application form, promising to get it filled in and returned to them by the end of the week.

"You may have trouble when you need to put down the names of two referees," Miss Webb explained. "As you don't have a previous employer. But perhaps you can find two people who could give you a character reference? The headteacher at your sons' school, possibly? Or another parent, preferably a professional who has seen you interacting with their children?"

"Um, not sure about that, but I'll think about it."

"Well, just do your best, but don't leave it blank or you can't be employed working with children." On her way home, Zena racked her brains for who she could ask to give her a reference. There was no point in using the headteacher at the boys' school as he knew absolutely nothing about her - Rob had made sure of that. Finally she came up with the leader of the Beaver group the boys had belonged to while they were still at home. She had been involved in lots of activities through them. And she could ask the headteacher of the infant school the boys had previously attended where she had also been very busy on the PTA committee. Zena waited until Rob had finished eating before she told him about the job. She explained how it would only be on those days that she was available. "You see, if they phone me in the morning to ask me to work that day, I can say no if we have arranged to go to the boat or if the boys are at home. It doesn't need to interfere with your life in any way at all."

"If you really want to then I suppose it's OK. But can we not broadcast the fact that you are a dinner lady. It's not the sort of thing that is expected of people of our status." Zena readily agreed, quite liking the sound of herself as a 'secret standby supervisor'.

Since their return from Stratford, Rob had been oppressed by feelings of remorse. The incident in Braunston had been bad enough but then to have allowed Rachel to come onto him like that was unforgivable. He was sure Zena must have guessed what had happened; it would not have taken much to work it out. He was overwhelmed by Zena's reaction to both incidents; there had been no recriminations or rows and she had continued to be a dutiful and dedicated wife. Although he sometimes regarded her as boring, he now realised how lucky he was that she could always be relied upon. He was also proud of her tenacity and initiative in finding herself a job that would not interfere with her role as wife and mother. He fully understood why she wanted to go out to work; she missed the boys and needed something to distract her. To make matters worse, he was often late home from the office and was hardly the best of company after a long and difficult day. Any other girl would probably have had an affair by now, he thought. With her amazing looks that would hardly have been difficult for Zena - she could have had whoever she chose. Instead, she had found herself a job, although he did not expect her to survive for more than a week in a school like that, full of layabouts, slags and druggies. Nevertheless, he admired her courage and genuinely hoped it would work out for her. He acknowledged that Zena was far more than he deserved. Although he had given her all the material comforts a girl could want, he began to wonder if that was enough. For the first time in their married life, he questioned if he had lived up to her expectations or if her marriage was a disappointment to her. He knew he could be such a selfish bastard sometimes, hardly surprising when he considered how spoilt he had been as a child. It was his mother's fault, he decided, for making him believe that he was the centre of the universe. He wanted to be at the centre of Zena's universe but feared that he had forfeited the right to be there. Once again he vowed to become a better husband. He must do something to make her happy and he decided that for once he would sacrifice his principles to bring her happiness. Although he was adamant in his belief that they should not visit the boys during term-time, he knew from the school newsletter that in a couple of weeks' time it was the Annual Spring Fayre. Since this would be the first year that both boys would be at the school, he thought that perhaps he and Zena should attend. "Why not make a weekend of it?" he declared loudly, excited at the prospect of pleasing Zena. He booked them into a suitable hotel where they could

101

stay overnight on the Friday and Saturday and take the boys for lunch on the Sunday. Zena's reaction to this news was everything he could have hoped for. She hugged him and kissed him and thanked him and almost immediately began to stock up the freezer with her contributions for the Cake Stall.

Jessica did not sleep well the night after the incident with Michael and at first light she left Abingdon and its associated memories behind. She soon reached the turning for Culham Lock, where she had to put away all thoughts of Michael in order to concentrate. There was a large weir ahead of her and the current and the wind were driving her towards it. When she arrived at the layby for the lock she guessed it was too early in the morning for any help from a lock-keeper. Jessica did not relish the prospect of waiting there doing nothing - she had to keep moving. There was no boat behind her so she would either have to wait or do it herself. These locks were so unlike the locks of the canal; huge hydraulic affairs that were large enough to hold several boats at once. She wished she had paid more attention the previous day when Michael and the lock-keepers were operating the locks. Exhausted from her previous night's insomnia, she could make no sense of the instructions on the control panel. She pressed buttons randomly, waiting in vain for paddles to open, until another early morning boater coming in the opposite direction arrived on the scene. The lady showed her what she was doing wrong. A paddle had been left slightly up on the bottom gates and this had to be dropped before the other paddles could be raised. Jessica watched the experienced crew as they operated the lock and when they had gone she gingerly steered Ragamuffin against the side of the cavernous space. She wound the middle rope around a bollard before letting the water out. The lock was deep and she had to continually loosen the rope as the water level dropped. Had she failed to do so, Ragamuffin would have been left hanging above the surface of the water until her weight caused the rope to snap. Jessica shuddered to think of the damage that could be done by such a simple mistake. After opening the gate, she climbed gingerly down the slippery steps and jumped aboard Ragamuffin, relieved to have completed the procedure successfully. On her way back to close the gates she paused to behold the beauty of the river in the early morning sunshine; with the lifting of the mist came the promise of a sunny summer's day. Jessica's heart was lifted by the spectacle of a cormorant flying overhead; with its massive black wings it brought back memories of the poster of a pteranodon that had been on her classroom wall during her final term at school. The bird landed briefly on the water before disappearing under the surface. It reappeared further downstream a few moments later and immediately dived again, surfacing almost out of sight just as Jessica had given up all hope of seeing it again.

As Ragamuffin was carried along by the current of the river, the countryside passed quickly by. It passed by Jessica altogether as she was so engrossed in her own despair. Over the water the mist may have cleared but inside Jessica's head was a thick haze. Her night of soul-searching had left her full of fury, fury that was directed at nobody but herself. She had used Michael badly; while she had not intended to lead him on sexually she could see now how she had given him the wrong signals. She had certainly enjoyed his company and up until the moment they had started kissing Steve had disappeared completely from her mind. She wondered what had brought on such an irrational fear of being raped and concluded that living alone on the boat must have made her feel more vulnerable. But her reaction had been extreme and she was mortified by her hysterical outburst. "Well that's blown it with Michael, that's for sure. How stupid. He was really quite nice."

Jessica's depression was so deep that she could remember little of her journey that day but by the time she reached Goring she was too tired to continue her journey. Reasoning that she had put enough distance between herself and the events of the previous day, she found a good mooring spot just beyond the lock, where there was a magnificent view of the bridge and the weir. She crossed over the bridge to get a better view of the stunning scenery surrounding her. She had read somewhere that this was an important river crossing in the olden days and she imagined what it must have been like before the weir, the lock and the bridge were built, when people crossed by ferry or rode across on horseback. She crossed the bridge into the village of Streatley where she found a footpath that took her up into the hills. Although the climb was hard, she was rewarded at the top with heavenly views of the Chiltern Hills on the opposite side of the valley. She gazed at the river, now reduced to a tiny trickle, and beyond that a train speeding through the countryside just like a toy railway. Seeing the twin church towers of the two villages, she managed to work out roughly where Ragamuffin was moored. Back in the village of Goring, she admired the old mill beside the church and the pretty brick flint cottages that lined the narrow streets. Too exhausted to shop for food, she returned to Ragamuffin and crawled into bed.

The following morning Jessica woke up very early, her deep sleep having healed and refreshed her. As she gazed across the river to the steeply wooded slopes beyond, she gave herself a firm talking-to. "I should try to forget about what happened with Michael and most of all I must stop waiting for Steve to call me. I'll find somebody else and until then I will be patient. It's time to concentrate on enjoying my cruise on the Thames. This is a designated Area of Outstanding Natural Beauty and I should make the most of it."

The next stage of the journey was picturesque and exciting and Jessica was beginning to enjoy herself. Now she had got the hang of these mechanised locks she found them less daunting. At the first lock of the new day, she chatted casually with other boaters. There were few narrowboats travelling this route; most of the boats were smart fibre-glass cruisers. 'Plastic bag jobbies' was how she used to refer to boats like this but these were much bigger and smarter than the ones she had seen on the canals. Jessica felt out of place in her scruffy clothes on her old boat. "The Narrow Escape would be much more in keeping here," she thought. "And Zena would certainly be dressed the part. I wish she was here.

Chapter 8

"Our life is determined for us - and it makes the mind very free when we give up wishing, and only think of bearing what is laid upon us, and doing what is given us to do." George Eliot (The Mill on the Floss)

As the river grew wider and deeper, Jessica found the change in her surroundings brought with it a sense of exhilaration. There was a greater variety of geese and ducks than could be found on the canal, and the steeply wooded hills to her left contrasted well with the water meadows on the far side of the river. Beyond Pangbourne, she was once again in the company of rowing eights in training. This time the coaches accompanied the rowers, cycling along the bank with megaphones. At one point, one of these coaches shouted at Jessica, telling her she was on the wrong side of the river. She felt rather aggrieved, having been forced over to this side of the river by the rowing boat sitting at ninety degrees to the bank. A little later on, Jessica had to steer close to the side to make way for a massive riverboat, packed with sightseers who waved cheerfully at Jessica as they passed. The sight of these tourists reminded Jessica that by travelling so quickly she was missing out on the places of interest along the way. At the rate she was going, she would reach London much sooner than she had anticipated. Having paid for a full three weeks on the Thames, it made sense for her to make the most of that time. She resolved to slow down and experience the places she was seeing instead of rushing on towards Reading so quickly. She moored up early in the afternoon and strolled along the riverbank, enjoying the boats and the countryside. Her phone rang as she was walking. Her heart leapt at the thought that it might be Steve and she scolded herself crossly. He would call when he was ready and she must just be patient. "Hi Jess. It's me, Karen. How are you?"

"I'm fine thanks. Just having a walk near Mapledurham," Jessica replied, trying to hide her disappointment behind a forced cheerfulness in her voice.

"Have you visited Mapledurham House?"

"Not yet. It's only open at weekends so I need to decide whether to wait here until Saturday. When are you coming to see me?"

"We thought perhaps we could come the weekend after next if that's OK?" Jessica was overjoyed. As it would be difficult to stop and pick them up on the tidal part of the river below Teddington, she arranged to meet her friends at Kingston on the Friday evening. She was so excited at the prospect of having company again that Karen's next question took her by surprise. "You sound a bit weird. Are you OK?"

"I'm fine."

"Only, I saw Michael yesterday. I gather things didn't go too well on Tuesday?"

Jessica steadied herself on a nearby tree. "You could say that. What did he say?" she asked sharply.

"Not much actually. He said he had messed up. I'm sorry you didn't get on with him. What happened?"

"I don't really want to talk about it if you don't mind. I messed up as well."

107

"OK. See you a week tomorrow then." As she ended the call, Jessica wondered if she had been too abrupt with her friend, realising that she should have been more grateful to her for trying to find somebody to replace Steve.

Because she had plenty of time to reach Kingston by the following Friday afternoon, Jessica decided to stay moored in Mapledurham for another couple of days to do some walking and take time to relax and think. Walking, unlike boating, would enable her to think without any distractions. She travelled for miles on the footpath on the high ground overlooking the Thames, where she discovered that looking down on the river gave her a totally different perspective than when she was cruising along it. Her life was like a map and she needed to look at the whole picture. Rather than constantly looking back at what lay behind her, she resolved to enjoy the place where she was and to look ahead positively to what was still to come. "Stop dwelling on the past and start living for the here and now," she told herself, "and the future has all sorts of happy surprises just waiting for you." She was feeling more optimistic by the time she moored Ragamuffin on the landing stage next to Mapledurham House on the Saturday afternoon. Although her visit to the House took her back into the past it was a welcome escape into a history unconnected with her private life and her imagination was full of Roundheads and characters from The Wind in The Willows. Refreshed and invigorated, she left the House and cruised past Reading to reach the village of Sonning before dark.

Before breakfast the following morning, Jessica had a leisurely stroll around the beautiful village and treated herself to the Sunday papers. As she returned to the boat she could see already that it was turning into a gorgeous day and she was filled with the warm conviction that good things were at last about to happen to her. She sat lazily on the front deck enjoying her toast and coffee, the papers spread out before her. Just as she was beginning to doze in the heat, a familiar voice brought her to her senses. "Lawrence, wait for Zac, please. And don't go too near the edge."

"Stop nagging them. They're old enough to look after themselves without a worrying mother on their case all the time."

Jessica spun around in her seat to see two young boys approaching her boat on the towpath and behind them the familiar figures of Zena and Rob. She stood up and called out breezily, "Hi there. You're a long way from Braunston."

"And so are you. Still enjoying your travelling?" replied Zena.

"Yes thanks. Are you here on your boat?"

"No, we've left it on temporary moorings near Stratford on Avon. We're going back next week to take it to our marina on the Grand Union. We are just down visiting the boys at school, aren't we, Rob?" Rob had already started to walk on past the boat when Zena spoke to him. He stopped reluctantly. Zena explained to Jessica that they had just been for a ramble along the river and were now on their way back. Rob had been invited to visit a yacht moored up beyond the bridge. It belonged to one of the parents at the boys' school. "And I don't want to be late," added Rob.

"So no time for a cuppa then?" asked Jessica.

"No there isn't," snapped Rob. Jessica thought what a rude and arrogant man he was and not for the first time she wondered what made Zena stay with him.

"Rob, why don't you and the boys go on and see the yacht and then meet me back at the hotel at twelve o'clock? I'd probably be in the way on the yacht anyway. End up knocking something over or damaging some essential piece of equipment," Zena laughed.

"OK then. Might as well leave the boys with you as well then." Wanting to talk to her friend alone, Jessica interrupted quickly. "Oh, I'm sure they would be far more interested in a grand yacht than a little old boat like this."

"Yes, that's true. I'll see you later then, Zena. Boys, wait for me - and come away from the edge!" Rob strode off along the towpath. Jessica and Zena stood looking at one another for a moment and Zena noticed the dark circles beneath Jessica's eyes. It was Jessica who spoke first; while Zena was settling herself on the front deck, she said plaintively, "You didn't phone me. I was hoping to hear from you."

"I'm sorry, I deleted your number. It was a mistake. Perhaps you could give it me again?"

"Yes I will, and give me yours as well this time."

After the two girls had put their respective numbers into their mobile phones and Jessica had placed a fresh pot of tea on the little table on the deck, they conversed comfortably together like old friends. Jessica told Zena about her adventures on the boat and her visit to Oxford, leaving out the part about Michael. Zena described the interview she had just had for her new job, thanking Jessica for getting her to question what it was that she needed. Her loyalty to Rob prevented her from telling Jessica about how Rob had behaved that night in Braunston or mentioning the incident at Stratford. Half an hour passed very quickly and as twelve o'clock approached, Zena became anxious. "I really must go. Rob hates it when people are late and he has booked a table for lunch at half past twelve. Would you like to join us?"

"That's kind, but probably better not. You don't get to spend much time with your sons and I don't want to be in the way."

"You're right. Maybe it's not the best occasion for us to talk. But I will phone. And please, please phone me," replied Zena.

"I can at least walk back to your hotel with you?"

"Yes that would be nice."

On her return from the hotel Jessica decided to it was time to leave Sonning. As she passed under the bridge beside the hotel she spotted what must have been the posh yacht that Rob had been visiting. She waved to the couple aboard who were drinking champagne and laughing loudly. Drawing level with the boat Jessica overheard the man saying, "Those poor boys. Fancy having a tosspot like that for a father."

"I know just what you mean," thought Jessica to herself. "And don't forget his poor wife. It will serve him right when she finally gets the courage to leave him."

For the next few days, Jessica travelled along a very busy stretch of the river. She admired the boathouses and expensive houses that lined the banks. "Each of these houses must be worth a fortune! I had no idea that there were so many wealthy people in this country. When I think about some of the homes of my children at school, it is just so unfair." By the time she reached Henley, she was more confident about her ability to avoid the canoeists and rowers, which was just as well as the river was packed with them and the little motorised boats that followed behind with rowing coaches barking instructions. In order to enjoy this scene properly without having to concentrate on steering Ragamuffin she moored briefly near Temple Island and walked back along the river bank. It was a stunningly sunny day and there were other walkers out enjoying the atmosphere. The July races were just over a month away and there was a sense of urgency among the rowers. Jessica tried to imagine what this place would be like with crowds of spectators lining the course. "I wonder where all the swans and geese will go?" she thought.

As Jessica was wandering back towards her boat her phone rang. It was a very excited Zena who just had to tell somebody that her contract had come through for her job as a relief lunchtime supervisor. Her DBS checks and her references had been returned successfully and now she just had to wait until the school called her. "Oh really? I'm so glad you've found something to do with your time," enthused Jessica.

"Yes, I am going mad with boredom and need to do something. It's not much but it's a start. Anyway, what are you doing?"

"I'm at Henley, walking along the regatta course. It's beautiful."

"Yes it must be. We went to the races there a couple of years ago. There was a fabulous atmosphere. I wish I was there with you. Anyway, I must dash. I have an appointment with the hairdresser in five minutes. But I will call you again soon."

The abruptness of the ending to their conversation left Jessica feeling deflated but she did not have long to speak to her friend again as Zena called her again the very next morning. Her excitement was childlike and made Jessica smile. "The school has just called me. They want me to work today."

"That's great! This is the start of your new career."

"I wouldn't call being a dinner lady a career exactly," sighed Zena modestly.

"Perhaps not. But it's a challenge. And it will help your self-confidence."

"That depends on how well I can do it."

"You'll be fine." Jessica guessed that she was the only person Zena could talk to about her job. "Will you ring me to let me know how you get on?"

At Kingston Jessica moored up outside Hampton Court Palace and waited for Karen and

Jack to join her. She was eagerly anticipating having company again but also apprehensive about questions that Karen might ask about Michael. As it turned out, Karen was less inquisitive than she expected, having news of her own that she wanted to share. The moment they arrived she showed Jessica her engagement ring. "We've been really lucky that there was a cancellation at the venue, so we can get married in August. Please will you be my bridesmaid?"

"Oh, how exciting! Of course I would love to be your bridesmaid. I can't wait. Congratulations, both of you!" squealed Jessica, giving enthusiastic hugs to both Karen and Jack.

Once they were settled on the boat, Karen gave Jessica an envelope, inside which was a letter from Michael. She waited until Karen and Jack had gone to their cabin to unpack before she opened it.

"Dear Jessica,

I am so sorry I frightened you so badly when I visited your boat. My behaviour was unforgivable, but do I hope that you can forgive me as I never intended you any harm. It was presumptuous of me to expect to sleep with you when you invited me to stay the night. It was just that there seemed to be a strong chemistry between us and I mistook your lovely hospitality for something more. After I left you that day, I realised that you must feel very vulnerable living alone on a boat and I totally understood your reaction. It was me that was behaving unreasonably, not you. My only excuse is I drank too much wine and I found you to be equally intoxicating.

114

I am sorry once again for the distress I caused you. I hope that we will meet up again in Oxford one day and that we can be friends.

With very best wishes, Michael. "

Jessica shoved the letter into a drawer to think about later. She was not going to let her guilt about Michael spoil her friends' visit. As it turned out, the weekend was one long celebration, starting with an exhilarating trip down the tidal part of the Thames from Teddington. The river was wide and fast flowing, carrying Ragamuffin rapidly downstream. Narrow boats, having no keel, are built for canals not tidal rivers and when Jessica pointed this out, Karen became quite scared. Jessica remembered that she should be carrying life jackets. She steered closer to the bank so that there would be less distance to swim if Ragamuffin should capsize. They soon passed under the very attractive Richmond Bridge and beyond that was the park. As they approached Kew Gardens, Jessica started to look out for the entrance to the Grand Union canal on the opposite bank. All too soon, the sign for the Thames Lock came into view and they entered the narrow channel. The first part of the Grand Union was a real anti-climax after the thrill of the Thames. "Ugh, nothing very grand about this," muttered Jessica, looking at the filthy water and abundant litter around Brentford. When they reached the flight of locks at Hanwell, Jessica was grateful for the help of her two crewmates so they could quickly leave this part of the canal behind. While Karen and Jack were busy operating the locks, Jessica had the opportunity to reflect on the contents of Michael's letter. She wished things had worked out differently and would have liked him as a friend at least. If only she had not spoilt it by inviting him back to the boat after lunch then none of it would have happened. It was so obvious now how Michael had been led to believe she wanted sex and the misunderstanding was her fault, not his. That evening she wrote her reply for Karen to deliver to Michael, choosing her words carefully to avoid making him think there would ever be a sexual relationship between them.

"Dear Michael,

Thank you for your letter. I fully understand the situation and I blame myself for not communicating better. Please don't feel bad about it. You did frighten me but that was due to my paranoia rather than your behaviour.

Perhaps I should have explained to you that I am just getting over an affair that has left me feeling confused and hurt. I am not ready for a relationship yet as I am still very much in love with somebody who I can't have. But if you can forgive me for my irrational behaviour I would very much like to be friends with you. Nothing more, just good friends, as I did not feel the chemistry that you described. But I enjoyed your company very much and you are welcome to come and visit me again on my boat, either for just a day, or staying overnight on the camp bed if you like. It would certainly be useful to have another pair of hands at the locks. Karen and Jack are with me now in London and I will be heading north along the Grand Union after that.

Best wishes,

Jessica."

Standing at Uxbridge station after her friends had left, Jessica felt very alone. She hoped that the letter to Michael would heal the rift between them and he would soon get in touch with her. It suddenly occurred to her that she had not given Michael any contact details and had no address for him or his phone number. Mortified that he would assume from this omission that her invitation was an empty gesture, she called Karen and asked her to write her number on the envelope before giving Michael the letter. Karen was pleased to hear that Jessica may see Michael again. "They would make a good couple," she said to Jack. "But to be honest, anybody would be better for her than Steve. I'm terribly afraid that she will go back to him. She's absolutely besotted with him still. I don't get it - from everything she's said, I think he's a bit of a pig."

"Too much time alone on that boat won't help either," replied Jack. "She needs to keep busy."

Jessica did not feel like going straight back to an empty boat so she decided to treat herself to a day out in London. She had always loved going into the city on a Sunday; although it was still busy there was altogether a different feeling about the place. She would not even need to change trains as the Piccadilly Line ran directly from Uxbridge to South Kensington, from where it was just a short distance to the Natural History Museum and the Science Museum. Then she could go to Hyde Park for a walk, possibly taking in the Serpentine Gallery. Excited at the prospect of doing something totally different and spontaneous, she bought her ticket and eagerly boarded the next train.

After a quick look around the Natural History Museum, Jessica decided to go for lunch at the cafe in the Science Museum. She had been there a couple of times with Steve. In fact, that was where it had all started. He had stayed to help clear up after the Friday night disco at the end of her first half term at the school and he had asked what she was doing during her week's holiday. She had replied that she was going to the museum to prepare for taking her class there in November. He had told her that he worked very close to the Science Museum and would love to take her out for lunch to thank her for all that she had done for his daughter Alice. "She absolutely adores you," he had told her. "We used to have such difficulty getting her to school in the morning but she is so happy in your class and won't have a day off even when she's really sick."

"I wish they all felt like that," had been Jessica's response. She had felt a bit embarrassed to accept his offer of lunch but had finally given in, thinking it would make a pleasant change. If she had known what was to follow, she would never have accepted. Over lunch he had told her how worried he was about Alice, since his wife had a drink problem and there had been a number of arguments between them which Alice and her younger brother Tom had witnessed. Jessica had promised to keep a close eye on both children and to let him know if they showed any signs of distress. When he had taken hold of her hands and thanked her he had gazed so intently into her eyes that she knew she had to do more to help him. That had been the first of several meetings; he would drop the children off with his parents for a few hours on a Saturday morning to give his wife a break while he supposedly went into the office. Nobody had suspected anything; his parents enjoyed their time with the grandchildren and Jessica was able to provide a listening ear. The listening ear had soon turned into a shoulder to cry on and by Christmas it had become an intense love affair.

While she was eating her lunch in the crowded cafe, Jessica watched all the families around her. She loved to observe the kaleidoscope of parenting styles in action. Of course, these were parents who had chosen to take their children to the Science Museum so it was certainly not a true cross-section of society. Supermarket queues and doctors' waiting rooms provided a broader perspective, she thought. A horrible thought suddenly struck Jessica - suppose Steve chose today of all days to bring his children to the museums? If so, he would be sure to bring them here for lunch. And Ali might be with them. It would be more than she could bear to watch them playing happy families together. Although she knew she was being paranoid, Jessica lost her appetite and made a rapid exit from the building. She was out of breath by the time she reached Hyde Park, where she threw herself down on to the ground to recover. There she reprimanded herself severely for her hysterical behaviour. "You need to get him out of your system. You know he's not going to leave her, and even if he does you are best out of it," her sensible self said. "But I love him," came the reply.

Jessica was making her way back to the boat from Uxbridge station when her phone rang. Despite her best efforts, she still clung to the hope that it would be Steve. "Hi Jessica, it's Zena."

"Oh hello. How did it go on Friday?"

"It was great. The kids were so much more responsible than I'd expected. When there was any trouble, all I had to do was to ask the right questions and it got them talking to each other. They genuinely wanted to sort out their differences for themselves," Zena gabbled gaily. She was like a child with a new toy.

"Are you working again tomorrow?"

"Yes. They expect the lady will be off all week, which will really give me a chance to get to know the kids. But there are so many of them I'll never remember all their names."

"You'll soon learn the ones you need to know," laughed Jessica.

They talked for a while and Jessica described the exhilaration of the cruise down the tidal part of the Thames. She told her about Karen and Jack's visit and her day out in London. Zena said how pleased she was that Jessica was having a good time and keeping herself busy. "It's great that you could spend time with your friends. I don't think it is good for you to be alone too much. Even somebody as independent as you needs to have company sometimes."

"Yes it does get a bit lonely. Perhaps I can meet up with you on the Grand Union before too long?"

"Yes, I'd like that. But I'm not sure when we will be back on the boat. Rob's very busy at work. But I could possibly drive over and see you one day when you get a bit closer to Aylesbury? Anyway, I must go now but call me when you reach our area and we'll fix something up." As Jessica put her phone back in her pocket, she reflected on the conversation. She was happy at the prospect of seeing her friend again soon. But she was also a bit jealous of Zena, so excited with her new job in a school. "Maybe, just maybe, I will go back to teaching one day."

Zena was happy to be back on the boat again. Rob was in an unusually good mood and the weather was warm and dry - so much better than the last time. The journey from Stratford to their permanent moorings would take them about a week and that would give her a chance to give the interior of the boat a really good clean. As she was working the locks, Zena spotted the changes on the canal in the short time since their last visit. Whereas before, the only ducklings to be seen were the tiny bundles of fluff whose frenzied flapping lifted them right out of the water when the passing boat separated them from their mother, now there were others, nearly full grown, swimming sedately behind their mothers and looking disdainfully at their younger counterparts. The leaves that before were just starting to sprout had now covered the trees with a dense curtain of green and the hedges were bedecked with creamy blossom. The cottage gardens were ablaze; some with paths edged by crimson tulips already past their best, others adorned with rampant clumps of forget-me-nots and many other flowers that Zena could not name. She could understand why Rob loved the canals so much and was sure the boys would have a fantastic holiday when the end of term finally arrived. "Just over a month and we will all be together again. I can't wait," she thought.

The improvement in the weather brought one unwelcome change however, as more boats on the canal meant they had to wait their turn at the locks. Unlike the locks on the Grand Union, which took two boats at a time, these were single locks. The old couple on the boat in front were painfully slow so Zena began to help them with each lock to move them along a bit faster. She felt sorry for the old lady who was scared to walk across the lock gate from one side to the other and who was finding it difficult to turn the paddle gears. She wondered why they were trying to do this at their age; there surely must be a point when boating holidays like this became too much for older people, she thought. The lady had told her that they had owned the boat for twenty years and they still used it every summer. They had travelled all over the country but this was one of their favourite canals. After the first two locks, Zena could see that the old lady was hanging back and letting her do all the work. Remembering that the couple had pulled out in front of them as they were approaching the locks, it occurred to her that this couple had been waiting there for another boat to appear to give them assistance. There were still another sixteen locks to go through before they reached Lapworth and it was clear that Zena would have to do most of the work for the entire flight while the old lady took things easy. She told Rob what was happening and he suggested they moor up for an early lunch to give the other boat time to get ahead of them. "I'm not having my wife wear herself out being taken for granted by some ungrateful nobody. We will stay here for a while and there may be more boats coming down this afternoon which will make it easier for you," he announced. The irony was not lost on Zena. "Thanks Rob. Now what can I get you for lunch?"

As Rob finished his final sandwich he asked Zena if she was ready to set off again. The elderly couple were out of sight and a boat coming towards them meant the next lock would be in their favour. They left eagerly, only to discover moored beyond the bend the boat they thought they had avoided. The old man was standing on the stern deck apparently waiting for them to catch up. But Rob was too quick for him and speeded up to overtake, dropping Zena off beside the open gates and steering straight into the waiting lock. For a moment Zena was afraid the old guy would fall off his boat, which was rocking badly in the wash created by The Narrow Escape.

However, he clung on to the tiller with one hand while shaking his walking stick at Rob with the other.

Chapter 9

"A supreme love, a motive that gives a sublime rhythm to a woman's life, and exalts habit into partnership with the soul's highest needs, is not to be had where and how she wills: to know that high initiation, she must often tread where it is hard to tread, and feel the chill air, and watch through darkness. It is not true that love makes things easy: it makes us choose what is difficult." George Eliot *(Felix Holt)*

As the Grand Union Canal runs alongside the main railway line from London to the Midlands, the fast trains are regular neighbours to their slower predecessors on the water. Each time one of these trains roared past Jessica it reminded her that her old life was not far away. As she watched the commuters heading for the stations in the morning and noticed the overcrowded trains thundering past, she wondered about all the people on their way to work and asked herself if they were as contented in their way of life as she was in hers. She knew she was not happy but the source of her misery was not the canal but her broken heart and she could think of nowhere else she would rather be while it mended. "And it will mend," she promised herself. "Just give it time."

When Jessica reached Hemel Hempstead she was ready for some home comforts and some companionship. She was missing her parents and decided to leave Ragamuffin on a fourteen-day mooring spot so she could spend some time at home. Studying the train timetable on her phone, she discovered that she could reach Birmingham in under two hours by train, a journey that would take her many weeks by boat. Her father was delighted when she called and he offered to pick her up from New Street station the following afternoon.

Jessica's visit to her home was a largely happy event; her mother, was pleasantly surprised to have her "little girl" back and set about spoiling her with all her favourite foods. Both Barbara and Bob commented on how well Jessica looked; they thought she had gained a little weight and her cheeks had a healthy glow. Jessica appreciated the effort her mother was making and was careful not to say anything that would upset her. Harmony reigned and for Jessica the healing process continued. On her last morning, while they were clearing away after breakfast, Barbara unexpectedly told Jessica to sit down as there was something she needed to tell her. "I know I found it hard to understand why you gave up that teaching job," Barbara admitted. "But I can see it now. You were having a much tougher time than we realised." Barbara wrapped her arms around her daughter and hugged her, which came as a great surprise to Jessica as they had never been the sort of family to give cuddles.

"That money from Auntie Joan came just at the right time," Jessica confirmed.

"Speaking of your Auntie Joan, we have a few things in the spare bedroom that we kept when we were clearing out the house. We thought you might like to have something to remember her. Come and have a look." As Jessica surveyed Auntie Joan's possessions spread out on the spare bed, she felt a lump in her throat. She had hardly given a thought to her aunt over the past few weeks. "I'm sorry, Mum, it must have been really hard for you, clearing out the house. I should have been here to help," she apologised sadly.

"It was OK. Gave me a chance to find out a bit more about her. She never spoke much about her younger days and now I know why."

125

"Sounds very mysterious," replied Jessica, hoping Barbara would expand on her last sentence but her mother remained stoically silent and Jessica put a check on her curiosity. Just then, she spotted an old windlass amongst the objects on the bed. She picked it up and looked at its well-worn handle. "Can I have this?" she asked eagerly.

"Yes of course. We expected you would want that."

Jessica also found a small badge with National Service written across the top and the initials IW underneath. She wondered what the letters stood for. Then she saw an old harmonica hidden amongst the other objects. She picked it up and blew softly and was surprised to discover she could play a tune of sorts. "I didn't know Auntie Joan played the mouth organ," she said.

"There are a lot of things you don't know about your Auntie Joan," muttered her mother, but once again she failed to follow up her comment with any explanation. Jessica took the windlass and the harmonica and a couple of pieces of jewellery that Barbara persuaded her to have and they walked solemnly back into the kitchen. "There is something else," Barbara said. "But I want to talk to you before you see them. You may be a bit shocked." She pulled out a bundle of old letters from the dresser and sat down opposite Jessica, placing the letters deliberately on the table in front of her.

"What is it?" asked Jessica, stifling her curiosity as she realised from the way Barbara was wringing her hands that she was finding this conversation very painful. "Take your time, Mum," she added gently.

"Well you know Auntie Joan never had any children? Now I understand why. It seems she was not attracted to men, if you know what I mean."

"Do you mean Auntie Joan was gay?" Barbara nodded and looked away from Jessica towards the window, where Jessica's father could be seen pottering around the garden. Jessica guessed that he had been told to stay out of the house whilst this conversation was going on. She studied her mother's face. Although she looked sad and awkward, Jessica could see no indication that she was either disgusted or angry. This surprised her as she knew how homophobic her mother was. "How do you feel about that, Mum?" she probed.

"I don't know. Shocked, I suppose. It's such a pity that she never had children, but this explains why. I'll let you read the letters yourself when you are ready. You can take them back to the boat with you."

"But don't you feel angry with her?"

"No not angry, just sad for her. She couldn't help the way she felt, I suppose. You have to respect her for being true to herself and honest enough not to pretend. It would have been hard for her. Nowadays, it's much more acceptable, but back then you were expected to have a husband and children. She must have been lonely." Jessica was amazed by her mother's acceptance. If she could be so understanding of Auntie Joan's lesbianism, perhaps there was some hope that her own affair with a married man might be forgiven? "Please don't read them now," Barbara requested. "It is too sad a story for us to think about and I don't want anything to spoil your last day at home. It has been so lovely having you here. "

127

Sitting in one of the several pubs in Long Itchington, Rob felt his rage rising as he listened to the group of lads at the next table who were talking to his wife. They were on a hire boat and were full of tales about their various mishaps, their banter and exuberance reminding him of the times when he went on boating holidays with his friends. One of the group asked Zena if she and Rob were on a hire boat too and she explained that they owned their own boat. The boy asked her what their boat was like and she told him it was exceptionally smart and that Rob had designed it. She beamed proudly at her husband. However, as soon as Rob started to describe The Narrow Escape, the boy remembered it was his turn to get the next round and interrupted Rob to ask what drinks everybody would like. When he finally came back from the bar and sat down again, Rob tried to resume the conversation. However, as it was apparent that this young man was not in the least interested, he gave up and talked to Zena instead. Throughout their meal he could tell that his wife was more entertained by the conversation at the next table than by anything he had to say. He decided he would stop talking altogether to see how long it would take her to notice, but Zena was so engrossed in the boys' jokes and stories that she was totally unaware of his silence. At one point she laughed so much that the tears were streaming down her face and he was embarrassed to watch her showing herself up in that way. The final straw was when one of the crowd was describing how to untangle fishing line from the prop shaft and his friend said, "This is a bit of boat you are talking about, isn't it, mate? For a moment then I thought you were teaching us how to fuck." The whole bar exploded into laughter, including Zena. Rob had heard enough and went to the bar to settle the bill. Zena looked surprised and disappointed when he came back and announced,

128

"Come on Zena, we're going."

By the time they arrived back at The Narrow Escape, Rob had worked himself up into a fury. He pushed Zena roughly down the steps of the boat and as she fell, memories that horrible episode in Braunston came flooding into her mind. "Surely he can't be jealous of those guys in the pub?" she thought. It struck her that he had been uncharacteristically quiet all evening and she remembered how at Braunston he had thought she was flirting with the boys at the locks. Seeing the similarities, she was very afraid. Never had that dreadful ringtone of Rob's phone sounded so melodious to Zena's ears as it did at that moment.

"Hello, Graham. Could you give me a moment and I'll call you back." The unexpectedness of the phone call was enough to bring Rob back to his senses. He was filled with shame and also with relief that he had on this occasion been prevented from going any further. He spoke softly to his wife. "Zena, I'm sorry. I shouldn't have pushed you like that. Those lads in the pub really wound me up, that's all. But I shouldn't have taken it out on you. It's all right - I'm over it now. Don't cry." Seeing Zena's tears and the pallor of her face, he was overcome with remorse. "I'm sorry. Please don't cry. I'm never going to hurt you again," he soothed, holding her tightly in his arms and tenderly kissing the top of her head. Once her sobs had subsided, Zena reassured him that she was all right and urged him to call Graham back.

Climbing back aboard Ragamuffin, Jessica found the cold damp air an unwelcome homecoming. As she lit her stove, she was aware of how much she missed the warmth of her parents' house and wished she had bought a boat with central heating. She wondered what it would be like living on the boat in really cold weather. It was still only the beginning of June so she had a few warm months to look forward to but she did not want to rely on this stove alone in the depths of winter. Before then she would have to make some decisions; she needed to start earning money if she was to have the expense of installing central heating and live on the boat through the winter. But she did not want to think about that now and turned her attention to Auntie Joan's letters. She had been impatient to read them ever since her mother had given them to her but had respected Barbara's request that she should wait until she returned to the boat. She could see from the postmarks on the envelopes that they were arranged in date order, so she started to read from the beginning. The first letter was very short.

24th May 1944

Dear Joan,

I hope this letter reaches you. I'm not going to write much until I know that you have received this letter unopened. I can't be sure that this is a reliable delivery address.

I am missing you so much already. I still can't believe you chose to stay and work on those wretched barges instead of coming here to Coventry with me. It's hard work in the factory but I know it's much harder for you. I couldn't have done it.

Your friend, Gloria.

130

Jessica guessed that the delivery address must have proved to be reliable as there were another dozen or so letters from Gloria, spanning several months. She wished she could have seen the letters that Joan had written in reply but those would either have been destroyed by now or else still in Gloria's possession. She guessed Gloria would have been about the same age as Auntie Joan and wondered if she was still alive and if so where she might be now. She moved on to the next letter.

10th June 1944

My darling Joan,

Thank you for your letter. We have had very little bombing although the air raid sirens still sound and we had a near miss at the factory yesterday. I have been on late shifts this week. I don't like travelling to work at night and I'm so glad we have a bus to get us there. It's terribly hard work in the factory, and so horribly loud that my throat aches at the end of the day from having to shout so loudly to make myself heard. But at least I am indoors, not like you, out in all weathers. I don't know how you managed when the canal was frozen over. Never mind, everybody says the war will be over before winter.

The hostel where I am staying is not too bad. There are fourteen of us in one dormitory. The Warden is a bit fierce, but I suppose she is only trying to look after us. We have a key to the hostel so we can let ourselves in if we go out at night. We have to be back by eleven, but as we are all so tired from the factory, that is no hardship. But I envy you your freedom; I guess you can come and go as you please. Some of the women here are not very nice; their language is foul and they spit like men. But there are a few quiet types as well so I suppose it is a good mix. You don't need to worry about me taking a shine to any of them, as I have promised to save myself for you. And I know you will do the same for me, even though you are living with two other girls.

The food in the canteen is rubbish and I don't think wartime rationing is the only reason. But there is a little shop where we can treat ourselves to some chocolate occasionally. But the best thing of all is we have our very own dance hall - it's nothing special, but it gives us something to look forward to. There's going to be a dance next week. I wish I had brought some better clothes with me - I shall look a right state!

I haven't had a chance to see much of Coventry yet but it looks a bit of a dump. But it's amazing how strong the Coventry people are after all that they've been through; they seem even more determined than us Londoners that it will be 'business as usual'. But I suppose we're lucky we're not in Stalingrad, poor devils. Some of the women in Coventry sent a message of solidarity to the women of Stalingrad and they received a reply. And they have embroidered a tablecloth for them. People have to pay sixpence to have their name embroidered and the money will go to buy medical supplies for them. There is much talk of rebuilding the cathedral when this beastly war is over. It's dreadful to look at those ruins and imagine what a terrible night that must have been. The bishop sounds like a lively character. He's very keen that the new building will be what he calls a "People's Cathedral". He used to be a housemaster in a boys' school, so I bet he's seen a thing or two! You can imagine what those boys got up to in their dormitory each night when they were missing their mothers. I wonder what he would say if he knew about you and me. But Jesus told us to 'Love

132

One Another' and that is what we are doing. I can't
see anything wrong with that even if it's not the usual
way of the world. But I don't want anybody to know,
ever, about those private things we do together.
Please promise me you won't tell those girls on the
boat. Please, I beg you! I worry so much about what
you gossip about when you are tucked up in that little
cabin at night. I know you wouldn't betray me on
purpose, but it is so easy to let things slip out,
especially when you are tired.

I have been rambling on a bit, haven't I? But
I miss you so much and I am hoping your boat will
come to Coventry before too long. I sometimes walk
down to the canal and watch the boats coming in,
and I always look out for you, even though I know
you are probably still very far away.

Write to me again soon and tell me more
about what it is like on the canals.

With all my fondest kisses,

Your loving friend forever, Gloria.

As Jessica finished reading the letter she
wiped a tear from her eye. She did not know if she
was crying for Auntie Joan or for herself. She could
imagine Auntie Joan reading the letter and it brought
back all her pain. Being separated from her lover and
not knowing if they would ever see each other again
must have been unbearable. The pain of separation
was something Jessica could understand all too well.
She had made it clear to Steve that he was not to
contact her until he had made up his mind once and
for all what he wanted. Either his marriage ended or
the affair did. It had been over two months now and
she had heard nothing. How much longer would she
have to wait? Should she assume from his silence

that he had decided to end it with her and had not bothered to tell her? That would be so typical of him, she thought, always retaining the upper hand by keeping her in the dark. She forced her attention back to the letter. Jessica guessed that her aunt must have been delivering cargo between London and other large cities such as Coventry and Birmingham so she would have been in danger from the bombing and rocket attacks. She had obviously survived but what about Gloria? There were no postmarks beyond the end of the war and Jessica began to speculate as to why this might be. The war had ended soon after the postmark on the last letter so perhaps they had stopped writing because they were quickly reunited. Maybe they had been a couple for years afterwards. Jessica could not imagine her aunt keeping a secret like that from Barbara. But neither could she imagine her aunt coming out to her family. A loud rumbling from her stomach interrupted her thoughts, reminding her that she should eat. She looked at her watch - four o'clock already. It was now too late for her to cruise anywhere so she would stay in Hemel Hempstead for one more night at least. She would have plenty of time to read the rest of the letters during the evening. But as she had no fresh food or milk on board she realised that she must visit the shops before she did anything else. She could not remember seeing any shops beside the canal as she had passed through the town but guessed there must be a large supermarket somewhere nearby. It was at times like this that Jessica congratulated herself on her extravagance in buying a mobile phone with Internet connection. She quickly found out what she needed to know; there were two supermarkets located close to one another to the north of the canal. She wondered how Auntie Joan had managed to find out things like the location of the nearest shops when she was travelling on the canals. She surmised that she would have asked other boaters. The wartime boating community would have been just as helpful as modern day boaters and probably even more so. Or perhaps not? She imagined the traditional boat people may not have welcomed these young girls on to the canal in place of the men who had gone away to fight. It would have been as Gloria described as "not the usual way of the world". Jessica paused for a moment to consider what Gloria had meant when she used those words to describe her love for Joan. Perhaps Jessica had read it all wrong and the relationship was not what she thought? It certainly appeared to her that they were having some sort of romantic and probably sexual affair but could there be a more innocent explanation? She guessed that the rest of the letters would make it clear one way or another and resolved to get her shopping done quickly so she could continue with her reading.

Preoccupied with thoughts of Gloria's letter, Jessica plodded along in a daze. She wondered what Gloria had meant when she wrote about "those private things" that she did not want Auntie Joan to share with the girls on the boat. She imagined two young girls kissing and exploring each other's bodies. Seeing the supermarket in front of her, Jessica reluctantly dragged herself away from her daydreams to concentrate on her shopping. The sooner that was done, the sooner she could return to the rest of Gloria's letters. Forgetting the long walk home, she allowed herself to fall into the trap of buying more than she could comfortably carry. On the long trudge back she cursed herself for succumbing to the 'Buy One Get One Free' offers. To make matters worse she was now heading straight into the wind, which must have been behind her on the way up from the boat. It was a great relief to get back aboard "Ragamuffin", her stove greeting her warmly as soon as she opened the door. She hastily unpacked her groceries and returned to her reading.

135

The contents of the next letter removed any remaining doubts as to the nature of Gloria and Joan's relationship.

1st July 1944

My Darling,

It was so good to see you again at the weekend but it seems months ago already. I hardly recognised you when you came to the factory, as you were so filthy and so thin. You looked more like a man than a woman! I don't know how we managed to smuggle you on to the bus and then into the hostel - I was sure we would get caught! Your poor hands were so bruised and rough and your fingernails so broken that I wanted to kiss them and kiss them over and over until they were healed. But after you had washed your hair and had a bath, I could see you are still as beautiful as ever. Your skin is much darker now and it makes your lovely teeth look so white. I hope you enjoyed the dance - it was wonderful that there were so few men that we could be each other's dance partners all night without anybody thinking anything of it. I loved being in your arms again. Wasn't it lucky that Doris was away for the weekend so you could have her bed? But do you know how much I longed to come and snuggle in with you in the middle of the night? Everyone else seemed to be asleep but I could not risk us getting caught. How I wish we could be alone together again! When this beastly war is over.......

I hope your journey back to Limehouse is going well. I expect you will be filthy again by now with all that coal on board. Please be careful - you frightened me with those stories you told me about how close you have come to falling in at the locks. I worry about you having to run along the top planks

136

with nothing to hold on to. Last night I had a terrible dream in which you were drowning and I was not there to save you. I woke up screaming, and woke everybody else in the dormitory. They were not very pleased with me about that.

The girls you are sharing with seem nice but don't let them make you do all the work. I know what you are like - always wanting to look after other people and doing more than your fair share. You should jolly well sit back and let them do it some of the time.

The factory work is so tedious that each shift feels like it lasts a whole week. Doing the same thing all day and every day makes your mind numb and your fingers ache. I can see now that you made a better choice. At least you get different experiences each day and it must be quite snug in your little cabin on the on the barge. Sorry, I mean your narrowboat - I remember how cross you get when I call it a barge! I wish I had been brave enough to come with you, but I just couldn't bear the idea of working outdoors in the winter. Sometimes I think I am going a little bit crazy, thinking about you all the time and wondering where you are and if you are safe. I have made up my mind that I am going to pretend to be ill so I can go back home and meet you when you arrive at Limehouse. I could be there for the whole of your week's leave. What do you think?

I must go now but I will see you again very soon.

With all of my love,

Gloria

Reading the letters, Jessica began to think of Gloria as an old friend and pictures of her were forming in her imagination. She felt as if she knew this girl, somebody she had never even met, even better than she had known her Auntie Joan. Gloria had indeed managed to get back to meet Joan at Limehouse and had written about her great relief when she discovered there had been no further bomb damage in her home street while she had been away in Coventry. But there was also such a a frustrating lack of information in the letters that it was like constructing a jigsaw puzzle with only half the pieces. For example, one letter described Gloria's pain about her father who was "missing in action" and although Jessica looked for further mention of him in subsequent letters she was unable to discover if Gloria's father had been killed or taken prisoner. But although there were still many pieces of the jigsaw missing, one thing was clear - Gloria's tone became more distant and less affectionate towards Joan as the months went by. Jessica speculated about the reasons for this. Did absence really make the heart grow fonder as it seemed to be doing for her, making her want Steve more than ever the longer they were apart? Or was it more a case of out of sight, out of mind, as she suspected it was for Steve? If only Jessica could see the letters that Joan had written she would know if she too had become less infatuated over time and if the relationship had come to a natural end.

No mention had been made of Rob's anger the night before although Zena could tell he was sorry by his gentleness that morning and the unexpected breakfast in bed. As she crunched her toast she wondered idly if she was about to receive another piece of expensive jewellery. They were due back at their marina the following day so Zena had an ample supply of locks to keep her busy. As the weather was awful, with torrential rain and side winds that swept the boat off course, there were few boats on the move. They went alone through both the Stockton and Calcutt flights with no boats coming in the opposite direction. When she finally came back aboard at the top of Calcutt, her waterproofs were dripping and the skin on her fingers was wrinkled and white. As Rob battled with the headwind along the meandering canal towards Braunston, Zena was grateful she was not steering. However she was not able to relax for long as a shout came from the stern deck. At the same moment, the boat leaned over at an alarming angle. "Zena, I need your help - now!" With no time to put on her waterproofs, Zena dashed up the steps to see what the problem was. A boat had slipped its moorings and the wind had blown it across the canal in front of them, forcing The Narrow Escape aground on the mud. Zena quickly but carefully made her way along the gunwale and climbed aboard the offending boat. She knocked on the windows and on the roof, calling out, "Hello there, anybody aboard?" There was no reply and she hurried along the roof to the stern, which was still tied to the bank. On her way, she kicked over a can of beer and its contents ran along the roof after her. There were countless more bottles and cans on the stern deck. Zena was concerned about the state the boat's owner must be in and knocked anxiously at the door, fearing him to be so drunk that he was unconscious and in danger. Still receiving no response, she pulled on the handle but the door was secured firmly. Grabbing the centre rope, she jumped to the bank and started to heave the boat to the side. Another boat had been following close behind them so Zena was soon joined by a burly man who helped

139

her to secure the rope to the sheet piling. She told him she was worried in case the occupant of the boat was unconscious and they peered through the windows until they were satisfied there was nobody aboard. "Probably gone to the pub," muttered her companion. Zena then looked back to see how Rob was getting on with The Narrow Escape. Thanks to his bow thrusters he had succeeded in freeing the boat from the mud and was now pulling into the bank where he could pick Zena up. "Thanks for your help," she shouted to the man as he walked back to where his boat was waiting. As soon as she had spoken, she was filled with dread that Rob might think she had been flirting with him. But he was more concerned about her welfare.

"Well done love," he said as she jumped aboard. "Now go and get yourself dry, quick". Zena did not need telling twice; she was wet through to the skin and her teeth were chattering from the cold. Typically, the rain had stopped by the time she had changed her clothes and she decided to join Rob in the sunshine on the stern deck and admire the beautiful rainbow that spanned the sky to their right. Braunston soon came into view, bringing with it painful memories of the last time they were here. Zena forced these unwelcome visitors from her mind and turned her thoughts instead to how she had met Jessica in this place and what a good listener she had been. Remembering that pleasant lunchtime with her friend, she recalled Jessica's question. "And what do I need? I need a man who will not threaten me with violence," she thought as she watched Rob on the tiller. She wondered what would have happened if Graham had not chosen that moment to call. The approach to the Braunston locks brought a further worry. "I hope there are no boys at these locks to upset Rob again. I could do with some help, but please God let there be some girls around this time."

140

As it happened, there were no other boats going up through the locks so Zena operated them single-handed. Throughout the process she was deep in thought, making no attempt to converse with the few people she met along the way. Sitting astride one of the lock gates, she tried to work out what it was that had brought out this uncharacteristic aggression in her husband. She wondered if it was his ownership the boat that had triggered this change in his character or if it was the result of them spending too much time together. She then considered the possibility that it was her, not Rob, who was behaving differently; perhaps she was inadvertently doing something to make him angry. After the locks were finished, Zena took her place at the bow end of the boat to hide in the comforting seclusion of Braunston Tunnel where she continued to contemplate the state of her marriage. For a while she considered the notion of leaving Rob but was apprehensive about how she would manage without him. She had never been alone, having gone straight from the safety of her parents' home to married life with Rob. She had no experience of working for a living and doubted if she could ever earn enough money to support herself and the boys. Grim reality struck her as she thought of her sons. The bonds of love that tied them to their father were as unyielding as those that would forever bind her to them. She could never leave Rob - losing her sons was too great a price to pay. Somehow she would have to make the marriage work. "But how can I stay married to a man who scares me?" she said to the black walls of the tunnel. Zena had still found no answer to this question when they emerged into dazzling daylight, and she sighed as she prepared herself for the Buckby locks.

Chapter 10

"We've got to live, no matter how many skies have fallen." D.H. Lawrence (Lady Chatterley's Lover)

Jessica had read and re-read Gloria's letters to Auntie Joan until late in the night so it was inevitable that her dreams were dominated by scenes from wartime Britain. Throughout the night incendiary bombs exploded around her, setting the world alight. Flames leapt high into the sky, with the dome of St Paul's cathedral encircled by a ring of fire. She saw boats ablaze and heard the screams of boaters leaping from the real flames into their burning reflections. Noisy munitions factories gave way in her dreams to crowded underground stations where women and children were crushed in the stampede to the exit. She saw the silhouette of a broken skyline amongst the pinkish glow of smoke clouds and the remains of Coventry cathedral reaching up to touch the Luftwaffe like fingers stroking a giant eagle. Then she watched, unable to move, as a massive barrage balloon exploded above her head and dropped down to smother her. She woke to find herself curled in a ball at the foot of her bed and it was not a barrage balloon that was suffocating her but her own quilt. She sat up, feeling far from refreshed, and the rain drumming on the roof of the boat did little to lighten her mood. Peering through a gap in the curtains, she saw the grey surface of the canal shattered like a broken mirror by the wind and the rain. She fell back into bed, pulling the duvet close around her for comfort. She spent the next couple of hours drifting in and out of sleep with the memories of Gloria's letters mingling with her dreams until she no longer knew what was real and what was imagined. She reached out for the bundle of letters and reread the final one. Its opening sentences were so cold and formal that it seemed hardly possible for this letter to have been written by the same person who sent those early lovesick messages. Jessica guessed that it must have been a very difficult letter to write.

16th April 1945

Dear Joan,

I hope this letter finds you well. This will be the last time you hear from me and I would appreciate it if you do not try to contact me at any point now or in the future. When I got your last letter, I was so shocked and surprised that you could write such mean things. I wanted to tear it up and never speak to you again. But I don't want us to part on such bad terms so I am writing to try to explain and I hope you will understand that it was never my intention to hurt you.

When you went to work on the canals, I promised I would wait for you, and I really did mean it. But you were the one who broke everything, not me. It was you who betrayed me first, telling those stupid girls about the things we did. Perhaps you didn't mean any harm, but the way they put their heads together and giggled when I came to you at Limehouse was just horrible. I couldn't stand it, even though you just laughed and shrugged it off. You didn't care how much it hurt me.

After that, I started to feel as if everybody was staring at us, and they probably were, because you told me about how quickly gossip spreads along the canals. I even felt it when I went down to the basin at Coventry - the old men and women were staring at me and whispering, as if they knew that I was the one they had heard about. *Why couldn't you keep our secret?* If only you had done that simple thing we could have waited until the war was over and then gone away together like we planned. I would have believed that everything would be all right if we pretended that we were sisters, like you said we would. But after the remarks those girls made I began to worry more and more about what other people would say if they found out the truth about us. I know I would go out of my mind if we had to live with ugly looks and remarks from everybody around us.

You are always saying that we should follow our dreams, but what if we have different dreams that are taking us to different places? You may not care if people give us strange looks, but I do. My dream is to fit in with society, not to be excluded from it. And although I have no desire to be with a man, I believe that I may want to have a baby when this war is over. And that is why, when I met a young man who was kind and considerate, I started walking out with him. It happened by accident - I was not looking for him but when I cut my hand in the factory he was the one who helped me and things just developed from there. I don't love him but I hope that one day I will. I don't know what the future has in store for us but Walter is the sort of man who would make a perfect husband - when you don't have a lot of money, the prospect of marrying a doctor is very inviting.

You and I were really only children when we met and we were playing a sort of game. I did love you, and perhaps I still do, but the game has to end now. I want to be a grown-up with a man to look after me and children to raise. And I want to be respected by my family and neighbours. So that is my *dream and I cannot follow yours. I am sorry to hurt you and I will always remember you with fondness.*

Yours affectionately,

Gloria.

Zena was in desperate need of something to occupy herself and was overjoyed when the school phoned to ask her to work again. She was further flattered when the deputy headteacher offered her some extra hours to cover for an exam invigilator who was ill. The following week she was sent on a first aid course, after which she took responsibility for all the youngsters who had hurt themselves on the playground at lunchtime. One day, when one of the teachers asked her if she had ever been a nurse, Zena laughed with delighted surprise. "It's just you seem to be a natural nurse," the teacher went on. "You stay so calm, even when there's all that blood, and you don't get agitated when they are screaming or crying. It's a gift you have. I know I would be absolutely useless at it."

This simple remark was the catalyst that jolted Zena into action; whatever Rob may think, she knew it was time for her to consider again a career in nursing. The following day she searched on the Internet to find out what it would involve and was excited to confirm what she had suspected - that she already had all the qualifications that were needed. There was an online personality quiz to find out which branch of nursing would be most suitable and Zena could not resist having a go at it. Her decision was already made when the results of the quiz indicated that she would be suitable for any of the four specialisms of nursing and she ferreted out further information about suitable courses at nearby colleges. She learnt that if she wanted to start a course in September her application should ideally have been made already but she may still be considered if she applied by the end of June. "But that's less than three weeks away! I need to get my act together quickly," she gasped. Without wasting another minute she set about making her application and when she had finished she revelled in the realisation that she had made a decision on her own. Normally the only decisions that she made without consulting Rob were about food, home furnishings and clothes. Full of new determination, she promised herself that she would see it through, although she had no idea how she was going to tell Rob what she had done.

Jessica continued her journey northwards from Hemel Hempstead in mostly good weather and as the residential landscape gave way to fields and woodland she remembered why she had chosen this way of life. There was so much to see and, best of all, there was time to reflect on those sights. For example, she studied the clever way a mallard washed himself. First he dived forward so that his front half was submerged. After that he flapped his wings vigorously and dipped the rear half of his body under the water. He continued to use his wings to splash water over himself for a while and then jumped out on to the bank to preen his feathers, fastidiously drawing each one through his beak until he was satisfied.

In the fields beside the canal, the lambs had grown nearly as big as their mothers and she wondered how long it would be before they were slaughtered. Jessica had often considered becoming a vegetarian but had never managed to last more than a month without eating meat. Watching the sheep follow each other across the fields and over an adjoining bridge, she was reminded that they were indeed quite stupid animals, which made her feel less guilty about her taste for roast lamb. Her attention was caught by a streak of colour shooting over the surface of the water and she identified the yellow wagtail immediately. She laughed at a pair of moorhens scrapping like adolescent boys and wondered where the female was that had aroused this display of aggression. "Do moorhens have testosterone?" she wondered.

The many locks leading to the summit at Cowroast were well spaced out and Jessica had help at most of these as there were plenty of boats around. She enjoyed meeting a variety of people and was once again conscious of the neighbourliness of other boaters. Some were on holiday so their cheery disposition was to be expected. But she also met continuous cruisers, people who lived on their boats full time and had a wealth of experience that they were only to happy to share. When Jessica stocked up on provisions at a supermarket at Berkhamstead, she noticed the stark contrast with those living their lives away from the canal. She felt sorry for her fellow shoppers who were generally in such a hurry that they were impatient and rude. While observing a particularly harassed mother moaning and nagging at her trio of lively children she was overcome by a compelling desire to interfere. She succeeded in keeping quiet, despite the compelling temptation to give this atrocious woman some advice about her parenting skills. As she wandered back to her boat she thought about her gentle friend Zena and imagined how different she would be when shopping with her sons; she was sure Zena would have actively involved her boys in the expedition, consulting them about which products to buy and asking them to lift items off the shelves and put them into the trolley. Zena had told Jessica how she missed her sons so dreadfully when they were at school and how she savoured every moment of their time at home. Thinking of Zena, Jessica realised that she was now close enough to Aylesbury to phone her and arrange a time for them to meet up. Zena answered at once and it was her suggestion that they meet for coffee in Aylesbury on the following Saturday as she was in school on most weekdays. Jessica was delighted to discover how Zena's job was expanding. "They must think very highly of her. All she needs to do now is to get away from that awful husband of hers."

Early the following morning while she cruised along the Grand Union, Jessica reflected on the content of Gloria's letters. She tried to imagine how Auntie Joan must have felt when she had read that last letter. From what had been written it was obvious that something must have happened to make Joan write "such mean things" in the letter to which Gloria was replying. Perhaps she had found out that Gloria had been seen in the company of a man? Or perhaps Gloria had written to her to tell her about Walter? Jessica really wished she could see the letter her aunt had written; it was so frustrating having to rely on guesswork. Making sense of it all was like trying to see the surface of the water through the silver mist that was hanging over the canal. Jessica had begun to like Gloria and was disappointed to discover such a weakness of character in her. Her real sympathy lay with her aunt. She had never married so it could be assumed that she had remained true to who she was. Jessica wondered if she had

148

ever met another woman or if Gloria had been her one and only love. When Auntie Joan had told her with such intense urgency to follow her dreams, was it Jessica she was thinking of or was she still remembering Gloria? She recalled that last conversation when Auntie Joan had told her she was waiting for her to find Mr Right. That had been the perfect opportunity for Jessica to confide in her about Steve and she had thrown it away. She would love to hear Auntie Joan's answer to the question she wanted to put to her: "Is it always wrong to have an affair with a married man or are there times when it can be justified?" She remembered having a lengthy discussion with her aunt on the topic of telling lies. Her aunt had taken the view that sometimes you have to tell little white lies to stop other people being hurt. "It all depends on the reason for the lie," was what she had said. Jessica doubted very much if Auntie Joan would have said, "It all depends on the reason for the affair". Although Jessica would have loved to have her aunt's approval, she knew deep down that Joan would undoubtedly have advised her to end it. "So much for following your dreams, Auntie Joan," she muttered. "If you can't follow your dreams without hurting other people."

Rob could not help being aware that Zena was frightened of him. He knew that she was resentful and unhappy and that he was the one to blame for her misery. He should have done more to put things right between them after his awful behaviour at Braunston. He had made himself a promise that he would be a better husband and he really had tried his hardest. Although Zena had led him to believe she would be in school only occasionally, right from the beginning she had volunteered to help in the classrooms and she was there nearly every day. His evening meals were now much more basic and unimaginative and his shirts

149

were not as pristine as they used to be. He had not complained but had taken an interest in what she was doing and had told her how proud of her he was. They had been steadily growing closer, he thought, until that stupid moment in Long Itchington when he had again allowed himself to be taken over by jealousy. He wondered why he should be filled with such uncontrollable rage whenever he saw Zena in the company of other men. He had no reason to believe that she had ever been unfaithful to him or that she ever would. Although he accepted that she could have anybody she wanted, he knew her too well to believe she was capable of betraying him. If she were ever to have an affair, she would be unable to hide it and would have to confess immediately. But then the marriage would be over. The explanation for his jealousy suddenly hit him - he was afraid of losing her. But ironically he was more likely to lose her as a result of his jealous behaviour. There was a new coldness in her eyes when she looked at him these days and she had stopped pretending to enjoy their sex life. He wondered if she had always pretended - perhaps he had never given her the intense pleasure that her cries and moans had suggested. Now her work at the school was bringing her into contact with new people and providing greater opportunities for infidelity. If he were not careful, it would be only a matter of time before somebody came along and stole her from him. He set about planning how he could make her love and trust him again. Rob always enjoyed a challenge and he was used to being on the winning side; he had every confidence in his ability to succeed in this matter just as he always did in business. Expensive jewellery was not going to be enough; he had to think of something better, something that she would find totally irresistible. Knowing how much she missed the boys, he came up with an idea that would certainly keep her away from all temptation.

However, he had to plan carefully when and how to broach the subject. He might need a period of uninterrupted time to talk her into the idea so it would be best done when they were on the boat. He set about the business of extricating himself from some of his commitments in order to take a few days off work at the earliest opportunity.

At Bulbourne, Jessica moored up for a couple of days to enjoy the reservoir and old canal architecture and to pass some time before meeting Zena in Aylesbury. On the Thursday afternoon she ventured down the Aylesbury Arm, a little used canal of delightful tranquility. In places the canal was so overgrown that she could see no water at all and it was as if she was travelling through a sea of reeds. Here Jessica spotted her first kingfisher and although she glimpsed the electric blue streak for only the briefest moment, the feeling of elation remained with her for hours afterwards. It dawned on her that she was not taking enough advantage of this great opportunity to watch bird life as she was always on the move. Her boat was in fact a perfect bird hide and if she allowed herself to stay still for long enough she would no doubt see many more wonders.

So the following morning, whilst moored in a particularly remote spot, Jessica opened her bedroom curtains and just waited to see what appeared. Just as she was thinking that she could not wait any longer for her breakfast, she spotted a heron in the field opposite. Jessica had seen many herons along the way, standing stock still at the water's edge and taking off with great flapping wings as her boat grew close. But this heron was totally different. It

151

moved through the field more like a cat stalking a harvest mouse, keeping a low profile to avoid being seen from the water. Then it struck, so fast that its prey did not stand a chance. The bird was only a couple of metres from Jessica and she watched entranced as the fish was swallowed, seeing its shape sliding down the heron's long gullet.

As Jessica moored in the crowded basin in the centre of Aylesbury her phone rang. It was Michael, hoping to meet up with her for a short visit that weekend. When she told him where she was, he suggested driving over there the following day. Jessica explained that she was meeting a friend for coffee in the morning but would love to see him at lunchtime or in the afternoon. "As long as it's not too far for you to drive for such a short visit?" she enquired tentatively.

"No, not at all. It's perfect, will only take about an hour. Don't worry about a boat trip. Let's just go and have lunch somewhere. I'll have to get back in time for the evening anyway." Jessica was relieved. Being alone on the boat with him might have been difficult and having just a short time together on this occasion would give them a chance to get over any awkwardness and make a fresh start. She guessed that Michael had been feeling much the same and had probably invented the excuse about getting back early. She wondered if it had crossed his mind that the friend she was meeting for coffee did not really exist. She considered introducing him to Zena so she could prove that she had been telling the truth. "Come to think of it, introducing him to Zena might not be such a bad idea. Michael would find her irresistible and having an affair would do her the world of good," she thought. "And it is just what Rob deserves."

Jessica arrived early at the coffee house suggested by Zena and selected a table near the back where the two of them would be able to talk quite privately. She was keen to hear how Zena was enjoying her job and if she had changed at all as a result of it. She found it difficult to imagine somebody reaching her age and never having been employed since she had left school - that first step must have been quite daunting. Jessica was pleased to have been such a positive influence; she doubted if Zena would ever have thought about her own needs without her prompting. She intended to help Zena work out what her dreams were and then encourage her to follow them. Auntie Joan had done that for her and it was only right that she should do the same for somebody else. Her reveries were interrupted by Zena's voice. "Hello Jessica. This is so lovely." The two girls hugged and sank down on the seat opposite each other. For the next forty minutes they were deep in animated conversation. Zena wanted to know all about Jessica's journey and insisted on seeing all her photos. Then she told Jessica about her job and the interesting people she had had met there. She was shocked by Jessica's question, "Any fit guys working at the school?"

"Jessica, I'm married!" she scolded haughtily.

"Doesn't stop you looking though, does it?"

"No, but that's all I would do. Rob may have cheated on me but I could never do that."

Intrigued, Jessica prompted Zena for more information and listened patiently while she told her all about her suspicions at Stratford and before that when the boys were little. Jessica was not at all surprised to hear that Rob had been unfaithful to

153

Zena but could not comprehend how her friend could tolerate it so easily. She was definitely going to introduce her to Michael now, however much she may protest that she could never cheat on Rob. Zena's next statement took her totally by surprise. "Actually, Rob and I may be splitting up. I've applied to university to do a degree in children's nursing."

Jessica gazed at her friend in astonishment and concern, worried that Zena may be moving too impetuously in pursuit of her dreams. It was a big jump from lunchtime supervisor to nurse. Then, remembering how she had felt when her mother had criticised her for being too impulsive in her decision to leave teaching, she resolved to give Zena her support and encouragement. "So when do you start?" she enquired.

"In September - if I'm accepted. I could have applied for either full or part-time study, but having wasted so much time since I left school, I decided to opt for the full-time course. The interview went very well so I'm quite optimistic."

"And when will you know if you have been accepted?"

"Any day now. I just have to keep checking online."

Jessica held up her crossed fingers and wished her luck. "I haven't told Rob yet," continued Zena. "I thought I would wait until I know if I've got a place first."

"And what do you think he will say?" Jessica was anxious, imagining Rob's hostility towards the idea.

154

"Well, he won't be pleased, that's for sure. To be honest, I'm a bit scared of telling him."

Zena went on to describe to Jessica the events of that night at Braunston and how she had been afraid of Rob ever since. Jessica was horrified. "So why do you stay with him?"

"Because up until then he had always been such a good husband. He says he's sorry for what happened and he will never hurt me again." Jessica was sceptical. She pointed out to Zena how Rob controlled her, how he would not let her see the boys during term-time, how she had to persuade him to let her go out to work and how he had been unfaithful to her. "But I love him," came the hoarse whisper as Zena fled to the Ladies. While she was gone, Jessica was hit by a horrifying realisation. There were undeniable similarities between the conversation she had just had with Zena and the one between herself and Karen when they had discussed Steve. Even worse, the picture she had just painted of Rob could very easily have been Steve. He too was quite controlling and he had been unfaithful to his wife. Although she had never experienced aggression from him, she could not be sure that he had never hit Ali. She knew they regularly had fights but she had only ever heard his version of them. Now that she was far enough away from the situation, it occurred to Jessica that Steve was so angry with Ali that he was more than capable of domestic violence. "But he would not hurt me," she told herself. "It's only because of the way Ali is."

When a more composed Zena returned from the Ladies with her make-up refreshed, Jessica apologised for upsetting her and explained that she needed to walk back to the boat soon because Michael was meeting her there. Zena was curious

155

about Michael and Jessica assured her that he was just a friend of a friend. As they walked, Jessica asked about the nursing course Zena had applied for and was surprised to discover that her first choice was in Oxford. "Not that university, the other one," laughed Zena. "I don't think my A Level grades are quite up to Oxbridge standards. I've put that as my first choice because I am still hoping to make it work with Rob. I could commute there from home."

"So, what will you do if Rob says no?"

"I don't know. I've still got to work it all out. I haven't been accepted yet, don't forget." Zena went on to explain about how worried she was about coping on her own and having to get to grips with things like bank accounts and insurance policies, things she had always left to Rob. She was also worried about moving to a new place where she didn't know anybody and Jessica told her about Karen and Jack.

"You must meet them. They are lovely and they know lots of people in Oxford who they could introduce you to. And now you're going to meet Michael and he lives there too."

Michael was apprehensive about seeing Jessica again. Although he wanted to put the past behind them and start again, he wondered if he was being realistic in thinking he could settle for a platonic relationship. He had found himself so strongly drawn to Jessica at their first meeting and had been devastated when he messed everything up in such a spectacular fashion. It was not as if he

156

hadn't been warned; Karen had already told him before he met Jessica that she had been hurt very badly and may not be ready for another relationship yet. "You'll need to be patient Michael," she had said. "She's the sweetest girl who has made a stupid mistake. What she needs is somebody just like you - but she may not realise it yet." That was why he had been so surprised when Jessica agreed that he could stay for the night. Without stopping to think he had interpreted it as an invitation to sleep with her. He should have known better.

As Michael approached Ragamuffin, tucked away in the corner of the basin, he noticed somebody sitting on the front deck with Jessica. "So she really was meeting a friend for coffee," he thought as Jessica spotted him and waved. Jessica climbed off the boat and walked to meet him.

"You're right on time," she said. "Zena is still here, I hope you don't mind."

"No of course not - she can join us for lunch if you like." Jessica gave him a quizzical look. Was he just being polite or was he trying to avoid being on his own with her? Zena could not stay for very long but she went to the restaurant with them and ordered just a starter. As they sat together at one of the tables in the garden, Michael noted how unlike one another these two girls were. What he liked about Jessica was how unaffected she was - no make-up or false nails, simple clothes that accentuated her natural beauty and sensible shoes that meant she could walk at his speed. Zena, on the other hand, was stunningly beautiful and although he did not usually go for "girlie girls" he found those eyes of hers quite mesmerising. He was pleased to have her company; there was something very calming about her presence that made it so much easier to talk to Jessica as if nothing untoward had ever happened between them. When Jessica told him that Zena was hoping to do a nursing degree, he was not surprised. "You do remind me of a nurse," he said. "I can see you being very good in an emergency." Zena gave him a warm smile.

"Oh thank you, Michael. Somebody else told me that as well. But I haven't been accepted on the course yet."

"So, where are you hoping to go?"

"Oxford."

"Oh really? That's a coincidence. I don't know if Jessica told you that's where I live. Take my number in case you need anything or want to meet up sometime," he offered quickly, handing her one of his business cards.

Jessica observed smugly how quickly Michael and Zena had relaxed in each other's company and congratulated herself on how well her little plan was working out. She noticed the slight blush on Zena's cheeks and the way she eagerly took Michael's card. It seemed that Michael could hardly take his eyes off her, even when he bent down to pick up the fork she had dropped on the floor. Jessica could think of nobody who was more unlike Rob than Michael; he was self-effacing and sincere and when he asked a question you could tell that he genuinely wanted to hear the answer. She understood completely why Karen had introduced her to him. He was just the medicine a girl needed after being hurt - an uncomplicated and honest man to gently kiss away all the pain.

After Zena had left, Jessica and Michael talked easily like old friends and Jessica felt a sense of peace. She told him all about her childhood holidays with Auntie Joan and how much she missed her. Although she wanted to tell him about Gloria's letters, she felt that would be a betrayal to her aunt. After all, she hardly knew him and it was too soon to share a family secret like that. However, Michael did not seem to have the same qualms when he described his grandmother who was evidently a very important person in his life. "She told me that she had once had a very special relationship with another girl, somebody called Joan, while she was working in a factory in Coventry during the war. She never disclosed any specific details but I definitely got the impression that they had been lovers in every sense of the word. Apparently the affair ended and she settled down with my grandfather."

Jessica concluded this must all be too much of a coincidence. "He wasn't a doctor by any chance, was he?"

"No, why do you ask?"

"Oh, never mind. It was just that your grandmother reminds me of somebody I know who was in Coventry during the war. Somebody who married a doctor," she responded casually.

"Well, Grandad was a baker, not a doctor. And he used to make the most delicious cakes. Speaking of which, would you like a dessert?"

159

"She had borne so long this cruelty of belonging to him and not being claimed by him." D.H. Lawrence (Sons and Lovers)

Back on the main branch of the Grand Union Jessica passed between Leighton Buzzard and Lindslade, where she found herself amongst a multitude of brightly coloured hire boats. She reprimanded herself for laughing at the poor steering skills of some of the novices who had just collected their hire boats. "We all have to start somewhere. I was probably no better than that when I first started. I must learn to be more tolerant," she thought. Beyond Linslade, as the navigation meandered to follow the contours of the countryside, Jessica could see the River Ouzel running along beside the canal. While she negotiated the tight bends, trying to keep on the deeper side to avoid going aground in the shallows, Jessica's mind went back to Auntie Joan's stories of how her boat used to regularly get stuck on the mud. Since Joan and her crewmates were always working two boats together, the motor-boat and its butty, it must have been near impossible to avoid going aground on these bends. She tried to imagine Joan, standing on the roof of the cabin, heaving on the long wooden shaft to push the boat out into deeper water. This must have been particularly difficult in the rain and she wondered if Auntie Joan's boots had ever slipped on the wet roof and sent her sprawling into the water below.

Jessica eventually left the meandering stretch of canal and reached the three locks at Soulbury where she had to wait for a boat that was turning around in the winding hole. Seeing the tables in the garden of the pub beside the third lock and inhaling the enticing aroma of fried food, Jessica decided it was time for the luxury of a pub lunch. Even this early in the year the garden was full of families enjoying the sunshine and the atmosphere. The speed of the cars on the busy road running beside the pub was an unwelcome reminder that not everybody was able to travel along at a leisurely pace and Jessica once again said a silent thank you to Auntie Joan for giving her this opportunity. There were a number of dogs in the garden and it amused Jessica to watch the owners trying to keep these lively creatures away from each other. One particularly handsome dog caught her eye and she went across to stroke it. It was a German Shepherd called Oscar and Jessica chatted for a while with the owners of the dog who were out for a day's walking. "Does he ever jump into the water?" she asked.

"He hasn't so far but it often looks like he is going to fall in when he goes after the ducks," laughed the woman as she tried to stop the dog from licking Jessica's face.

When she was once again on her way, Jessica considered the possibility of getting a dog herself. She knew that having a dog would make it difficult to leave the boat and go off for a few days to visit her parents or friends but she would certainly enjoy having a furry companion. And she would feel much safer when she moored up at night if she had a dog like Oscar on board. But she would need either a much smaller dog or a bigger boat - a German Shepherd like the one she had just seen would take up far too much of her space. She could hear her mother's voice telling her how impulsive she was and reminded herself that getting a dog was too big a decision to make on the spur of the moment. She put it out of her mind as she travelled on towards Milton Keynes. She planned to stop at Fenny Stratford, which was close to Bletchley Park, the home of the famous code-breakers in World War Two. She remembered her Auntie Joan telling her about this place and decided it was one she must visit.

It was already warm by the time Jessica set off on her walk to Bletchley Park the following morning. The two miles from the canal at Fenny Stratford to Bletchley seemed to last for ever and Jessica was relieved when she caught sight of the railway station which she knew was quite close to the museum. She was hot and breathless so she stopped to buy herself a cold drink in the small shop in the station. On her way out of the shop she noticed some teachers trying to control a sizeable crowd of children who had just got off a train. A young boy with ginger hair and a cheeky freckled face was arguing with one of the adults who was preventing him from going to buy a drink from the station shop. Seeing this school party, Jessica's first instinct was to turn around and walk in the opposite direction but, wanting the fun of watching other teachers at work in a situation where she had none of the responsibility, she followed behind them as they set off along the road to Bletchley Park. Jessica thought that the children must be aged about eight, which would put them in Year Three or Year Four at school. The teachers arranged themselves so that two adults were at the front of the group, two were bringing up the rear and the rest were spaced out between them. This arrangement should have been enough to keep the children safe but Jessica spotted one of the group as he broke free from the rest. Beside the pavement was a patch of land with horse chestnut trees and various saplings growing amongst the long grass and wild flowers. It was here that the child was hiding behind one of the bushes as the adults at the rear of the group walked past. Jessica tried to call out a warning to them but they were so deep in conversation that her shouts went unheeded. Approaching the spot where the child had evaporated into the long grass, Jessica detected a slight movement in the cow parsley. She stopped and waited, not wanting to find herself accused of abduction but anxious to make sure the child was safe. After a while she noticed the cow parsley on the move again as the child doubled back towards the station. She followed slowly behind until she saw the boy emerge from his hiding place and dart behind a tree trunk, where he stood watching until the school party had disappeared from view. Jessica recognised him immediately as the little boy who had been arguing at the station and this gave her an idea. As his eyes met hers she held out the bottle of orange drink she had just bought. The boy looked surprised and wary but when she smiled at him he stepped forward and took the proffered bottle. As he drank, Jessica told him he should hurry up and join the school party before they missed him and he got into trouble. "I don't want to go to a stupid museum, it's boring," he said.

"Well, I'm going there and I do hope it won't be boring. What are you going to do instead?"

"Shopping," he replied.

"Have you got any money?" Jessica asked and he held out a shiny two-pound coin. "Well, that's not going to last very long and there aren't any good shops around here anyway. There's a really good one in the museum that sells lots of things you would like. Why don't you come there with me now?" Jessica held out her hand and to her great astonishment the boy took it and allowed her to lead him towards Bletchley Park. Going through the large security gates at the entrance to the museum, Jessica could see the school party and hear the panic in the teacher's voice. "That's only thirty three - there's somebody missing. Children, can you see who is missing?"

"It's all right, he's here," called Jessica. "He decided he would rather go shopping." The teacher gave Jessica a big smile and thanked her for bringing him to them before turning her attention to the boy. "Ricky, what did we tell you? You must stay with the group and not wander off - it could be dangerous." Jessica smiled wryly. How typical that it was another Ricky. And yet this Ricky had readily responded to her request that they should go to the museum. She wondered if it was because he was a less challenging child or if it was because he did not know she was a teacher. Or perhaps she had changed? Perhaps she was now the sort of person with whom even her Ricky would have cooperated.

Throughout her visit to Bletchley Park Jessica kept bumping into this school party, which had been split into four smaller groups. She found herself observing the children more than she was looking at the exhibits and was delighted to see how much they were enjoying themselves. She was not surprised to see that the display of old toys was especially popular with the girls while the boys seemed generally more excited about the old vehicles. On one occasion she caught sight of Ricky who was looking rather rebellious as one of the teachers was trying to stop him running off. He saw her and gave a little smile so she went across to talk to him and his teacher. "Hello Ricky," she said. "Have you seen anything that you like?"

"No it's all boring," he muttered. The teacher looked at Jessica suspiciously.

"How do you know his name?"

"I heard your colleague call him that when I brought him back."

"Oh, you're the one who found him. Sorry I didn't realise. We just have to be careful about letting them talk to adults we don't know, you see."

"I understand. I'm a teacher too," explained Jessica. Suddenly aware of her mistake, she corrected herself. "Or at least I used to be."

"Well please feel free to come along with us, if you like. I could do with some help keeping Ricky in line. I wouldn't normally invite a complete stranger to join us, but since you brought him back, I guess we can trust you! We are off to a talk now about evacuees in the war." Jessica did not need to be asked twice and on the way to the hut where they were due to have the talk, she found out a little more about the teacher who had invited her to join them. He was called Chris and was newly qualified. Jessica could not help noticing that he was very fit; his bright blue eyes shone with enthusiasm as he spoke and his well-toned body suggested the track suit and trainers that he was wearing were regularly put to good use. He was softly spoken and had a calmness about him that immediately put Jessica at ease.

During lunchtime, she found herself surrounded by a group of girls, all curious to find out more about their new helper. When she told them that she lived on a boat their eyes opened wide with disbelief. They all wanted to come and visit her but Jessica knew that was inappropriate and quickly put them off, explaining that there would not be room for them all. Later, when it was time for the group to return to the station, Jessica walked with them, keeping a close eye on Ricky to make sure he did not wander off again. He was keen to show her the things he had bought in the shop. There was a tea towel and mug for his mum, a key ring for his dad, a painted tin for his sister, a shirt for his big brother, and a pack of cards, rubber and pen for himself. Sceptical about how far two pounds would go, Jessica calculated that shoplifting must have accounted for a significant part of his hoard. She said nothing about it, thankful that it was not her responsibility. When it was time for the school party to board their train, Jessica was thanked by the teacher in charge, a plump middle-aged woman called Kate. "Thank you for all your help today."

"I should be thanking you. I've really enjoyed it."

"You know what? We are always looking for volunteer helpers in the classroom if you could spare us any time. Here's the phone number of the school if you'd like to call the Head and speak to her." Since the school was located not too far from the canal in Milton Keynes, Jessica promised that she would see them all again very soon.

Back on Ragamuffin, Jessica thought about all she had seen at the museum. She was upset by one thing she had learnt there. The great mathematician Alan Turing, whose brilliance and hard work in developing improved methods for breaking German codes had saved probably thousands of lives and shortened the war by at least two years, had been later prosecuted for homosexuality. Convicted of criminal behaviour in 1952, he had allowed himself to be chemically castrated rather than being sent to prison. He died of cyanide poisoning just two years later at the age of forty one. Jessica was appalled by this revelation and it made her regard Auntie Joan's relationship with Gloria in a different light. She wondered if lesbianism was also illegal at that time

166

or if the law applied simply to male homosexuality. "Either way," Jessica thought, "I judged Gloria too harshly. If society in those days was that narrow-minded, it is no wonder she was so afraid to be discovered as gay." Jessica then imagined the thousands of people, mostly women, working in great secrecy at Bletchley Park to break the German codes. She wondered if their lives had been any easier than Auntie Joan's and Gloria's had been. She wished she could remember more about what her aunt had told her about her wartime experiences. It was so long ago when Jessica was only a little girl that Auntie Joan had told her about her time on the canals. She had probably spared her many of the details on account of her age. If only Jessica had asked her more questions when she was older. There was so much she wanted to know and now it was too late. Joan would have been a girl of eighteen - younger than Jessica was now. What must it have been like for her to work in such hard and dangerous conditions? She thought again about that last letter written by Gloria to Joan. She would never know if her aunt had found somebody else or if she had spent the rest of her days living in loneliness. If Joan had been unable to follow her own dreams it would explain why she was especially keen for Jessica to follow hers. "But first," thought Jessica. "I have to know what those dreams are." She felt so alone and confused and was overcome with an overpowering need to speak to Steve. They had an agreement that she would never phone him in case Ali was within earshot but he would call her back if she sent him a text. She had done so well in resisting temptation up until now. It had been a major achievement to have actually been in London and resisted the impulse to text him to meet up with her, she thought. But the further away from London she travelled, the more it felt like she was leaving him all over again. A short conversation on the phone wouldn't hurt anybody, she reasoned. The text was very short. "Missing you. Call me if you'd like to talk xxxxx."

Jessica telephoned the school the next day and arranged to go for a visit at the start of the following week. It then dawned on her that none of her clothes or shoes were suitable for school wear so she stopped off near the centre of Milton Keynes to buy herself some black trousers, a couple of shirts and some shoes. She was afraid she would get lost in the massive shopping centre and the story of Jonah and the Whale came into her mind - she felt as if she too had been swallowed up. It was like a huge indoor town and Jessica was puzzled by the effect it had upon her. Although she was used to living in the tiny space of her narrowboat, this cavernous vastness was strangely claustrophobic and her initial instinct was to escape outside. However once she had become accustomed to the echoing noise of hundreds of voices and the harsh clip-clopping of heels on the hard surface beneath her feet, she began to relax. It had been such a long time since she had wandered around shops like this and the novelty was really quite enjoyable. She hunted down some good bargains and silenced the voice inside her that reminded her she should not be spending money on clothes that would be of no use on the boat. Her purchases complete, she strolled back through the park to the canal, wondering what the school would be like and hoping she could find a secure mooring spot not too far away.

The canal circled around the edge of the town and Jessica found its monotony rather tedious. Although there were plenty of green parks and tree-lined paths, the housing estates all looked much the same and she welcomed the return of countryside on the northern outskirts. Here she moored for the night and in the morning she enjoyed the freedom of a long walk across open fields to the River Great Ouse. She then cruised further along the canal to the village of New Bradwell where she found rows of old Victorian terraced houses looking so out of place among their modern surroundings; it was like finding a couple of old Dickens' characters hidden amongst a crowd of teenagers on prom night. She pictured what it must have been like in this spot when Auntie Joan had travelled this way, long before the new town of Milton Keynes was built. The canal would have been full of working boats and the iron railway bridges would have resounded with the clattering of steam trains.

Jessica dreaded the prospect of another full day on her own before her visit to the school. Still there was no reply from Steve and she could bear this silence no longer. If he wanted her, she thought, he must tell her. If he did not want her, it was too cruel of him to keep her in ignorance any longer. She knew she had to keep herself busy or she would lose all her self-respect and send him a second text. She phoned her parents and invited them to come and visit her for the day. It was short notice but as they had nothing else planned they were only too delighted to be invited. They arrived quite early the following morning as the roads were quiet and their journey easy. Bob, Jessica's father, found the stretch of canal around Wolverton particularly fascinating with its railway bridges and a large black and white mural of a train. Jessica had been told this mural was supposed to represent the past, present and future of the town of Wolverton. She teased Bob about his love of trains which she argued was in conflict with her love of the canals, for it was the coming of the railways that had brought an end to the prosperity of the working boats. Beyond Wolverton, they passed over the old iron aqueduct that carried the canal high over the Ouse valley. As they neared the point where the aqueduct crossed the river, Bob left the boat to walk along the towpath and take photographs. Barbara, on the side of boat away from the towpath, was terrified as she looked down at the long drop below. "Be careful, Jessica," she said. "Mind you don't steer over the edge." Jessica reassured her that it would be impossible to do that even if she tried and they soon crossed the river and continued towards the lock at Cosgrove. Jessica, steering the boat slowly and carefully past all the moored boats, took advantage of the opportunity to talk to Barbara about Auntie Joan.

"I could see what you meant about Auntie Joan's letters telling a very sad story," she said.

"Yes, it was so sad and what a shame that she never had children of her own. She was a natural with kiddies, as you know."

"Yes she certainly was. But do you know if she had any other relationships after Gloria?"

"Not for sure, but I think she probably did. When I was sorting through her photographs, I found a few snaps of her and another girl. I've brought them for you to look at. They're on your bed. There's also an old diary of Joan's that I thought you would like to see."

"Thanks Mum. Those will be really interesting."

Jessica moored Ragamuffin at the end of the aqueduct, and although she had given her father clear instructions for how to operate the lock she was a little apprehensive as she watched him winding up the paddles. It was a relief when a boat came up behind them, bringing help and advice from an experienced boater. Watching her father nattering away to the man from the other boat, she thought how good it would be for him to have a proper boating holiday and she mentioned this to Barbara. To her surprise, her mother was in full agreement and said that next time Jessica invited them to visit, they would bring a suitcase and stay a few days. "We used to go camping before you were born, you know," she told Jessica. "I am capable of living without my home comforts."

They stopped in the pretty village of Cosgrove, where they discovered an old horse tunnel that led under the canal, connecting one part of the village with the other. Sunday roast dinner at the pub was good value and Jessica managed to forget that the roast lamb she was tucking into had once been one of those fluffy creatures that grazed in the fields beside the canal. After lunch they travelled north for a few more miles, passing under a beautiful old stone bridge before turning around and returning to New Bradwell.

After Barbara and Bob had gone, Jessica thought about what a strange day it had been. Never having entertained her mother before, she had given Ragamuffin an extra good clean in preparation for the inspection. She had expected negative remarks from Barbara and was pleasantly surprised to be told that it was a lovely boat and how homely she had made it. Barbara told Jessica that this life was obviously suiting her although she was pleased to hear about her planned visit to the school as she could not live this life forever. She was also a little concerned by the dark circles under Jessica's eyes and wanted to know if she was sleeping properly. As Jessica could not tell her mother about her sleepless nights waiting for Steve to call she said the circles were the result of too much reading late at night.

Barbara seemed satisfied with this but when she left she made Jessica promise to get some early bedtimes.

The photos that Barbara had left for Jessica had the dates written on the back. One of these, a black and white photo taken in April 1946, showed a figure she recognised as Auntie Joan standing with a bright-eyed girl with dark curly hair. Auntie Joan had her arm around this girl's shoulder and they both looked very happy. There were other photos, taken later in the same year, that seemed to confirm that the two girls spent a lot of time in each other's company and had possibly been on holiday at the seaside. However, there was nothing after 1946, so Jessica could only guess at what had happened next. She turned her attention to the diary, which was old and hardly legible. She recognised it as the one Auntie Joan had shown her when she was a child. The vivid memory of sitting in Auntie Joan's sitting room listening to extracts being read to her from this very book filled Jessica's heart with fresh grief. If only she could see her aunt again, just one more time, to say all the things she wanted to say to her and to thank her for enriching her childhood. Her death had come too unexpectedly and Jessica had failed to see her as often as she could have done in recent years.

Once she had dried her tears, Jessica gingerly opened the precious diary. Reading through the yellowing pages, she realised why Auntie Joan had only selected a few extracts to read to her as a child. As well as giving an account of the events that had happened on the boat, it contained many references to Gloria. Jessica turned to the back of the diary to see if she could find out more about how the relationship had ended, but to her disappointment, the last entry was written a month before Gloria's final letter and contained no mention of her friend. Instead, Joan had written about how they had spent nearly a whole day untangling rope from the rudder, which had involved climbing into the cold water and sawing away at the rope with a knife. Joan had cut her hand and it was troubling her, which was clear from the illegibility of the handwriting. Jessica guessed that Joan's hand had probably become worse the next day which would explain why she had not continued the diary. "Perhaps after that she just got out of the habit of writing," thought Jessica, sadly resigning herself to the fact that she would never know what happened next. "If only she were still alive. There is so much I want to talk to her about. And I need her to tell me what I must do about Steve."

The Headteacher, Mrs Jones, was a friendly lady who greeted Jessica warmly. Although Jessica did not have a copy of her DBS certificate with her, she was at least able to remember the contact details of her previous school so the Headteacher could ask them for a reference. As Mrs Jones gave Jessica a tour of the school it was clear that she loved her job and it was also apparent that the teachers and children liked and respected her. Jessica knew at once that this was a school where she would be made to feel that she belonged. She explained to Mrs Jones that she would not be able to commit herself to anything long-term, but would love to come in for just a week or so before she continued her travels and she readily agreed to come back and help them the following week. The school were having an Arts and Crafts Week in connection with their topic on "Britain since the 1930s." They would be harvesting vegetables and cooking them, baking cakes with dried eggs, and making things such as rag rugs and peg dolls. Jessica was happy to fit in with wherever there was the greatest need for her help. She anticipated this would be an interesting diversion and was delighted to think that she had none of the lesson

173

planning to do but could still take part in the activities without having to organise anything herself.

Jessica was buzzing with excitement when she returned to Ragamuffin and wondered how she would pass the time until the following week. She decided to stay moored where she was for a few days and then she would take a trip to Stoke Bruerne where there was a canal museum that may be worth a visit. As the sun was shining, she considered it would be a good time to clean some of the brass work on Ragamuffin. She was polishing the tiller handle and quietly humming the tune of "We'll meet again" when her phone rang. The sun was so bright that she could not see who was making the call, but her hopes were high. "Steve?"

"Sorry Jessica, it's Zena. Who's Steve?"

"He's my boyfriend. Or maybe I should say my ex-boyfriend."

"Oh, I see. Do you want to talk about it?"

"No, not really. He's married, you see."

"Oh. You poor thing - probably best out of that one. Er, the reason I was calling is that we're on the boat heading down towards Blisworth. I was wondering if you were anywhere near us?"

"I'm in Milton Keynes. I plan to head north to Stoke Bruerne next and should be there in a day or two," Jessica explained.

"Well that's a coincidence. We are going to Stoke Bruerne too. Rob wants to visit the Canal

Museum before we turn back. Could we see you there? Say on Friday?"

"That'd be cool. I'll see you there." After exchanging a few pleasantries with her friend, Jessica slipped her phone back into her pocket and resumed her work on the brassware with even more vigour; if she rubbed hard enough perhaps she could rub Steve out of her life as well as the tarnish.

The journey to Stoke Bruerne was a pleasant diversion. Jessica stopped in Cosgrove for a couple of nights and enjoyed some strenuous walks around the area. On her second night she met up with a family of friendly boaters who were moored beside her and they chatted casually for about an hour before they all disappeared to the pub and Jessica went back inside Ragamuffin for the evening. She would have loved to go to the pub too but was aware that she needed to economise; it was better to live cheaply for a few days now and treat herself in Stoke Bruerne at the weekend. Beyond Cosgrove there were some spectacular views across the rolling countryside. There was a sense of isolation for several miles, there being no villages directly beside the canal, but Jessica spotted church towers and a busy road to her left. Turning her attention to the other side of the canal, she spotted a tall church steeple in the distance. The canal was on higher ground than the land beside it so she had uninterrupted views of this striking landmark, which completely dominated the flat landscape. Since the steeple never seemed to get any closer Jessica guessed that it must be built some way from the canal. "I wonder where that church is and if it is too far away to walk there," she thought. "It was obviously built at a time when this was an area of greater prosperity. What was it that made the people here so rich? The sheep in the adjoining field provided one possible answer. The wool trade perhaps?" She contemplated how this landscape might give meaning to her musings. If Steve was that steeple in the distance, her life was the flat landscape around it. She had to make that landscape more interesting. She must fill it with something else, something that would stop her aspiring for the unattainable. "I need a friend. I wonder what Michael is up to this weekend."

Chapter 12

"It was as if thousands and thousands of little roots and threads of consciousness in him and her had grown together into a tangled mass, till they could crowd no more, and the plant was dying. Now quietly, subtly, she was unravelling the tangle of his consciousness and hers, breaking the threads gently, one by one, with patience and impatience to get clear." D.H. Lawrence (Lady Chatterley's Lover)

When Rob had told Zena they would be going down to the boat for a few days she had been afraid. But she had persuaded herself that one more journey on the boat would clarify matters one way or another. She fervently hoped that she and Rob might re-establish their love and trust. If not, she could at least be certain that she had made the right decision. A trip on the boat would also help to pass the time until the boys came home for the summer and would distract her from worrying about how to tell Rob that she would be starting university in September. Now the blackness of the Blisworth Tunnel seemed to be longer than its 3000 or so yards. Having heard that this tunnel was very wet in places, she had chosen to stay below decks while Rob, dressed in waterproofs, steered the boat. Sitting where she was inside the rear cabin, Zena was unable to look for the light at the end of the tunnel. But knowing that Jessica would be waiting for them at the other end, she sensed a brightening of her own dark prison. Jessica was a source of strength and independence from whom she hoped to empower herself as if by osmosis. Just being close to Jessica she believed would be enough to help her through this final stage of escape.

Rob looked for moorings as soon as they came out into daylight to avoid what would probably be a very crowded spot around the museum at Stoke

177

Bruerne. He soon found a good place just beyond a winding hole where he could easily reverse back the next day to turn the boat around. He guessed the museum would be closing soon but he would have a good look round it in the morning. In the meantime he wanted to book a table at the restaurant. This evening he would tell his wife about his exciting plan to make her happy again. "I'm going to walk down and have a look at the village, Zena. Do you want to come?"

"Yes, that would be good. I have seen some photos of the locks here and they look quite pretty. I'll bring the camera." Zena's voice was full of excitement as she had received a text from Jessica to inform her that Ragamuffin was moored just two locks away and that Jessica would be walking up towards the centre of the village. Not wanting anything to spoil her reunion with her friend, she was working especially hard at keeping Rob happy, laughing dutifully at all his jokes as they walked along the towpath towards the village. Out of the blue, Rob gently took hold of her hand and told her they would be going out for dinner that evening and he had a lovely surprise for her. She wanted to tell him about the nursing course – it felt so wrong to be keeping such a big secret from him when he was trying so hard to treat her well. But she would prefer to talk to Jessica first. As a teacher, Jessica must have experience of family break-ups and would be able to advise her on what she should do to minimise the effect on the boys if she had to leave Rob.

Jessica sat at one of the tables outside the old pub, watching all the people around the cafe and the lock. The gongoozlers (a term used among boaters to describe the people watching the boats) were busy studying a pair of boats that were making their way upstream. She wondered if The Narrow Escape would come down this far or if Zena and Rob would moor closer to the mouth of the tunnel. When she spotted her friend, over on the far towpath, she was disappointed to see that she and Rob were holding hands and laughing together like a pair of young lovers. From the few casual remarks that Zena had let slip on the phone, she had rather got the impression that the marriage was almost over. One of her reasons for inviting Michael to come and stay on the boat for the weekend was so that he and Zena could get to know one another better.

Zena was in such a hurry to get across the lock gate that she lost her footing and almost fell into the churning water below. It was fortunate that she had been holding firmly on to the rail; she didn't care that her jacket had a nasty smudge of black oil from the paddle gear. By the time she reached the far end of the lock gate Jessica was there, holding out her hand to help her descend. "Look, there's a bridge at the end of the lock. Silly girl. Why didn't you use that instead of climbing over the lock gates?" shouted one of the gongoozlers.

Rob came out of the restaurant as Jessica and Zena strolled back over the footbridge. He was pleasantly surprised to see that Zena had bumped into an old friend as he had no plans for the rest of the afternoon. So when Jessica invited Zena to come back for a cup of tea on Ragamuffin he said that he would come along too as he would like to have a look at her boat. The spectacle of some novices trying to open the lock gate then caught his attention so he failed to spot the disappointed look on Jessica's face and the slight blush on his wife's cheeks. Once aboard Ragamuffin, Rob soon found there was little to interest him as it was indeed a very basic design. However, he was keen to find out about Jessica's journey down the River Thames. "We must do that trip soon, love," he said to his wife who was sitting very meekly beside him. "Although I think I would prefer to go all the way down to Limehouse instead of Brentford." While Jessica was talking, Zena was trying to work out a way to meet up with Jessica away from her husband. She wanted him to leave and go back to The Narrow Escape but could think of no excuse for staying behind without him. Jessica was also hopelessly trying to think of a way to get rid of Rob. As Rob had booked a table for two at the restaurant that evening, she and Michael were not going to be able to spend an evening with them in the pub as she had hoped. In the end she asked, "So what are your plans for tomorrow?"

"We are going to look at the museum first thing and then we will have to turn round and make our way back, I'm afraid. I need to get back to work in a couple of days to check on this big contract we're working on," Rob declared importantly.

"I was planning to go to the museum myself," said Jessica. " A friend if mine is arriving this evening. Perhaps we could all meet there?"

"Oh Rob likes to take his time in museums and I think he would find our chatter a bit irritating," interrupted Zena. "Why don't you bring your friend for a coffee while Rob visits the museum and then you two could go and visit it on your own when we have gone." Rob was surprised by his wife's excellent intuition. He had not only made this trip to Stoke Bruerne to tell Zena about his plan to save their marriage, he also really wanted to visit the museum. The prospect of being accompanied there by Zena's friend had certainly not appealed to him. He would have been quite happy for Zena to come along but this girl had rather too much to say for herself and would almost certainly have spoilt the experience.

The bar was crowded but Jessica and Michael managed to find a table tucked away at the back, where they hungrily devoured a large and unhealthy meal. Whilst they ate, Jessica finally told Michael about her affair with Steve. "Deep down, I suspect it can never work out between us. I think he's actually a very controlling sort of person. At first it was quite exciting having somebody else make all the decisions for a change. He always dictated when and where we would meet, he even chose my food and wine for me at the restaurants. I'm not used to being told what to do but I was very happy to bow down to his superior experience and judgement. But then we didn't get to spend very much time together - if we were in each other's company all the time I certainly wouldn't have wanted him deciding everything for me. I know I'm really better off without him but I just can't let go. I can't stop myself from hoping that he will phone me and tell me that his marriage is over and he wants to be with me."

"But it's been months now since you left the school. Haven't you called him at all?" Michael was trying hard to hide his dismay and disillusionment. He was saddened that Jessica was with somebody as he still hoped there might one day be room for him in her life. But his greatest disappointment was in her – he had believed Jessica was a better person than this.

"I can't carry on as it was before," Jessica continued, totally unaware of Michael's distress. "He needs to choose and I'm not going to put pressure on

181

him. If he wants to stay with Ali, then he can't have me as well. If I call him it's like saying I've changed my mind and he will persuade me to start seeing him again."

"And how do you feel about Ali?" Michael's question took Jessica by surprise.

"What do you mean?" she asked defensively.

"Don't you feel guilty about sleeping with her husband?"

Jessica did not know how to answer this question. Because Steve had always told her his marriage was effectively over and he was only with Ali because of the children, she had not really considered her to still be his wife. She had been worried about being found out of course but after that first night she had not felt ashamed. She had been consumed with such a passion for him that their being together was the only thing that mattered. When she tried to explain this to Michael, she realised how amoral it made her sound. She asked him if he thought she ought to feel guilty. "Well to be perfectly honest, yes I do. I'm actually quite shocked by what you've told me this evening. I thought we shared the same values but obviously not. I regard marriage as something special and I could never have an affair with a married woman. I thought you were better than that."

Jessica felt the heat in her cheeks. Not only did she resent being told off, she also realised this was the end of her plan to pair him up with Zena. She choked back the tears. "Perhaps we will have to agree to differ on this one," she muttered.

"Yes, I think so. I didn't mean to lecture you but you did ask me what I thought."

"Yes I did. And thank you for being so honest. But let's change the subject before we fall out."

The sun was just breaking through the clouds as Rob entered the museum. Jessica and Michael watched him go inside on their way to The Narrow Escape. Zena had been waiting for them and the coffee maker was already at work. She was curious about the friend was that Jessica was bringing with her - perhaps it would be Steve? She wanted to meet this mystery boyfriend of Jessica's. When she saw it was Michael, the blood rushed to her cheeks. "Oh hello. When Jessica said she had a friend coming for the weekend, I didn't realise it was you." Michael gave her a peck on the cheek and said it was good to see her again. Her blush deepened. But Zena was not the only one who was overcome with surprise. Jessica was rendered speechless by the immaculate interior of The Narrow Escape. She knew it was an exceptionally smart boat but had never anticipated anything on this scale.

"Wow! What a boat," she gasped.

"Rob's pride and joy," replied Zena and enthusiastically showed them around. Arriving back in the rear saloon Jessica asked her, "When will Rob be back?"

"Oh I expect he'll be a couple of hours yet."

"Good. That gives us plenty of time." Jessica settled herself beside Zena on the sumptuous sofa. Michael sat in the plush armchair opposite the two girls.

"Sorry Michael, I've got something I must tell Jessica before I explode," said Zena, turning to her friend. "I was dying to tell you yesterday but couldn't because Rob was there. I've been offered a place on the nursing course in Oxford and I've accepted it." Jessica put down her coffee cup and gave her friend a big hug. "But I haven't told Rob yet," continued Zena. "And now there's an unexpected problem." She stood up and wandered over to the window to watch a boat that was approaching too quickly. "He told me last night that he wants us to have another baby."

"Is that what you want?"

"No, I want to have a career. If I have another baby now, I know I'll never train to be a nurse. I'm going to have to leave him." She turned to face Jessica. There were tears in her eyes and her lip was quivering. Michael felt awkward and wondered if he should leave the two girls to have this conversation in private.

"So what did you tell him?" Before Zena could reply, a sudden movement of the boat caused her to fall back down on to the sofa and Rob appeared at the doorway. His face was red and sweaty and he was visibly agitated. He glared suspiciously at Michael. Zena and Jessica exchanged anxious looks, each wondering how long he had been there and what he had heard. Zena went pale as Rob announced, "Zena, we've got to leave now, the taxi will be here any minute." To Zena's relief, Rob's agitation appeared to have nothing to do with what she was telling Jessica. Something had gone badly wrong with the big contract he was working on and he had been called back to the office to sort it out. The taxi would take him and Zena back to the marina where their car was parked and Rob would drop Zena off at home on his way into work.

After leaving The Narrow Escape, Jessica suggested to Michael that they should go for a walk. Michael was very quiet as they strolled slowly down the path past the top lock, still packed with gongoozlers, and past the pub where families were already gathering for lunch in the garden. Going down the flight of locks, they paused along the way to open and close the gates for other boaters. Once they were alone again, Michael started to ask about Zena. Jessica explained that she hoped Zena would not let Rob persuade her to have another baby. She said it would be better for her to leave her husband. "Why are you so keen for them to split up?" he asked.

"Because he is a bully and she is unhappy."

"But surely that's up to her to decide. You can't go around persuading your friends to end their marriages just because you don't like their husbands." Jessica could sense storm clouds gathering on the horizon.

"Michael, I know what you think about marriage but believe me, Zena has been used very badly by Rob. The marriage suits him perfectly well but it has been at the expense of her happiness. He has sent their children away to boarding school and won't even let her speak to them on the phone. He controls her life completely. And he's been unfaithful to her."

"Like Steve you mean?" Jessica stopped walking and stared at Michael. She hated it that he was right. His words merely confirmed what she already knew. Leaning against the heavy beam of the lock gate, she held her head in her hands. As she reflected on Michael's words she could no longer hide from the truth; the way Steve had treated her and Ali was actually no better than the way Rob had behaved towards Zena. Michael came and stood beside her.

"I'm sorry. That was below the belt." He put his arm around her hunched shoulders and she began to cry. He pulled her close and she broke away from him.

"Don't be nice to me," she snapped. "That'll make it worse. You're right. But that doesn't help." She moved away from him and wandered over to look at the red brick wall of the pumping house that took the water back to the top of the flight of locks. After a moment's solitude, she returned to Michael and they crossed over to the other side of the canal to begin their way back towards Stoke Bruerne. They walked in silence, Jessica stewing over the irrefutable truth of Michael's remark and Michael wondering what he could possibly say that would not make matters even worse. He had realised the previous evening that he had sounded too judgemental and he had promised himself that he would not mention Steve again. But he was too impatient for her to be free from her unhappy past, ready to start a new life and maybe even a relationship with him. As they approached the village, they stopped to admire the view of the imposing church tower amongst the trees. Then they left the towpath to walk through a field and from there up the hill to the church and on to a footpath beyond. This led them across another field to a stile where the cattle-churned mud was too much

186

for their footwear. They retraced their footsteps to the church and back down the hill towards the canal. As they neared the pub, the smell of cooking reminded them that it was lunchtime and they made their way back to Ragamuffin.

Their afternoon visit to the museum provided a welcome distraction for Jessica and Michael. Jessica discovered that there was much about the canals that she had never known before. It was crammed full of displays and models taking them back in time to when the canals were first built. The display on the building of the Blisworth Tunnel was of particular interest to Michael. The men excavating the tunnel not only had no machinery to help them but also had to work by candlelight. There was a small model showing legging boards that stuck out from each side of the boat; on each board lay a man who worked the boat through the tunnel by moving his feet along the wall. "That must have been incredibly hard work," he thought and automatically began to calculate the number of joules that would be needed to move a fifteen tonne boat for half a kilometre.

The museum reminded Jessica of her Auntie Joan, especially when she discovered a board and display case all about the work of the women on the canals during the war. Amongst memorabilia such as clothing coupons she spotted a badge just like the one she had found among her aunt's belongings. She had learnt from reading the diary that the initials stood for Inland Waterways, but people jokingly called them the Idle Women. As Jessica read about the bombing that had taken place mostly during the early years of the war, she was thankful that Auntie Joan had not started work until 1944. The canals were too easy a target for the bombers with the moonlight reflected on the water. Since many industrial areas were situated beside them, the German pilots would use the canals to help them navigate. Jessica was really excited when she found photographs and information about Sister Mary - the same woman who was mentioned in Auntie Joan's diary for nursing and caring for the boat people for many years. When they left the museum, Jessica stopped to point out to Michael the brick house where Sister Mary had lived and had her surgery.

Back aboard Ragamuffin, once they had finished discussing the museum, Jessica and Michael found conversation difficult. Awkwardly avoiding any mention of Zena, Rob or Steve, the silence was stony. They discussed plans for the following morning and agreed that they would make an early start so Michael could do the flight of locks with Jessica before walking back to his car, which was parked at the top. Although Jessica needed to go downstream to Milton Keynes, Ragamuffin was still facing upstream. They would need to go up through two locks before there was a place where Jessica could turn Ragamuffin around to face in the right direction. As it was a lovely evening they agreed to do those two locks, turn round at the top and return to the same mooring spot. That would leave just five locks for the following morning. Michael asked if he could steer the boat and swap over at the top after he had turned the boat around. Jessica was amused by his confidence; as she walked ahead to prepare the lock she chuckled to herself at the number of gongoozlers who would be there to witness Michael's inexperience. They turned it into a bit of a game to amuse the crowds, with Jessica covering her face in mock horror as Michael steered too close to the side and then Michael shouting up to her to "Put your back into it" while she was raising the paddles. She was hoping that Michael would struggle to manoeuvre the boat at the top and she would have to jump aboard and help him. But he was annoyingly good and handled the boat as if he had done it a hundred times before. "That was fun," he said, as they moored once again in the pound below the second lock.

"Yes - although I think you might have made more of an effort to entertain the gongoozlers when you turned around."

"I would have done if I hadn't been shitting bricks that I was going to bump your boat." Jessica smiled smugly to herself - so Michael was not as cool and collected as he had appeared.

Zena's phone call came just as they were preparing to go to the pub. Michael took the boat keys from Jessica and locked up the boat for her. He then walked off ahead to give Jessica some privacy. Zena told Jessica more about Rob's suggestion they should have another baby. "He knows how much I miss the boys and he thought that another baby would make me happy. He would also love to have a little girl, if we were lucky enough for that to happen. Not that we don't love the boys, of course, but having a girl would complete our family somehow." Jessica remembered Michael's words from the day before. If Zena wanted to stay with Rob and have another baby, what right did she have to try and change her mind?

"And are you absolutely sure that you don't want a baby? You're still young enough to train as a nurse later," she suggested.

"I'm absolutely certain. I have been so bored at home and I think I would still be bored if I had a baby to care for. It's taken me so long to get round to applying to university and now I've been accepted I just want to get straight on and do it."

189

"So you need to tell Rob. And soon," Jessica insisted.

"Yes I know. But if he can't accept it and we decide to split up, it will ruin the boys' holiday. I was thinking of waiting until they went back to school in September and then leaving immediately after I had told him." Jessica recommended that she should not wait until September. Her advice was to get the difficult part over and done with before the boys came home for the summer. She may even find that Rob was willing to consider the idea and then she would have spent the whole holiday worrying for no reason. It might still be possible to save the marriage, she argued.

"No, that's not going to happen. You are right about Rob - he's a bully. I should have listened to you before. I'm not sure I even want to stay with him anymore." Zena went on to explain about how worried she was about coping on her own if she left Rob. She would have to get to grips with things like bank accounts and insurance policies, things she had always left to Rob. She was also worried about moving to a new place where she didn't know anybody. "But thanks to you I've met Michael now. He's really lovely. Did you say he was single?" Jessica's stomach gave a lurch. Her plan to get Michael and Zena together now seemed such a childish idea. "What on earth was I thinking of?" she asked herself.

"I've ordered for you," said Michael as she joined him at the bar. "I presumed you would like your usual wine?"

Jessica was stunned. "And what if I want something different?" Her tone was hostile.

"No problem. I'll drink the wine. What would you like instead?"

"Well actually I would like the wine, but that's not the point." Jessica felt outmanoeuvred. Just as she thought Michael was trying to control her like Steve did, it appeared that he was after all being perfectly reasonable. Of course, he liked the same wine as her it would have been fine if she had wanted a different drink. She thanked him and slumped down on a bench in the corner.

"Do you mind if we sit outside?" he asked. "I want to talk to you and it's a bit public in here." Jessica wondered what he might have to say that he didn't want other people to hear.

"Is this OK?" she asked, choosing a table close to the lock and away from the smokers.

"Perfect." He asked if Zena was all right and Jessica explained that it was looking quite likely that the marriage was over.

"But I didn't encourage her," she added. "I've been thinking about what you said yesterday and you are right. Nobody should try to split up a married couple." She smiled at Michael and he decided to take a risk. If they were going to be friends there was no way he could avoid the subject.

"And does that include Steve and his wife?" Jessica's silence seemed endless. At last she replied.

"Their marriage was in trouble before I ever arrived on the scene. Steve was at his wits' end and to begin with I just wanted to support him. I didn't plan to fall in love with him. But I was wrong to let it go beyond a friendship, I can see that now."

191

"So where do you go from here?"

"I just wait. He will eventually decide what he is going to do. He knows I will be waiting for him if he leaves her. I'm not going to put any pressure on him."

"But in the meantime your life is on hold? You really can't waste the rest of your life waiting for him, Jess. End it now, once and for all, and then you can start living your life again." Jessica could see the sense in what Michael was saying. Even if Steve did leave Ali, there was no guarantee that she would be happy with him. Given that he had been unfaithful to his wife, how could she ever rely on him to be faithful to her? He had not even bothered to reply to the text she had sent him over a week ago although he must know how unhappy she was.

The following morning, as Michael helped Jessica to go down through the remaining locks, he noticed how distracted she was. She looked as if she had not slept much either and he was quite worried. As he was about to leave, he asked her if she was all right and she told him that she had been thinking very hard about what he had said about Steve. "You are right," she said, "and I can do it. As soon as I get back to Milton Keynes this afternoon, I am going to call him. I can't wait any longer for him to make up his mind. And, to be honest, I don't even know if I want to get back with him now, after all this time. Seeing how miserable Rob has made Zena has got me thinking that Steve is not the sort of guy who would make me happy anyway. He's too much like Rob I think." Michael put his arms around her. He did not know what to say, but just stood holding her quietly for a few minutes until she pulled away. "Thanks, Michael. But go home now. I'm fine, or at least I will be once I have made that phone call."

192

"If you don't like it, alter it, and if you can't alter it, put up with it." D.H. Lawrence (Sons and Lovers)

The song of the cheerful blackbird perched on the branch above her head caused Jessica to forget for a moment why her head ached so badly. Then the awful truth hit her - she had lost Steve forever. One stupid phone call and the splinters of all her dreams had come crashing down around her like shards of broken glass. Pulling the quilt back over her head, Jessica buried herself in the murky depths of her despair. Her pillow was sodden from the million tears she had shed during the night. She could not erase from her mind his sarcastic tone when she had told him that she was not prepared to wait any longer and he should consider the affair to be finally over. "So much for you caring about Alice and Tom. You expect me to just leave them with Ali and come running to you? I never knew you were such a cold-hearted bitch." He had informed her that he had already told Ali he was leaving and that if Jessica had only been patient for just a few more days he would have called her. He accused her of emotional blackmail and said there could never be a future for them as she was too manipulative. Remembering their argument in the cold light of day, Jessica could not believe that she had completely humiliated herself by begging him to change his mind. She then directed her anger at Michael - why did he have to persuade her to end it with Steve? What right had he to pass judgement on her relationship anyway? Saint Michael the Moronic Moraliser. As the alarm on her phone rang, reminding her it was eight o'clock, she crawled out of bed like a creature awakening from a long hibernation. As she rinsed her aching body with cold water and pulled on her smart clothes, she gave herself a lecture as if she were scolding a naughty

193

child. She was not going to lie there all day, feeling sorry for herself and wishing things could have been different. She had a school to go to. The week ahead was just the medicine she needed, offering her the opportunity to get to know new people and a chance to find out how she felt about working with children again. Going up on deck for some fresh air, she perceived the almost invisible outline of a pale sun attempting to penetrate the mist, like a knife cutting through cotton wool. It was a spectacular sight and one which Jessica thought a perfect reflection of her own situation. She had been lost in a mist of despair so dense that it felt as if nothing would lift it, but if she could just focus her attention on that dim circle of light she could find a brighter future ahead.

Jessica was surprised how nervous she felt as she stepped into the entrance foyer of the school. But this feeling was short-lived, as she was soon greeted by Chris, the teacher she had met at Bletchley Park, who told her she would be working with him that morning and in the afternoon she would be with Kate, the other teacher she had already met. Chris had split his class into four groups, one of which would be working in the garden with him while she and two other volunteers worked with one group each. Jessica was to make peg dolls with her group and there was an assortment of fabrics and threads, wooden pegs and pipe cleaners, already set out on the desk, with some sheets of clear instructions. While the children were in assembly, Chris explained the tasks to the volunteers. "Please get them to study the instructions first," he requested. We have been looking at instructional writing in Literacy so they should be able to tell you what the key features are."

"Yes, I can do that. The first word is a verb, sentences are short, importance of sequence, numbers or bullet points to help the reader."

"Oh, I can't tell you how good it is to have a qualified teacher as a helper," enthused Chris. "And then perhaps you can talk about why peg dolls were made. No money for non-essential items, factories making weapons not toys, fabric would have been scraps from old clothes etc."

"Do you want them to make clothes in the style of the nineteen forties or can they dress the dolls how they like?"

"I hadn't really thought of that. What do you think?"

"I think we should let the children decide," replied Jessica. The morning went really fast, with Jessica having one group before playtime and a different group afterwards. At playtime, Chris was on duty so she went out on to the playground with him. Some of the girls she had met at Bletchley came over to talk to her and she felt a real sense of belonging. Watching Chris dealing with a group of boys who were fighting, she was not at all surprised to see Ricky in the midst of it and she caught his eye as he was arguing with Chris. Surprised to see her there, Ricky stopped arguing and stomped across the playground to slump on a bench. With his hunched shoulders and bowed head, he looked like a little old man trying to shelter from the cold. Jessica walked over to him and listened as he told her that it was not his fault and how it was always him who got the blame. Once he had calmed down she asked him what he had been doing that morning. "Nothing much. We had Literacy and then Numeracy. Why can't we do interesting things like they're doing in Mr Allen's class?"

"Well, I happen to know that Mr Allen's class are having their Literacy and Numeracy this afternoon, and your class will be doing what they were doing this morning."

"Will you be coming to help in our class then?"

"I think so but I don't know if I will be with your group. That's up to your teacher."

"I bet she doesn't let me do anything fun. I never get to work with anybody new. It's not fair." As it turned out, it was the following day before Jessica worked with Ricky. She was amazed how knowledgeable and co-operative he was, eagerly answering her questions about instructional writing and showing great creativity while making his peg doll.

On her third day at the school, Jessica was thankful that she did not have to make any more peg dolls. Having done the same activity with over sixty children, she was ready for a change. On the third day, the children all dressed up, some with cardboard boxes holding imaginary gas masks strung over their shoulders. Jessica was amazed how much effort had gone into the children's outfits and could tell that the parents must be very supportive. She had already met a couple of mums who were also volunteering in school during the week and they had been full of praise for the school. If she had been teaching here instead of where she was, her teaching career may have had a very different start, she concluded.

The whole of the third day was taken up with a simulation of the evacuation of children during the war, with role play on imaginary train journeys and the meeting of the evacuated children with the local country children at the pretend village school. Jessica was astonished at the willingness of the children to enter into this drama, and watched Ricky enthusiastically telling a "London" child to go back to where he came from. In the discussion at the end of the day, the children showed highly sophisticated levels of empathy, and it was evident that much had been learnt during the activity. The entire day had been planned and led by Kate and at four o'clock she sank down next to Jessica in one of the armchairs in the staff room. "That went well," Jessica told her.

"Yes it was a great success. But I'm absolutely whacked now. I haven't slept properly for weeks, worrying about whether it would work or not."

"Well it certainly went very well. I couldn't believe some of the things the children came up with in that last session."

Jessica's final two days were taken up with cookery, again working with one group at a time, making rhubarb crumble and gooseberry tarts with fruit that had been grown in the children's garden. She was full of admiration for this school, where there was so much creativity and commitment. Mrs Jones was regularly in the classrooms, asking children what they were doing and what they had learnt, and eagerly watching all that was going on. Jessica noticed how relaxed the teachers were in her presence and thought what a lovely school this must be to work in. There was no doubt that everybody had worked hard to set up this Arts and Crafts Week, but because they were enjoying their work so much, nobody seemed to mind being exhausted. This must be the "buzz" that she had heard about from teachers in her school but it was the first time she had experienced it for herself. On the Friday afternoon, Jessica was invited into the Headteacher's office and they discussed how the week had gone. Jessica told her how much she had enjoyed helping in the school and Mrs Jones asked her if she would like to come back in September. "I would love to, if I am in this area," said Jessica. "But I'm afraid my money will be running out by then and I might need to go and get a job."

"Well, I can't offer you a permanent job as there are no vacancies," replied Mrs Jones. "But we are always in need of supply teachers so if you are in the area, give us a call. The teachers are all very committed and drag themselves into work when they are not well so we don't have a huge amount of sickness cover. But there's always somebody going on a course. I could also put in a good word for you with other schools in the locality so you should be able to get one or two days most weeks. The teachers have been very impressed with you so we would love to see you back here." Jessica was taken aback by this, not having realised that she had been under observation, but was also very flattered.

"I'm really not sure yet what I will be doing in September, but if I did choose to go back to teaching this is a school that would really suit me."

"Well, have a think about it and give me a call if you want to talk some more. And thank you once again for all your help this week. We couldn't have managed without you."

That evening, Kate and Chris invited Jessica to meet up with them for a drink. They were still buzzing from the success of the week and full of stories about how children who were normally quite reserved had blossomed during the activities. Listening to these two talking, Jessica knew that her decision was already made. She would return to teaching But she would do it slowly by working part-time to begin with. That way she could have both the boat and a career, earning just enough to keep herself and Ragamuffin afloat and taking time off for cruises in between. Chris was keen to persuade her to come and work as a supply teacher at the school. "It's a great place to work. And you did so well. Look at how easily you handled the difficult ones like Ricky. And there's no doubt that it has been good for you - you look so much happier than you did at the start of the week. I hope you don't mind me saying, but you looked dreadful on Monday morning - so bad in fact that I wondered if you were fit to be in school. But now look at you - you've got no right to look that good on a Friday evening!"

"Well, thank you for those kind words. Yes, I wasn't feeling too good on Monday morning. It's very tempting. I could see myself fitting in really well there."

"So, what are your immediate plans?" asked Kate.

"I shall set off north tomorrow, I think. While you poor things are seeing out the last couple of weeks of term, I will be enjoying the fresh air and sunshine."

"Oh, you lucky thing. Wish I was coming with you," said Kate, She finished her drink and headed off to the bar to get another round.

After Kate had left, Chris moved to sit closer to Jessica. She was alarmed by an unexpected feeling of electricity passing through her. He asked her about Ragamuffin and he seemed genuinely interested in finding out what it was like to live on a boat. Jessica was flattered for a moment to have the full attention of this gorgeous guy and was tempted to invite him back to see Ragamuffin when they left the pub. But memories of what had happened with Michael reminded her to be cautious. However lonely she may feel and however gorgeous Chris was, she was not ready for any more misunderstandings. She needed to get over Steve first anyway. "But perhaps in September?" she thought as she inched her body a bit further away from temptation.

After one more drink Jessica left Chris and Kate in the pub. They were obviously prepared for a long session. She had succeeded in buying one round of drinks but could not really justify the expense of another. Besides which, she was tired and could already feel the effects of the alcohol. She hugged them both goodbye, promising to see them again in September and made her way to the towpath. Although it was the beginning of July, the air was still quite cold and Jessica zipped up her jacket and thrust her hands into her pockets as she walked through the car park. She was glad they had chosen a pub that was beside the canal and it was only about a fifteen minute walk along the towpath to where Ragamuffin was moored. There was a clear sky so Jessica looked up in wonder at the stars as she walked. Although the street lights of Milton Keynes made it difficult to spot some of the more obscure constellations she could still pick out the Plough quite easily. She felt tired but content, thankful that she had been too busy to think very much about Steve during the week. She was disappointed but not surprised that she had heard nothing from him since their last terrible argument. She still harboured a tiny hope that by now he would have forgiven her for putting pressure on him and that he would beg her to come back to him. Since several hours had passed since she had last checked her phone, she could not help herself. She had to take one last look, just in case, and she promised herself that if there was still no word from him, she would accept that it was finally over between them. If she could not change the way things were, she would just have to deal with her disappointment and move on. She reached inside her bag and pulled out her phone. As she went to take the next step along the towpath, instead of feeling the ground beneath her foot, Jessica experienced the scary sensation of falling forwards. She was in the water in an instant, the strange gurgling in her ears confirming what had happened. She was not afraid as the canal was not deep, nor did she feel cold. All she could feel was anger at herself for being so stupid. She had known the towpath was close to the edge of the canal, so why on earth had she not been watching where she was going? Jessica pulled herself to the side and held on to the sheet piling while she recovered from the shock. There were a few boats moored nearby on the bend of the canal and as there were lights on inside one of these she could shout for help if she needed it. However, acutely embarrassed, she would prefer to get herself out of this predicament without being seen by anybody. Her feet were on the mud at the bottom of the canal and the water was up to her shoulders, so she tried to jump up and at the same time heave herself out with her arms. But after several minutes of desperate struggling, it became apparent that this was not going to work. By now Jessica was beginning to shiver and she reluctantly accepted that she must swallow her pride and get some help. She waded along the edge of the canal, holding on to the corrugated piling, until she came to the first of the moored boats. It was strange to see the boat from this angle. When you were actually in a narrowboat, it seemed to be very low in the water, but looking up at the steel bows from where she was now standing, Jessica was surprised how high she would have to jump to get aboard. She let go of the piling and moved out

201

towards the middle of the canal to continue along the side of the boat. The uneven surface of the bottom of the canal and the weight of her wet clothes slowed her progress as she waded through the water and once or twice she stumbled. She wondered what she was stepping on and hoped she had not swallowed any of the filthy water when she fell in. There were no lights showing at the windows of the first boat so she continued to the next one, a brightly painted craft called Ruby where she could see signs of life behind the thin curtains. She knocked loudly on the side of the boat, hoping the people aboard would be friendly. "Who's there?" shouted the angry head that appeared through the hatch.

"I'm sorry. Can you help me?"

"Oh, my goodness. Wait a minute. I've got a step ladder somewhere here."

Within minutes, Jessica was pulled aboard and stood dripping on the deck. "Come below. Margaret is running you a hot bath. You need to get out of those clothes and into something warm." Jessica, reluctant to undress in front of strangers, insisted that it was all right and she could manage get back to her own boat. But they were persistent and as she was in no mood to argue she allowed this kindly old couple to take care of her. When she explained to Margaret that Ragamuffin was moored further along the canal, this warm-hearted lady took her boat keys and hurried along the towpath in search of some dry clothes for her. Jessica, meanwhile, sat wrapped in a blanket, sipping tea. "Are you feeling better now my dear?" asked the man, who had introduced himself as Roy. "You gave us quite a shock."

"Yes, I'm fine now," she replied. "I gave myself a bit of a shock as well. I had been at the pub but I'm not drunk. I just wasn't concentrating. I don't know what I would have done without your help. Thank you so much."

"Oh, it's very easily done. Most of us have fallen in at some time or another. Did you lose anything in the water when you fell?" Jessica picked up her bag that was sitting in a wet heap on the floor and began to check its dripping contents. Thank goodness she was in the habit of hanging it diagonally over her shoulder, she thought, otherwise she would have surely lost it. Margaret had already taken her keys to Ragamuffin. Her purse was still there, which was the important thing, as it contained not only money but her credit card. She would be able to dry out the notes later. Then she noticed that her phone was gone and, remembering that it was in her hand as she fell, she realised it would almost certainly be somewhere in the mud at the bottom of the canal. Now she could not find out if Steve had tried to contact her and return his call if he had. So it really was over between them. She had been holding herself together very well until this point but now she let go and heaved loud, uncontrollable sobs, much to the embarrassment of herself and her companion.

Michael was concerned that he may have said too much on that last evening with Jessica and had encouraged her into ending the relationship with Steve before she was ready. Having reprimanded her for trying to persuade Zena to leave Rob, his own behaviour seemed rather hypocritical. He was tempted to call her to find out if she had spoken to Steve. However, he realised that this may be too pushy and he persuaded himself to wait for her to contact him. However, he was so besotted with her that he could not put her out of his mind and he caught himself thinking more and more frequently about her and hoping he had not completely blown his chances by being so openly disapproving of her behaviour. Why she had ever allowed herself to have an affair with a married man, and even worse the father of one of the children in her class, was beyond his understanding. Steve had obviously taken advantage of her good nature and naivety, first winning her sympathy and then seducing her. He was incredibly angry with Steve, believing the bastard should have known better than to put Jessica in that impossible situation, jeopardising her career as well as breaking her heart. Michael hoped that by the time they met again, Steve would be completely out of the picture and he could try again to build more than just a friendship with Jessica. Although they had agreed to meet at Karen's wedding, by the end of the working week he knew he could not wait that long to see her again. He tried to phone her at regular intervals throughout the weekend, each unsuccessful attempt fuelling his frustration and anxiety. He could not understand why she was not answering her phone and guessed she must be avoiding him. Or perhaps her battery was flat and she hadn't bothered to charge it? Michael became increasingly worried that Jessica may be unable to answer the phone because she was ill or there had been an accident. He pictured her lying alone on her boat unable to move, listening to the ringing of a phone that was beyond her reach. By the time Sunday evening arrived, he could bear it no longer and called Karen to enquire if she had heard anything from Jessica and to request her to call her as well. If she answered a call from Karen, at least he would know she was all right and was just him she was avoiding. In which case, he would have to assume that there was no future for them; he would just have to swallow his disappointment and move on.

As soon as it was daylight, Jessica walked back along the towpath to have another look for her phone and to thank Roy and Margaret, the couple who had rescued her the previous night. She carried out a thorough search of the towpath where she had fallen in but had to accept that her phone must have gone into the canal with her. Roy and Margaret emerged from below decks while she was bent over the grassy verge and they were pleased to see her. They dismissed her expressions of gratitude with reassurances that it could have happened to anyone. But they also asked her to try to be take more care in future in case she found herself in even greater trouble. "You need to be careful when you are walking the towpath on your own at night," Margaret warned her. "It's not just the danger of falling in - you also need to watch out for possible muggers when you are moored in a town. You are very vulnerable on your own." Jessica promised to be more sensible in future and as she left them she expressed a hope that they would meet again one day. Margaret asked where she was heading and she told them of her plans.

"I would not recommend the Erewash," Roy warned her. "We went there once and said we'd never go again. There's shopping trolleys and all sorts in the canal and the only really safe place you can moor is Sandiacre. And there's nothing at Langley Mill - it's not really a canal basin at all."

Margaret saw the disappointed look on Jessica's face. "Hang on Roy, Jessica might have a reason why she particularly wants to go along the Erewash." Jessica explained to them that she was a D.H. Lawrence fan and had been hoping to see some of the countryside where his novels were set and visit his birthplace museum in Eastwood.

"You would do much better to go along the Trent towards Nottingham. It's non-tidal there and you've got miles of beautiful river," continued Roy. "And you could probably catch a bus from Nottingham to Eastwood." Jessica agreed that this might be a better option and thanked Roy for warning her about the Erewash.

"Be careful where you moor in Leicester - probably best to use the pontoon moorings at Castle Gardens," added Margaret. "The river is really wide there so don't worry about double mooring - or even triple mooring if it's full. They lock the gardens up at night so it's perfectly safe, but there is one gate where you can use your BW key to get in and out if you want." After thanking them again for all their advice, Jessica asked where they would be travelling. "Oh, we'll probably stick around here a bit, and then I think we may head off towards Stratford," Margaret told her. "But our paths may cross again sometime. It's quite staggering how you bump into the same people as you move around."

Jessica was relieved to leave Milton Keynes behind and resume her travels. It felt as though she had already been too long in one place and the embarrassment of falling into the canal had been the final straw. She had enjoyed her week in school and looked forward to returning again in September, but she felt as if the cut were calling to her, reminding her that her journey was not over. She had decided to moor in Leicester and take a train to Oxford. Karen had asked her to arrive a week before the wedding in time for the hen-do which had been organised by the other bridesmaid. Jessica would the stay at Karen's flat for the entire week to have her bridesmaid's dress altered and her hair and nails made presentable for the big day. Jessica pitied the poor stylist and manicurist who would have to work some kind of miracle in order to make her look elegant before the wedding. She wondered what she had let herself in for by agreeing to be a bridesmaid. Fancy frocks and make-up had always been unnatural to her and these weeks of living on the boat had alienated her still further from the world of style. She had agreed to be a bridesmaid because of her fondness for Karen and Jack but formal weddings had never been to her taste. She predicted that she would trip over as they walked down the aisle or something equally stupid to ruin Karen's big day. What had seemed like a good idea when she was cruising down the Thames became more ridiculous as the day approached; now all thoughts of the wedding and the week leading up to it filled her with dread. She consoled herself with the fact that she would not have to make a speech so as soon as the ceremony itself was over she would be able to relax. Then, having done her duty, the several weeks of cruising the canals before September would be all the more enjoyable. After the wedding Jessica planned to continue travelling North along the River Soar to the Trent and Mersey Canal. She could then either go east towards Nottingham, north along the Erewash Canal or west towards Birmingham. Despite Roy's attempts to persuade her to go to Nottingham, she favoured the third option as it would take her past the places where she used to walk with her Auntie Joan as a child. It would be strange to view Fradley Junction and Alrewas from a boat instead of the towpath. Jessica decided she would make up her mind when she got there – she loved the freedom of not having to make decisions in advance but just to go where the fancy took her.

As Jessica cruised back through Wolverton and over the aqueduct at Cosgrove she thought back to her parents' visit. It seemed ages ago already. She really must have them to stay with her for a few days and wondered if they might like to join her for an excursion to Nottingham. She would call them as soon as she could find a payphone. Fortunately her parents' number was ingrained in her memory otherwise she would have been in a mess. Losing her mobile was a real nuisance as she now had no contact details and no Internet connection. She needed to replace it as soon as possible and guessed that Leicester would probably be the best place. "More unnecessary expense. I'm so stupid. I will have to look after the next one more carefully," she muttered. At least her bank balance was still remarkably healthy and she now had a plan for earning money in September.

Chapter 14

"There is something sustaining in the very agitation that accompanies the first shocks of trouble, just as an acute pain is often a stimulus, and produces an excitement which is transient strength. It is in the slow, changed life that follows - in the time when sorrow has become stale, and has no longer an emotive intensity that counteracts its pain - in the time when day follows day in dull unexpectant sameness, and trial is a dreary routine - it is then that despair threatens; it is then that the peremptory hunger of the soul is felt, and eye and ear are strained after some unlearned secret of our existence, which shall give to endurance the nature of satisfaction." George Eliot (The Mill on the Floss)

On reaching the bottom of Stoke Bruerne locks, Jessica was inevitably reminded of that phone call she made to Steve when she was last in this spot. She waited miserably at the water point for another boat to accompany her through the seven locks and before too long she was pleased to see the arrival of a big boat with plenty of crew. The guy on the tiller called across to Jessica, "It's been another lovely day," as they entered the first lock. He was evidently was keen to talk to Jessica as they journeyed through the locks and since it was his crew that were doing all the work she made the effort to converse with him.

"Did you see the mist hanging over the water this morning? It was quite a sight." Jessica spoke cheerfully although her heart was in turmoil. She could not help remembering how happily she had worked these locks with Michael, before she had made that stupid phone call. If only she could go back in time. "If only, if only, if only," the words went round her head in perfect time with the sound of the paddle being raised. She had forgiven Michael by now, telling herself that he had only done to her what she had done to Zena. He was a good friend and she knew he had her best interests at heart. She hoped he no longer harboured any romantic or sexual feelings towards her as she could not reciprocate them. She wondered if she would ever be able to love anybody again after Steve. As they travelled into the third lock, Jessica turned her attention back to the guy on the boat alongside her. He was a really friendly man who had recently bought the boat and was full of enthusiasm. He was hoping to travel down to the Thames and when Jessica told him she had done that, he plied her with questions about such things as VHF radio and lengths of chain for the anchor. Jessica tried to give him as much information as she could but explained that she had only travelled the Thames as far as Brentford. If he planned on going downstream to Limehouse, he would need to talk to somebody more knowledgeable than her. The boats parted company at the top lock and Jessica was soon plunged into the black nothingness of the Blisworth Tunnel. Jessica thought about how the villages of Blisworth and Stoke Bruerne were separated by the 3057 yards of this tunnel. With no towpath, the only way to walk between them was over the top of the hill. Jessica was excited at the prospect of entering new territory, which was always more interesting ing than travelling along familiar parts of the canal. Searching for the tiny white dot at the end of the tunnel, Jessica tried to focus her thoughts on the new places and new experiences that lay ahead. However, as she manoeuvred her way through the damp darkness, Steve intruded once again into her thoughts. She could not rid herself of the notion that he may be trying to call her and apologise; having lost her phone, she was now as estranged from him as the two villages at either end of this tunnel.

210

Upon reaching the other side of the tunnel Jessica stopped for the night and in the morning she explored the village of Blisworth. She found a call box and rang her parents. As there was no answer she left a message. "Hi Mum and Dad. Just to let you know, I've dropped my phone in the canal so there's no point in you trying to call me. But I am safe and well and will get another phone in a few days. I'll ring again when I've got it." Having been unable to speak to her parents and with no phone or Internet connection Jessica felt strangely isolated from the world. For the next few days, yearning for human contact, she chatted to everybody she met along the way, grateful for the friendliness and warmth of the boating community. However there were occasions when she had less comfortable encounters. From time to time she would come across miserable individuals who were not suited to life on the canals at all; she also witnessed the effects of too much alcohol or other substances on some people. On one occasion she had a run-in with some ill-tempered fishermen who had chosen a spot just beside a bridge where she had to wait for an oncoming boat to pass. The fishermen, not at all pleased when she used reverse gear to stop the boat, shouted obscenities at her. Jessica chose to ignore them, telling herself that they were probably envious of her way of life and she simply looked away as if she hadn't heard. But these were the exceptions and Jessica had many positive encounters with fellow boaters, anglers and other people who were just cycling or walking along the towpath. Just beyond Weedon, she came to a place where the canal and motorway were close together and she marvelled at the speed of the cars and lorries as they whizzed along. She wondered how it would feel to travel on a motorway now; would it seem so reckless to move so quickly if she were sitting in a car rather than on a boat?

When Jessica reached the bottom of the Long Buckby flight at Whilton she had the good fortune to meet a delightful family who were having their first holiday on the canals and she accompanied them up through the flight. They had two little girls, Amy and Becky, who were sensibly wearing life jackets as they assisted with the locks. Because these locks were unusually deep, the gates were heavy and the girls were too small to move them but that did not stop them from trying, much to Jessica's amusement. With such lively companions, the journey through the flight of seven locks passed very quickly. The final lock of the flight was beside a busy road, under which was built a useful pedestrian tunnel where boaters could cross safely from one side to the other. The little girls had great fun making their voices echo as they stomped through this tunnel. Waiting in the top lock beside the busy pub, Jessica remembered that this was the setting of one of her favourite stories from Auntie Joan. While they were waiting for the lock to fill, Jessica recounted to Amy and Becky Auntie Joan's story about Winston the cat, delighted that they were as enthralled as she had been when she first heard it. Jessica parted company with her companions as they left the top lock; they were heading down towards Braunston while she was branching off on to the Leicester section of the Grand Union.

Passing a couple of marinas, set in tranquil surroundings amongst open fields, Jessica soon came close to the motorway again and found the noise of the traffic and smell of exhaust fumes an unwelcome change from the countryside through which she had just cruised. At one point, the canal actually ran alongside the lorry park of the motorway services; all she had to do was climb over the fence and she would once again be amidst crowds of people all rushing around the shops and cafes like a swarm of ants. Jessica concluded that she was much happier on this side of the fence using the mode of transport of her choice. Soon after this came Watford Locks where she had to wait in a queue with other boaters as the middle three locks were in a staircase. The helpful lock-keeper was on duty to ensure boats coming from different directions did not attempt to enter the staircase at the same time. He also taught Jessica how to operate the paddles in the staircase, using their red and white colouring to help her remember. It was important to open the red one first to empty water from the side pond into the lock below before opening the white paddle to send water from the higher lock into the side pond. It was an ingenious system for saving water and Jessica wondered why the side ponds at other locks were no longer used for this purpose. It was a pretty scene with its colourful tubs of flowers adorning the footbridges and when Jessica reached the top lock she was amused to see a picnic bench painted in the traditional black and white of the balance beams and paddle gear. She admired the magnificent view from the top looking back over the Northamptonshire countryside. It was like a painting, except that it was constantly on the move, the lively breeze rippling the surface of the water in each of the three side ponds and causing the grasses to dance. On the other side of the canal, the motorway spoilt what must once have been a breathtaking landscape. The fields were dotted with majestic old chestnut trees, amongst which the cattle grazed.

Leaving the locks and the motorway behind her, Jessica was once again in peaceful countryside and as the canal was swallowed up by the rolling landscape, she passed through a short tunnel. Beyond the tunnel was the village of Crick where she shopped for provisions and spent a pleasant evening in one of the pubs enjoying a pint of beer and some friendly company.

The next day started well. After giving herself a long lie-in, Jessica did not set off until after midday. She cruised peacefully through a long stretch of rural countryside with no villages beside the canal and no locks either. Jessica had no idea if Auntie Joan had ever come this way but she thought what a relief it would have been for her to have had such a long section without any locks. Joan and her crew had few opportunities to stop and rest during their trips so stretches like this must have been very precious. The three-women crew would have taken it in turns to have a break and Jessica remembered her aunt's description of how they used to swap over. She pictured her aunt jumping off the butty boat at one bridge hole and running ahead to the next one to climb aboard the motor boat before going down into the cosy cabin to put the kettle on the primus stove or else to sit on her bunk and write a letter. The canal continued along the contours, meandering past open fields and wooded cuttings. In places, the alder trees grew down to the water's edge, their limbs reaching right across the canal. On one of these branches Jessica spotted the iridescent bottle green head of a male mallard and laughed at its gaudy orange webbed feet as it left its perch to plop into the wash of water created by Ragamuffin. Soon afterwards she watched a squirrel dancing precariously along the higher branches above her head. "I wonder if they ever fall off?" she asked herself and pictured a funny scene with a squirrel running along the roof of the boat desperately trying to find its way ashore.

Towards the end of the afternoon, after passing through another short tunnel, Jessica began to look for somewhere to moor up for the night. Suddenly sensing that her engine smelt hot she

214

looked at the water temperature dial. It showed over a hundred degrees so had no choice but to cut the engine immediately. The bank was too overgrown with weeds for her to pull into the side so she switched off the engine where she was and allowed herself to drift while it cooled. The wind coming from behind caught Ragamuffin, pushing her into a position diagonally across the canal. Jessica hoped no other boats arrived while she was blocking their path but there was little she could do until she could get to the bank and tie up. Having no mobile phone was a real issue now; she would be unable to call out an engineer if the problem proved too much for her limited motor maintenance skills. Whilst she let the engine cool, Jessica consulted her guide-book to find the nearest boatyard. She was not sure exactly where she was; it had been some time since she had been aware of any signs of civilisation and she had not taken notice of the numbers on the bridges. But wherever she was, she must get the boat to a place where she could at least tie up so she climbed up on to the roof and lifted the heavy pole. She used the pole first to straighten Ragamuffin and then tried to push herself further along the canal to where there were fewer reeds. Once she got the boat moving again Jessica began to feel she was once again in control but her jubilation was short-lived as she heard the tell-tale scratching sound of Ragamuffin going aground. The sweat was pouring down her face and her arms ached - however hard she pushed, the boat would just not budge. The wind was driving Ragamuffin further on to the mud and it seemed like a losing battle. She contemplated attempting to jump to the bank where she could use the rope to pull Ragamuffin, but even if she succeeded in reaching the bank, getting back aboard would be almost impossible. Her only hope was that another boat would come along and help her but it was late in the day and she suspected all sensible boaters would have tied up by now as heavy rain was forecast. "I can't stay like this all night," she moaned. "Please, somebody come and help." She was angry with herself for not replacing her phone immediately; it would have been so easy to go shopping in Milton Keynes if she had not been in such a ridiculous hurry to set off after her misadventure. Still standing on the roof of the boat, she scoured the landscape for signs of nearby villages but all she could see were fields. One of these fields had cattle grazing in it, which was at least a good sign as there must be a milking shed somewhere nearby. Perhaps somebody would come walking along the towpath and she could throw them a rope. "Or perhaps not," she muttered, the long grass growing on the towpath clearly demonstrating that it did not get a great deal of use. Jessica was beginning to despair when she spotted another boat approaching her in the distance. "Thank goodness. Let's hope they've got an engineer on board, or at least a mobile phone." She stood on the roof, waving frantically to the helmsman of the oncoming boat so he could see there was a problem. She hoped that whoever was on the tiller was paying attention, as there was no way that she could move Ragamuffin out of their path. Fortunately the boat spotted her in good time and pulled into the bank quite some distance ahead where it looked like there was a better mooring place. Jessica waited for what seemed like hours while the helmsman of the other boat knocked in a couple of stakes so he could tie up his boat and leave it. She was greatly relieved when the figure finally approached her along the towpath. As this person drew near, Jessica could see that it was not a man but a woman. She too was apparently travelling alone as nobody else had appeared from within her boat. "Hi there, thanks for stopping," called Jessica, realising straight away what a stupid thing that was to say when Ragamuffin's position across the canal had left the other boater no choice.

216

"What's t'problem, ducks?"

"Engine's overheated and I've gone aground."

"How long ago did it overheat? D'yer think yer would be able to start it for a short while now?" the woman enquired, her calm, no-nonsense approach giving comfort to Jessica.

"Yes, it might be cool enough now. I'll give it a go."

"Throw me yer centre rope anyway. If yer could use yer engine just fer long enough to reverse off the mud, yer can switch off while I pull her along if needs be." So the two women worked together to release Ragamuffin and in a remarkably short time she was tied up next to the other boat. Jessica was overwhelmed with gratitude.

"Thanks so much for your help. I don't know what I would have done if you hadn't come along," she said.

"Ah, it's nowt ducks. A lot of people have helped me in t'past," came the affable reply. The woman stayed to watch while Jessica lifted up the decking board and examined the engine. She warned her against taking off the water cap until the engine had cooled down properly as it had heated up again whilst Jessica was reversing off the mud. They decided to have a drink while they waited and while Jessica was filling the kettle, the woman introduced herself as Sue. She suggested that it was too late in the day to call out an engineer but reassured Jessica that she would stick around in the morning until it was all sorted. She had a mobile phone and the guidebook would have the number of the nearest boatyard. Jessica's relief was so great that she started to cry. She felt like such a baby. "Don't worry. Let it all out me ducks. You had a bit of a fright, that's all. Did yer think her were going to be stuck there all night?" Sue said sympathetically.

"Yes, it was beginning to look that way. I'm sorry for being such a wimp." She blew her nose and dried her tears and sat down at the table with Sue, watching the rain hammering on the choppy surface of the canal. They agreed that it would be best to leave the engine until the morning as it was beginning to grow dark and the rain showed no signs of stopping.

That evening Jessica managed to forget about her engine troubles as she had such an enjoyable time playing cards and chatting on Sue's boat. It was a traditional boat with an engine room and bedroom at the back and the living space at the front. It was beautifully kept, with proper lace curtains and shining brasswork. Jessica discovered that Sue had been travelling around on her own since she had retired four years ago. She was a widow with no children so she had decided to rent out her house and have an adventure while she still could. There was nothing to keep her at home and the last thing she wanted was to spend the rest of her life feeling sorry for herself and waiting to die. "I thought I would only do it fer about a year but t'time has passed so quickly and it's been such fun. It's a grand life and I've been to most places in t'north of England. Now I'm on my way down south to London and then mebbe head west to Bath."

"Oh that means you'll go on the Thames. You'll love it - it's really exciting," Jessica told Sue all about her trip from Oxford and in exchange she learnt about the Huddersfield Canal that crossed the

218

Pennines and Sue's journey through the Standedge - the longest and deepest tunnel in the country.

"So what's it like living on a boat in winter?" asked Jessica, wondering how she herself would cope if she was still living on the boat once the weather grew cold.

"Once that stove's going, it's real cosy in here," Sue replied. "And it's so pretty in t'snow. When t'canal is covered in ice everything comes to a standstill and it's unbelievably quiet."

"Don't you ever leave the boat - not even in the winter?" Sue explained to Jessica that she had a nephew called Carl who lived in Birmingham with his wife Emily. She had arranged for all her mail to be delivered to his house and he would come and collect her every few weeks or so to take her home with him.

"It's strange being on land again after yer've been on the boat. Even though there is so much more space in Carl's house, I must admit I do get a bit claustrophobic when I'm shut up indoors all day. It makes a nice change fer a few days but I wouldn't like to be there all t'time." Jessica asked how well she got on with Carl's wife and Sue said, "Aye, she's a lovely girl and she always makes me feel so welcome. If I had a daughter I would want her to be just like Emily. Her mother died couple of years back - it were very sad. But now Emily's pregnant and it's going to be so lovely for them. That's another reason fer me to head south. I don't want to be in t'way when babby comes. They only have two bedrooms so I don't think it will be so convenient fer me to stay with them anymore. I've arranged t'have my post readdressed to post offices where I can collect it meself so Carl won't have to bother about that neither."

"But won't you miss them?"

"Yes terribly, but I'm not going to be a burden to anybody. They've done so much fer me already. Anyway, that's enough about me. I want to know what a young thing like you is doing travelling all alone." Sue listened patiently to Jessica's tale of her woes at school. She agreed that it had been a wise decision to take time out to reconsider her future, especially as Auntie Joan's inheritance had come along at just the right moment in her life. She told Jessica her aunt would have been proud of her if she could see how she was using the money.

"But I do get so lonely," confessed Jessica. "Don't you feel that too?"

"Aye, that I do. But then I'd be a darn sight more lonely stuck at home on me own. At least this way, I do get t'see folks. But it's different fer me - being lonely is just part of getting old. You shouldn't be though, at your age. Yer need to do summat about it." Jessica told Sue about her plans to return to Milton Keynes in September to do some supply teaching.

"I'm really looking forward to it," she enthused. "You never know, I may even go back to full-time teaching if it all works out. I'd like that."

"It's good yer have a plan. Now yer can enjoy a long holiday for the rest of t'summer. And who knows, summat else may come along in the meantime. I always think it's t'unexpected things that come along which make life so interesting. If yer knew exactly what tomorrow were going to bring, where's the excitement in that?" she declared.

Although the following morning was damp and grey with a cold northerly wind, Jessica was in a more positive mood. Her evening with Sue had been so interesting to the extent that she was really quite pleased to have broken down. Reflecting on Sue's suggestion that something else may come along before September she concluded that it might not be such a good idea to have the future too neatly mapped out. All sorts of possibilities lay where they were least expected. While she had a plan of sorts she must remember to keep her mind open to other opportunities. She thought back to when she was teaching; she always had a lesson plan, but often a child would say or do something to make her abandon her plan and do something different, generally resulting in a better outcome than it would otherwise have been. That was good teaching. Now she needed to apply the same principle to living.

Once Jessica examined her engine in the clear light of day she was able to diagnose the problem. She found a leak in the large rubber hose that ran from one skin tank to the other. It was not something she was going to be able to repair herself but she calculated that she should reach the nearest boatyard if she kept stopping the engine and topping up the water level every mile or so. Sue arrived on the scene and agreed that this was a good plan except that the nearest boatyard was two miles behind her with a tunnel to go through. "I must have cruised straight past it yesterday without noticing."

"I expect yer were daydreaming like I do when I'm on tiller. Never mind, I can give yer a lift up there in Mucky Duck. We'll take t'old hose with us to make sure we get right size. There's a junction just past the boatyard, where I can turn round and bring us back again," Sue suggested helpfully. Jessica hesitated before replying anxiously,

"Are you sure? That's going to take up a lot of your day. I could just call them out if I can borrow your phone."

"What, and deprive me of all t'fun? I'm not in any hurry to get anywhere. I told yer before, it's these unplanned things make life so much more interesting. Besides, yer don't want to go shelling out good money on call-out charges if yer can help it."

"But will I be able to fit the new hose myself?" Jessica procrastinated.

"If yer have the right tools yer will. I'd find it mighty difficult getting down there at my age but a young thing like you should manage it. And I've got plenty of tools yer could borrow." So Jessica agreed to accept help from Sue and once she had disconnected the old hose they set off in Mucky Duck to the boatyard. All seemed to be going too well, Jessica thought, and she was right. As they were about to enter the tunnel, Sue was dismayed by the discovery that her headlight was not working. So Jessica had to kneel on the front of Mucky Duck, holding up a torch to light the way. This cast just enough light for Sue to steer by and fortunately they did not meet any oncoming boats. But Jessica's back, still sore from the previous day's exertion, ached from the strange position she was in; she was relieved that it was only a short tunnel, not like Braunston or Blisworth. As they came out into the daylight she rejoined Sue at the stern.

"You see what I mean? It's t'unplanned things that make life better," laughed her friend. "If I hadn't bumped into yer, I would have had t'travel through that tunnel with nobody to hold t'torch fer me."

The people at the boatyard were very helpful and they fitted Sue with a new headlight bulb as well as supplying a hose of the right size for Jessica. The couple journeyed on to the junction with the Welford Arm, where Sue was able to turn Mucky Duck around for the return trip. This time they passed through the tunnel without incident, after which Sue let Jessica have a go on the tiller. She found steering the sixty foot narrowboat more challenging than manoeuvring Ragamuffin; it was slower to respond and the thought of damaging somebody else's boat was quite unnerving. She realised now how nervous Michael must have been when he was steering Ragamuffin, even though he hadn't shown it. At last the familiar sight of her boat came into view. Jessica found fitting the new hose considerably more difficult than taking off the old one as the bilges were now full of cold water that had drained from the system. She used her bilge pump to get rid of most of this but there was still enough residue to make it messy work. When she lost the jubilee clip in the water, she was afraid Sue may have been shocked by her bad language. Eventually though, she was finished and able to top up the system with fresh water. She could not spot any leaks and after running the engine for twenty minutes there seemed to be no signs of overheating. Jessica felt elated that she had achieved this task herself and she thanked Sue for all her help.

"Yer'll need to keep an eye on temperature gauge for the rest of t'day," Sue reminded her. "Yer may find yer've got an airlock in t'system. It's nothing serious, but yer will need to let t'engine cool down and then take off t'cap to release any trapped air. It may need doing a few times."

Before the two women set off on their separate ways, Jessica invited Sue aboard Ragamuffin for lunch. Although she was running out of fresh provisions she still had some tinned tuna and part-baked baguettes, which were much appreciated after their busy morning. When it was time for them to say goodbye they both felt quite sad, having developed a good friendship. Sue wrote down her phone number for Jessica, who promised to give her a call when she had a new phone. Mucky Duck was now facing the wrong way so Sue had to travel north for a mile or so to the next winding hole. Jessica, following behind on Ragamuffin, watched in admiration at how neatly Sue manoeuvred her boat. She waved sadly to her friend as the two boats passed one another, wondering if they would ever meet again.

"Thanks again for all your help. Hope you enjoy London," she called.

"I'm sure I will. Be careful yer engine don't overheat in t'Foxton Locks."

Foxton Locks were a real treat after so much isolation and Jessica decided to moor at the top so she could spend some time exploring the area. The locks were in two staircases of five, with a small pound between where boats could wait. To the side of each lock were large side ponds like those at Watford and Jessica spotted the same red and white markings to indicate which one should be opened first. Once again there was a lock keeper in attendance to help boaters through. The view from the top was incredible, but as the sky was overcast Jessica decided to take photos in the morning, which promised to be much brighter. Next to the flight of locks was the site of Foxton Inclined Plane, where in days gone by boats could be carried down the slope in large crates to bypass the locks. Jessica had seen a model of this in the museum at Stoke Bruerne and was delighted to see the site of the real thing. A steam-driven winch would have heaved the crates up to the top of the slope, with one crate going down as the other came up, rather like a ski-lift. It was such a shame it was now derelict with the chimney long gone and the boiler house turned into a museum. But Jessica still found it fascinating to look at the slope where the rails could still be clearly seen and to let her imagination fill in the rest.

"Michael would have loved this," she thought, remembering the interest he had shown at the museum. " He would have told me exactly how much energy would be consumed in raising a boat to the top, and probably how much it would have cost per boat as well. It's such a pity he's not here now." Her anger with Michael had now dissipated completely and she accepted that he had done her a big favour, setting her free from Steve to live her own life. Deciding it was time for a treat, she went for a meal in the pub at the bottom of the locks where she found an abundance of displayed photographs and memorabilia from when the Inclined Plane was in regular use. She wondered if Auntie Joan had ever been on the Inclined Plane but guessed that she had probably not or she would surely have told her about it.

The following morning was bright and chilly and Jessica had plenty of time to admire the view as the lock keeper explained that she would have to wait for two boats coming up the flight before she could go down. A family of swans approached her in search of food, the cygnets grown nearly as big as their parents, and she laughed at the high pitch squeaking of the youngsters.

"You sound more like a tiny moorhen chick, not at all like the big bird you are," she said to one of the cygnets as she threw some pieces of bread into the water. When her supply was finished, the swans slid away and Jessica strolled down to the bottom of the flight, where one boat was just entering the first lock and the second was still waiting to start the ascent. The boat in front was a hire boat full of novices and the lock keeper was patiently explaining to them how to use a windlass. It was obviously going to be a long wait. To pass the time, Jessica had a lengthy conversation with a lovely couple on the second boat, which was called Along Shortly. Although she was quite accustomed to the friendliness of other boaters by now, Jessica could still not get over how easy it was to strike up a conversation with complete strangers. Witnessing the light-hearted banter between this couple Jessica longed for companionship; she was tired of travelling alone. When the woman told her they had just celebrated their Golden Wedding on the waterfront at Market Harborough, Jessica was impressed. She doubted if she would ever find somebody special enough to want to spend fifty years with her. Then an unexpectedly chilly blast of wind made Jessica bid a hasty farewell to her companions and look for a warmer place to wait. She was lucky enough to find a bench that was sheltered from the wind but still bathed in sunshine. She basked like a lizard in the warmth of the sun, contemplating her solitary state.

226

As her body warmed, so her spirits rose again. Loneliness was a state of mind, she told herself, and being alone gave her the freedom to please herself. Besides, a spoonful of solitude was just the tonic she needed to put the past behind her. She tipped back her head and closed her eyes, allowing the sun to soak her face and neck.

"This is sublime. Enjoy it. No more self-pity," she commanded.

Chapter 15

"What destroys us most effectively is not a malign fate but our own capacity for self-deception and for degrading our own best self." George Eliot (Adam Bede)

Finally the summer holidays had begun and although Zena was overjoyed to have her boys home, she found the first week of the holiday somewhat challenging. The boys were impatient, eager to try out all the new fishing tackle that Rob had bought for them. During that first week at home they were bored and irritable and Zena was dismayed to see how quarrelsome they had become. Zac had changed beyond all recognition during his first year at boarding school and she hardly recognised the obstreperous nine-year old as the same child that used to be her little boy. He no longer wanted cuddles and would not share a book with her at bedtime, preferring to read on his own or play on his computer. Lawrence, at eleven years old, was more like a teenager and had learned to slam doors and sit in a sullen silence when he did not get his own way. Zena put down his bad moods to hormones and probable anxiety about moving from the Junior Department to Senior School in September. Rob was working long hours in the office attempting to wind up a contract before they went away on the boat. He had their three-week cruise all mapped out. They would go via Birmingham and Wolverhampton to Worcester and then return to the Grand Union via the Tardebigge Flight. Zena was looking forward to the hustle and bustle of Gas Street Basin and the excitement of travelling down the River Severn. She hoped they might visit a few museums along the way and possibly take a trip on the Severn Valley Railway.

A few days before they were due to set off, Zena took the boys shopping for clothes and shoes for the holiday. Rob had given her a generous sum of money for this purpose but Zena resented paying top prices for designer clothes that would only get spoiled or grown out of in no time. But when she led the boys into unfamiliar shops where she hoped to find better value for money, they were shocked and there were sulks and tantrums. Compromises were reached and purchases made, after which they went for ice cream to celebrate. Just as Zena was beginning to think that her boys had forgiven her for economising on their clothes, Lawrence's words were was as cold as the ice cream he had just eaten. "Is it because you don't love us that you are making us wear these horrible cheap clothes?" Zena stared at her son in disbelief. How could he possibly say such a thing? And since when had he become such a snobbish little brat? She did not know whether to blame the school or his hormones but of one thing she was certain - he was growing up to be too much like his father. Although she knew it was up to her to put it right she had not the faintest idea how. It was something she would have to think about. In the meantime, having had much practice in the art of appeasement, she settled for reassuring him.

"No, of course I love you! You know I do. It's just that I have been economising recently and I don't want to waste money on clothes that are more expensive than they need to be for a holiday on the canals. With these clothes, you can relax without having to worry about spoiling them. When we get back from holiday, we will be buying you new uniform for September and I promise you will have only the best of everything that you need for Senior School."

"Why are you economising? Is there a problem with Dad's work?" Zena could hear the alarm in Lawrence's voice but it was impossible to tell her son the real reason for her new thriftiness. She quickly reassured him that there was plenty of money and the boys had no need to worry on that score. "But if our boarding school fees are too much, you would tell us, wouldn't you?" Lawrence persisted.

"Yes, of course. But honestly, there is nothing to worry about. Dad is earning tons of money. Just wait till you see the boat - you will see then how well-off we are."

Zac had been sitting very quietly throughout this conversation and Zena asked him what he was thinking. He did not return her gaze but kept his eyes fixed seriously on the empty dish in front of him. His voice was hoarse. "I don't mind not going to boarding school if we can't afford it."

"Of course we can afford it. Don't be silly. But don't you like the school?" Zac explained to her that he got homesick and sometimes in bed at night he would start crying. Zena felt terrible and reached across the table to hold his hand but he snatched it away sharply. She was trying to reassure him that he would get used to school when Lawrence interrupted to complain that they never went home at weekends, unlike the other boys. He informed her that other parents visited and telephoned their children, while he and Zac did not even receive any letters from home. They had discussed it together and had come to the conclusion that Rob and Zena just did not love them as much as other parents loved their children. They had been sent to boarding school in order to get them out of the way. "But I would have you home every weekend if I could," replied Zena. "It's just

230

Dad knows more about these things than I do and he says it is better for you if we don't come and see you or bring you home for weekend visits."

"Well, Dad's talking out of his arse," said Lawrence. Zena was shocked, not only by Lawrence's choice of language, but by the truth in his last remark.

"Lawrence, don't talk about your father like that. He works very hard to earn the money to send you to one of the best schools in the country," she reprimanded firmly.

"Sorry," muttered Lawrence, and Zena squeezed his hand.

"Well I promise you that things will be different next term. Now I know how you both feel, I will certainly phone you or visit you every week."

Zac's eyes lit up. "Really?" he asked.

"Yes, really. I can't promise that Dad will do the same as he is absolutely convinced that it is better for you to have no contact with us in term time. But that won't stop me from coming on my own or at least phoning you when he is not around."

Lawrence fidgeted in his seat and looked worried. "So will it be like a secret?" he asked hoarsely. Zena explained that secrets were not a good idea and promised that she would talk to their father about it. She asked them to leave it to her to choose the right moment, which would probably be when they came back from the boat. By this time, both boys were smiling and the immediate crisis seemed to be over, but Zena took advantage of the opportunity to ask one more question.

"If you didn't have to go to boarding school and you could go to a school near home, what would you say?" There was a very long silence while each boy considered the question. It reminded Zena of the time Jessica had asked her what it was that she needed. Just like her, the boys were not used to being consulted about what they wanted. She made herself a promise that she would no longer allow Rob to stop her asking her sons about their dreams; without that information how could she possibly do the right thing?

"I'd still like to go to boarding school," said Lawrence. "As long as we could come home sometimes at the weekend."

"What about you Zac?"

"A lot of the boys do part-time boarding. I would quite like that. But I don't mind really. It would be cool to live at home and go to a day school. I don't know, I will do whatever you think is best for me." Zena longed to hug her youngest son, but aware of the embarrassment this would cause him, instead she flashed him a massive grin to demonstrate how much she appreciated his flexibility.

"Well, let's just leave it like that for now. But if either of you want to talk to me about it later, we can think about different possibilities. I just want the pair of you to be happy."

"And what about Dad?" asked Lawrence.

"Well, I suppose I want him to be happy as well, but we can't have everything. You two will always come first."

After the Foxton flight, the locks were once again doubles and Jessica was lucky enough to find a friendly couple on their way to Leicester who were happy to travel with her. On the stern of their boat was a platform upon which a motorbike balanced precariously and they needed a travelling companion who would treat their boat with respect. Although Jessica was slow because she was travelling alone, they were content to have somebody who would go first into each lock and use the rope to haul their boat well over to the side. Then they could bring the other boat alongside without fear of the bike being knocked. It required patience and consideration, but once they got into a rhythm the three of them worked well together and they decided to moor alongside one another overnight so they could journey together the following day.

After more meandering around the loops and tunnels of isolated countryside, the canal was finally swallowed up by the River Soar. Although the delicate pink and lilac flowers along the riverbank provided some residual charm, the hefty pipe bridges and cooling towers loudly proclaimed that the countryside was over and the serious business of industrial development had arrived. Electricity pylons, like massive monsters, stood guard at the entrance to the city. On one side of the river was a new housing development that Jessica thought resembled a prison block; on the other side was a large weir, clearly marked by orange warning buoys. A flock of Canada Geese occupied the crest of the weir, appearing to be walking on water as they charged each other along the wall, whooping loudly. As Jessica operated the lock, she wondered if the geese were trying to compete with the noise made by the crowd at the impressive Leicester City stadium that lay just beyond. She journeyed towards the centre of the city and found the good moorings at

233

Castle Gardens that Roy had described. This was in a convenient spot near the cathedral and museums but before Jessica could do any sightseeing she had to do some shopping. For the past couple of days, having used up all her fresh supplies, she had been living off tinned food. She also needed to buy herself a new mobile phone.

The first call Jessica made was to her parents as she guessed they would be worrying about her. It was Barbara who answered the phone and she told Jessica that Karen had rung them to find out if she was all right. Barbara said that Karen had also mentioned somebody called Michael who wanted her to get in touch with him as soon as possible. Jessica could hear the unspoken question in her mother's voice but chose not to say anything that might encourage her to put two and two together and make five. Barbara made no secret of the fact that she hoped to be a grandmother before too long. Barbara gave Jessica the phone numbers of Karen and Michael, and by the time she had written these down, it was her father's turn to talk to her so she escaped her mother's curiosity for the time being. Bob's first question was predictable. "How did you manage to lose your phone?"

Jessica paused for a moment, not wanting to tell an outright lie but not wishing to worry her father unnecessarily. "I reached into my bag to take out my phone while I was walking near the edge of the canal. It fell out of my hand."

"Well, it's better for your phone to go into the canal than for you to fall in," he replied philosophically. Jessica kept quiet. "Well your mum and I have decided that we are going to pay for your new one. Call it an early birthday present."

"You can't do that - it's way too expensive."

"Yes we can. Tell me how much it cost and I will transfer the money into your account." Jessica could tell from Bob's insistent tone of voice that she was not going to win this argument and she gave in gracefully. She resolved instead to blow her budget on spoiling Bob and Barbara when they came to stay with her.

As soon as Jessica had finished speaking to her father, she phoned Karen and they talked about how the arrangements for the wedding were progressing. Karen sounded amazingly calm about it all, seeming more intent on letting Jessica know just how concerned Michael had been about her. So Jessica's next phone call was to Michael. She expected it to be quite a brief call just to reassure him that she was all right but Michael was keen to hear all about her week in school and she found him so easy to talk to that they chatted for over an hour. When Michael finally rang off, Jessica discovered that her apprehension about Karen's wedding had given way to eager anticipation. It would be so good to see Michael again.

A very bubbly Karen picked Jessica up at Oxford station on the Friday afternoon and drove her back to the house, all the time talking incessantly about the wedding. Jessica, nervous to be once again travelling at a speed greater than three miles an hour, had to bite her fingers to stop herself telling Karen to be quiet and concentrate on her driving. She was beginning to dread the week ahead and wondered what she had let herself in for. It was something of a relief that Karen had insisted on just a very simple hen-night, not one of these crazy affairs that lasted all weekend involving spas and all-sorts. "Completely OTT" was how Karen had described such pre-nuptial bonanzas. A long-legged blonde girl called Angela was waiting for them at the house and Karen introduced her to Jessica as one of the other bridesmaids, the one who had arranged the hen-night. Karen worked with Angela and they had become very good friends since she moved to Oxford, often going out to see a film together or meeting up for a shopping expedition. Looking at Angela's polished nails and designer jeans, Jessica felt rather intimidated. The trousers and shirts she had bought in Milton Keynes were the only smart clothes she had with her and she possessed no make-up or nail varnish. Fortunately, Karen had anticipated this and told Jessica she had laid some clothes out on her bed that she could borrow for the hen-night if she wanted. Jessica chose to wear the black trousers she had brought with her, which were transformed when combined with one of Karen's tops and some shoes with heels. It was lucky that she and Karen were the same size; they had often borrowed each other's clothes and shoes when they were at college. Jessica soon discovered that Angela was a really lovely, easy-going type of girl and she could understand why Karen had become such good friends with her. So she was not in the least offended by Angela's offer to give her a makeover. Although she was not used to wearing make-up, Jessica was so pleased with the way she looked that she asked Angela if she would help her again on the morning of the wedding. Angela was only too happy to agree; another friend would be doing the bride's make-up so she would have plenty of time to sort Jessica out.

When they all went out together that night for the hen-night, Jessica was surprised by how much fun she had. She had not danced or drunk excessively in such a long time that she actually enjoyed the novelty of letting go of her inhibitions and just going along with everybody else. She liked Karen's new crowd and there were a few familiar faces from college as well so it was a good group of people. Most of all she enjoyed the sense of belonging; she had expected to feel like a fish out of water but had very quickly become absorbed into the group. She particularly liked Angela and thought what a pity it was that she would not see her again when the wedding was over. She was such a warm and funny person that Jessica felt envious of Karen having such a close friend to hang out with. Then she remembered Zena; if only she still had her phone number, she could have introduced her to all these lovely people in Oxford.

The following morning, Jessica's throbbing head and nauseous feeling in her stomach told her that she had the huge hangover she deserved. She was relieved that the dressmaker was not due to arrive until the afternoon so both she and Karen could spend the morning recovering. She thought about the previous night; although she had drunk way too much, it had been a successful evening and it had been wonderful to see Karen enjoying herself so much. Jessica had never seen Karen so excited about anything before but she hoped desperately that the wedding would not be the sole topic of conversation during her stay. She lay in bed contemplating the week ahead. Jack would be away from the house as he had already gone to stay with the Best Man until the wedding. Although Karen would be going into work during the daytime from Monday until Thursday she and Jessica would be able to spend time together in the evenings. Jessica could not recall which evening they would all be going down to the church for a run-through, but she did remember that Karen's parents were due to visit them on Sunday and they were all going out for a meal together. Jessica liked Karen's parents, especially her dad who had a wicked sense of humour. She was eager to see them again since they had not met since Graduation Day. The rest of the week should be fairly quiet until Friday. The dressmaker would be back on Friday morning and then there was the manicurist in the afternoon. They were going to the hairdresser on Saturday before returning to the house to have their make-up done and put on their dresses for the wedding. She had not yet seen the wedding dress and hoped it would be as beautiful as it sounded from Karen's description. Jessica resolved to make the most of the peace and quiet while Karen was at work for the next few days; there were plenty of books in Karen's house that she could borrow and she could go into Oxford if she felt like a change of scene.

That afternoon Angela arrived, along with Jack's two nieces aged eight and six. Jessica was apprehensive about trying on her bridesmaid's dress although she did not need to worry as Karen knew all too well the style that would suit her. She was deliriously happy with the off-the-shoulder style dress in royal blue taffeta fabric. Although she found the shoes pinched her feet terribly, the discomfort was worthwhile when she looked in the mirror and saw how her boyish looks had been totally transformed. The dress flattered her figure, enhancing her curves to make her look more like a woman. She had lost weight since had she sent her measurements to Karen but the dressmaker reassured her that it would fit perfectly with just a few tucks. Angela looked absolutely stunning in her identical dress, which needed no alterations, and the two little girls were like angels in their matching blue chiffon dresses. Just as Jessica was beginning to think that formal weddings might not be so bad after all, the youngest girl threw a terrific temper tantrum about the blue hairband she had to wear. Jessica would never have guessed that such an innocent-looking child could possess such a vocabulary. The little angel continued to scream hysterically at her mother and when this did not have the desired effect, she bit her older sister who then started to shriek uncontrollably and tugged fiercely at the younger girl's hair. The mother had great difficulty in prising her fingers open, and was rewarded with a scratch on the face from her youngest daughter and being kicked in the shins by the older one. Jessica surveyed the scene calmly, thankful that this was not her problem. It was such a relief that she no longer had to deal with ill-behaved children. However, her complacency was soon shattered by Angela's reminder that because Jessica was a teacher, Karen had suggested that she should be responsible for looking after the younger bridesmaids. "I got the hen-night to organise," she said, "and you get those little darlings."

Jessica's phone rang soon after the dressmaker and fellow bridesmaids had left. "Hi Jessica, it's Michael. I was wondering when you would be arriving in Oxford. Perhaps we could meet up for a drink before the wedding?" he suggested.

"I'm here already. I came on Friday for Karen's hen-night and will be staying here until the wedding. Yes please, I would love to meet up," Jessica responded happily. Since she wanted to make herself available in the evenings for anything Karen might wish to do, they arranged to meet on Monday lunchtime. She hoped he would not mention Steve; although she should be grateful to him for encouraging her to end the relationship she really wanted him to forget it had ever happened. She valued Michael's opinion and was still upset that he thought less of her for having had an affair with a married man.

239

Karen, seeing that Jessica was in a world of her own, became quite concerned and asked her if she was worrying about being a bridesmaid. "No, not at all. I was before this weekend. But now I have met all your lovely friends and been reminded what brilliant people your parents are, I feel so much more comfortable about it all. I'm really looking forward to the wedding in fact."

Michael was already in the pub when Jessica arrived and he jumped up to get her a drink. As they scanned the menu together, Jessica asked him what time he had to get back to work and was pleased to discover that he was in no particular hurry. "I went in very early this morning and I can work late this evening so we can take our time," he reassured her. "What about you?"

"Well, I need to get back in time to cook a meal for Karen but I haven't got anything else planned." Michael grinned, revealing those lovely dimples in his cheeks. "Good. It seems ages since we were in Stoke Bruerne." They placed their food orders and settled down for a good gossip. Michael wanted to know if she had heard from Zena and she told him that when they last spoke, Zena had decided to postpone telling Rob she was going to university until the last possible moment. Jessica had told her she thought this was a mistake and it would almost certainly mean the end of the marriage. They had not spoken since and Jessica explained that she had lost all her contact details when her phone went into the canal. "As you know, I've kept the same number, so she could call me. I was hoping you might have heard from her?"

"No, I'm afraid not. I wouldn't worry though. She strikes me as the sort of girl who only gets in touch when she needs something, so I guess she will phone one of us before too long," he replied cynically.

"I have a horrible suspicion that she's given in to Rob about having another baby and she's too embarrassed to tell me. Oh sorry, do you mind if I get this? You never know, it might even be Zena." Still having very few contacts stored in her phone, Jessica was unable to see who was calling her.

"Hello Jessica." The familiar voice was unmistakable and blood rushed to Jessica's face.

"I can't talk right now, I'll call you back later .... Calm down.... Steve, listen - it will be all right. Just take a deep breath and don't do anything yet.... No, Steve, I can't.... We'll talk later OK?" She pressed the key firmly and turned back to face Michael, smiling apologetically. "Sorry about that."

"So you're still seeing him?" Michael's tone was accusing.

"No, that's the first time we've spoken in weeks. The last time was the day you left Stoke Bruerne and I told him it was over."

"So why is he phoning you now?" Michael asked suspiciously.

"I'm not sure. He was in quite a state. It seems he has finally left Ali and she is denying him access to the kids. He needs a friend."

"Just be careful. You know where it ended last time you gave him a shoulder to cry on. Unless that's what you want?" he asked, studying her face intently. Jessica looked away.

"I don't know, Michael. I will have to call him back later but I'm not planning on getting involved with him again."

The arrival of their meals put an end to the conversation for the time being, giving them both time to think. Michael was thoroughly deflated; optimistic that Jessica would have ended the affair with Steve and got over the worst of it by now, he had hoped Karen's wedding would mark the beginning of the next stage in their friendship. But with Steve still very much on the scene there was no chance of that. Jessica was even more distressed. And angry. Angry with Steve - why had he chosen that particular moment to call? All those weeks of waiting for him and then just as her life was getting back to normal he had to mess everything up for her. Angry with herself for answering the call - whoever it was that was calling her, even if it had been Zena, it could not have been so important that it would not wait. By answering the phone she had unwittingly signalled to Michael that she would rather be talking to somebody else than to him. They both attempted to shove Steve to the back of their minds while they made small talk but the mood had shifted beyond salvation. They were polite but reserved as they parted company.

Jessica returned Steve's call as soon as she was back in Karen's house. She told him that the state of his marriage was no longer any of her business and reminded him of all the nasty things he had said to her the last time they had spoken. "So why are you calling me back then?" he asked. "I know you still love me, otherwise you wouldn't have made this call. Come on Jessica, we can be together now, isn't that what you wanted?" Steve's voice sounded as sexy as ever and Jessica's resolve began to weaken. She reminded herself that they had been so happy once. For months, all she had wanted was for him to leave Ali and be with her. Now that he had, there would be no more waiting alone in her studio flat for him to call, no more sneaking around, no more lying alone in a bed that he had deserted to return to his wife. They could be together, properly together. She could even take him home to meet her parents, she thought. But as they talked, it dawned on Jessica that Steve's voice was calm and he was in complete control of his emotions. So what was that earlier agitated state all about? She had seen it too often before - an act to win her sympathy and to manipulate her. Common sense overcame desire and she explained calmly that things were different between them now. The relationship was over; she was willing to be a friend if he needed someone to talk to, but no more. He then told her that he had been speaking to his solicitor and was in the process of fighting for custody of the children. The penny dropped.

"And you would be in a stronger position if you were in a steady relationship?"

"Yes, but that's not why I want..." Jessica rang off before he could finish.

"So that's why he called. The selfish pig just wanted to use me to get his children back. No way."

Chapter 16

"Why, oh why must one grow up, why must one inherit this heavy, numbing responsibility of living an undiscovered life? Out of the nothingness and the undifferentiated mass, to make something of herself! But what? In the obscurity and pathlessness to take a direction! But whither? How take even one step? And yet, how stand still? This was torment indeed, to inherit the responsibility of one's own life." D.H. Lawrence (The Rainbow)

The wedding went smoothly and it seemed that everybody was infected by Karen and Jack's happiness. Jessica worked wonders with the younger bridesmaids, keeping them entertained while they were waiting before the ceremony and even managing to shepherd them into the correct places for the many photographs. Karen was radiant in her simple white satin wedding dress while the permanent smile on Jack's face proclaimed him as the happiest man alive. Jessica could not help shedding a tear as they were exchanging vows. Instead of dabbing daintily with a tissue she rubbed her eyes fiercely, forgetting that she was wearing mascara. Fortunately it only smudged a little and, as everybody was looking at the bride and groom, it did not much matter. In the car that took them from the church to the hotel where the reception was being held, Angela cleaned her up and reapplied more mascara and lipstick. Jessica admired Angela's steady hand as the car jolted over bumps in the road, knocking the two of them into each other. When Angela had finished she thanked her for her kindness. "Oh it's nothing. Can't have all the photographs ruined can we?"

Jessica was disappointed that she was not sitting anywhere near Michael at the wedding breakfast. She was on the top table with Karen and Jack, their respective parents, the Best Man and Angela. To her great relief the younger bridesmaids were seated with their parents at another table. Michael was tucked away towards the back of the room where Jessica was unable to make eye contact with him. She left her seat to visit the Ladies and check on her make up, going out of her way to pass by his table on her way back. She hoped to stop and talk to him for a while but he did not notice her. He was deep in conversation with a petite redhead who looked absolutely gorgeous as she placed her delicate well-manicured hand on Michael's arm. Jessica felt unaccountably jealous.

Angela was in extremely good form and Jessica was pleased to be sitting next to her - if Michael was not to be her companion then Angela was the next best thing. She had a raunchy sense of humour and their lively conversation was punctuated with raucous laughter. When the speeches started, as usual some were rather predictable while others were hilarious. The Best Man was particularly funny, having known Jack since their school days together and possessing a plethora of secrets to tell. But none of the speeches lasted too long and Jessica and Angela moved into the next room, where there was music and dancing. Jessica tried to catch Michael's eye, wanting an opportunity to talk to him and to assure him that it really was over with Steve. But Michael seemed to be avoiding her, chatting for ages with friends at the bar and not coming anywhere near Jessica until she was dancing with a group of old college friends. However, when it was time for her to take the taxi back to Karen's house, she went over to speak to him and he said he would come outside and wait with her. Whilst they were waiting, she told him why Steve had phoned and what her answer had been. She persuaded him to spend another weekend on the boat after her parents had stayed.

"That would be really good, yes please, I'd like that. Actually, I'm owed some time off work. Would it be all right if I came for a bit longer - four days perhaps?"

"That's cool. Come by train so I can pick you up in one place and drop you off in another. Come for as long as you like." Jessica gave Michael a quick peck on the cheek before climbing into the taxi that whisked her away into the darkness.

Jessica locked up Karen's house late the next morning and posted the key through the letter box as instructed before heading off to the station. Her phone rang when she was on the train. "Steve, there's nothing else to say. It's over." Jessica was conscious of a general pricking up of ears amongst her fellow passengers. She sat forward in her seat, dropping her head so that she was talking to the floor. Steve's velvet voice was persistent.

"Just hear me out, please Jess. I understand why you are angry. I have treated you very badly and I'm sorry. But for Alice's and Tom's sake, please listen. I've got to get custody - they are not safe with their mother. Her drinking is worse than ever and she's very unstable. I've got to get them away from her."

"Then phone Social Services and tell them." Jessica answered abruptly and sat back in her seat. As she did so, the couple sitting opposite quickly shifted their gaze.

"But then they will get put into care whilst it's all sorted out. That's not fair on them," Steve continued.

"But at least they will be safe in the meantime. Look Steve, I really can't talk now. I'm on the train. Call me again in a couple of hours." As she put her phone back in her bag, Jessica avoided the sideways glances of her companions, pulling out a book she could pretend to be reading.

Jessica was delighted by how excited her father was when she met him and Barbara a few days later at Leicester station. He told Jessica that the city was full of history going back to Roman times and he was very keen that they should visit one of the museums near Castle Gardens. They went to have a look at Newarke Houses, a charming little museum of local history. Jessica was surprised at how interesting she found the display about the Royal Leicestershire Regiment, something she would never have given a second glance if she were not with her father. For some reason she tended to only associate the army with the two World Wars and modern conflicts such as Afghanistan so it was a surprise to learn that the regiment had been in existence since 1688 and had served in the colonies. Jessica thought the museum as a whole was delightfully put together with the 1940's reconstruction of a Leicester street being particularly memorable. She began to think about the exciting possibilities the museum offered for a school trip until she remembered the hard work and anxiety involved in organising such a visit. While Jessica was silently remonstrating with herself for romanticising teaching, Barbara interrupted her reveries. She complained that she was finding the museum too crowded and stuffy and was going out into the garden. Jessica left Bob enjoying the history of hosiery manufacturing and accompanied her mother outside. Jessica thought the garden was delightful, with its formal beds and old stone wall dating from before the time of the Civil War. Barbara commented on the garish colours of the towering university buildings surrounding the garden. Jessica thought the contrast between the old and the new was actually a vibrant and interesting additional feature, but resisted contradicting her mother.

After visiting the museum, they left their moorings and headed towards Mountsorrel, a village to the north of Leicester where Jessica planned to stop for the night. On the way they passed a short stretch of industrial canal where the water was black and full of litter. Jessica knew this was just something you had to live with; in order to appreciate the true beauty of the open countryside, it was necessary every now and then to encounter some unpleasant stretches like this. Barbara, however, did not share Jessica's philosophy and her racist remarks caused Jessica to regret her decision to invite her parents to stay on the boat for a whole week. While they had got on remarkably well that day in Cosgrove, staying overnight on the boat was another matter entirely. Fortunately, as they reached Birstall, Barbara's mood changed with the scenery and Jessica was relieved to hear her approving comments about the views across the lakes on either side of the canal and the neat modern houses with their well-tended gardens. By the time Mountsorrel came into view the mood was jovial and Jessica dared to hope that the holiday might after all be a success.

Barbara did not sleep well in Jessica's double bed as she disliked being squashed against the side of the boat when Bob rolled over in his sleep. She was also unhappy about being unable to get up and make herself a cup of tea in the middle of the night as this would have woken Jessica. So the following day she remained in bed for much of the morning. Jessica did not want to move Ragamuffin for fear of disturbing her, so she and Bob went for a walk around the village. She was quite pleased her mother was not with them; it was good to spend time alone with Bob, telling him all about her travels. For a while, she could forget her worries and pretend to be his little girl again, instead of a grown woman with her own life to sort out. They browsed happily in the shops together until it was time to return to the boat. Jessica was pleased to see that her mother was much happier that afternoon. She even had a brief turn at steering Ragamuffin and apologised to Jessica for her earlier anti-social episode. "That's OK Mum. You don't need to say sorry. It's your holiday and you should do as you please. You can stay in bed all day if you want to, it won't bother me," Jessica reassured her.

"I just had a bad night, that's all. I'm sure I will soon get used to your bed."

But Barbara did not get used to the bed and the following morning she was ominously quiet during breakfast. When she did not appear on deck, Jessica assumed she must have gone back to bed. She sat with her father on the stern of Ragamuffin, taking it in turns to steer, and as they went through Zouch he pointed out Ratcliffe power station in the distance. "The chimney looks like a giant cigarette coming out of the ground," commented Jessica, "and the white bit on the top is the filter." Bob chuckled at the analogy.

249

"And the giant also has eight egg cups," he added. As they neared the power station, Jessica noticed the tall chimney had disappeared - the eight cooling towers were still there, but the giant appeared to have smoked his cigarette. She was puzzled - how could you lose a chimney that size? But her question was answered as they rounded a bend and she glimpsed tiny fragments of chimney peeping through gaps in the clouds of steam from the cooling towers.

Bob had by this time learnt to steer Ragamuffin so well that when they reached Ratcliffe Lock, Jessica let him take the boat in on his own while she operated the gates with the crew from another boat that was travelling along behind them. It made a pleasant change for Jessica to have somebody else looking after Ragamuffin while she talked to other boaters. They had a long discussion about Leicester, a woman from the other boat saying how she hated the city because the water was so dirty. When Jessica told her about the lovely moorings close to the museums and the cathedral, she replied that perhaps she would moor there the next time they were passing that way. Then another member of the group pointed out a warning sign and Jessica called down to Bob, "Dad, it says there are strong currents from the right when you go out of the lock. Will you be OK or would you like me to take her out?"

"I'll be fine. And if I can't stop to pick you up, I'll see you in Nottingham," he joked.

"No, seriously though Dad, if you can't stop, the river is plenty wide enough for you to turn round and come back again." Jessica need not have worried; her father managed remarkably well, skilfully throwing a rope onto the landing stage where he could wait for Jessica to arrive when she had finished at the lock.

They soon reached the junction with the River Trent where the expanse of water was so vast it was more like a lake than a river. The navigation was clearly labelled, with marker buoys preventing boats from going down the wrong route. They moored soon afterwards in a pretty spot on the Cranfleet Cut and Bob pointed out a coot with its unmistakable white beak and striped head. They could not decide if the loud metallic "pinkt pinkt" cries were telling them to go away or requesting food. As Jessica spoke gently to the bird she realised how happy she was feeling; it was so good to have company again. But when she went below to organise lunch she discovered that Barbara had reorganised all her belongings. "Why have you moved everything, Mum?" she asked in exasperation.

"The cupboards needed a good clean, so while I was doing that, I decided to rearrange things a bit better."

"But now I can't find anything!" Jessica wailed.

"Well, if that's all the thanks I get for cleaning this pigsty, I wish I hadn't bothered."

"Yes, I wish that too. It's my boat and you need to respect that. You can't just come here and start organising everything."

After lunch, determined that her mother was not going to spoil her father's holiday, Jessica invited Bob to steer the boat again. They soon arrived at an amazingly beautiful stretch of river. As it was so wide they were able to ride along on the current at an exhilarating pace and Jessica was thankful that Roy had persuaded her to come this way rather than along the Erewash as she had planned. They stopped at

Beeston in the late afternoon and the three of them enjoyed a walk along the riverbank before dinner. As they walked, Jessica could feel the antagonism emanating from her mother. She shrugged off her feelings of resentment and tried to make conversation with her, asking her what she would like to do when they reached the centre of Nottingham the following day. Her mother was quite non-committal so she persevered. "You could go shopping or you could visit the castle or the caves. Or a museum perhaps?"

"We'll see," was all she got in reply so Jessica gave up and talked to her father instead for the remainder of the walk.

Later that evening, Barbara brought up the topic of Michael. "Did you call that young man back?"

"What young man?"

"Michael. The one who was worrying about you." Barbara gave Jessica a look that said she was not going to be fobbed off. Jessica explained that he was a friend of Karen's who she had seen a few times but that he was just a good friend, nothing more. She told Barbara not to start reading things into her friendship with Michael.

"He's nice, Mum, but I don't fancy him."

"So how will you meet somebody that you do fancy then? Not on the canals, surely - you need to find somebody respectable. It's time you grew up. You need to go back into teaching properly instead of messing about with supply teaching. There must be a school somewhere in the country that is desperate to recruit a teacher for September. It's not too late to stop this nonsense, you know," Barbara urged.

"It's not nonsense Mum. I'm happy and I'm working out what I want to do with my life."

"But you are becoming more like a dirty gipsy every day," Barbara lashed out. Jessica was furious. She had expected her mother to be pleased about her decision to try supply teaching, and this vicious attack took her off guard. Ignoring her father's warning look she replied angrily, "It's my life, and I will live it my way. I'm sorry if you don't approve and if you think I'm dirty, but if you don't like it you know where the door is." There followed a long silence between the two of them for the rest of the evening and there was nothing that Bob could say or do to lighten the mood. When Barbara took herself off to bed, Jessica sat up with her father for a while and he tried to placate her. "Your mum worries about you. She shouldn't have said that about gipsies, but it's only because she doesn't understand why you should want to live like this."

"But do you understand?" Jessica asked plaintively.

"Yes, I think it's a grand way of life, for a while. You should be enjoying yourself while you can. But you also need to prepare for your future. There will come a time when you need to think about getting yourself on the property ladder and to start saving for your pension," Bob counselled.

"But not yet, surely? The future scares me. I really don't want to think about it."

"You certainly need some time to sort out who you are and what you want to do. Personally I think the supply teaching is a good idea. It will give you the chance to find out if you really want to teach and also to discover a school that would be right for you. But don't feel you have to be a teacher just to please your mum if it's not right for you. Just believe in yourself - you could do almost anything you choose to do once you have decided. I'll talk to your mum and I'm sure she will come round in her own time."

The following morning Bob shuffled out of the cabin alone and made a cup of tea to take to Barbara in bed. He looked dreadful, Jessica thought. She had heard voices late into the night and could imagine what a hard time her mother had been giving him. "Morning, Dad. Did you manage to sleep?"

"Eventually. Your mum is really quite upset. Jess, would you be terribly offended if we got off when we reach Nottoingham? I don't think we can manage a full week on the boat after all." But Jessica, having been busy on the Internet, had a better idea.

"There's a station just a short walk from here with frequent trains to Birmingham New Street. She could be home in a couple of hours," she declared.

After her parents had left, Jessica put back all her belongings in their proper places and continued towards the centre of Nottingham. At Beeston Lock they had left the river and she was now cruising along a part of the Nottingham canal that had been built in response to the opening of the collieries. She remembered that this was the same canal that had been constructed across the Brangwens' land in "The Rainbow", cutting the farm off from the town of Ilkeston. Recalling the scene in the book where the canal burst its banks, she was reminded of her own misadventure. But she had

254

fallen into still water within reach of the reassuring bank, unlike the dark swirling blackness that had overcome the unconscious body of Tom Brangwen. She wondered what it was that drew her to scenes of drowning in books like "The Rainbow" and "The Mill on the Floss". Was that to be her destiny? She made herself a promise to be much more careful, reminding herself that water can be deadly despite the beguiling innocence of its softly rippling surface. A blow to the head as you fell in and you would have no chance.

Jessica was cruelly conscious that she was no longer "Daddy's little girl" when she made the mistake of walking into the centre of Nottingham that evening and watched gaggles of giggling girls tottering along the street in what she considered were ridiculous shoes. "On no, I sound just like my mother," she thought. It was not so many years ago that she had dressed just like that and gone to bars with her university friends but now she could think of nothing that she would like less. "Is this what I have become? A recluse, old before my time? I feel like I haven't even grown up yet but I'm acting like an old woman," she thought. "I suppose it's hardly surprising when you consider the average age of boaters must be at least fifty. The sooner I spend some time with people of my own age the better." She wished she could contact Zena but she still did not have her number. She must ask Michael if he had heard from her. Her spirits lifted with thoughts of Michael and the realisation that it was now only a week until he was coming to visit her. Perhaps the future was not so bleak after all. She wondered whether to stay in Nottingham and ask Michael to visit her there. She decided instead to return to Leicester and travel from there back towards Milton Keynes where she could try to meet up with Chris or Kate again before the start of term. Jessica was sick of being alone; having overdosed on solitude she was now in desperate need of company.

Zena wondered why Jessica had not answered her calls; she had tried several times every day for a week to speak to her to find out how her volunteering in school had gone. Finally she had left a voicemail message, followed up with a text, asking Jessica to get in touch. "Hi Jessica. it's Zena. Nothing to worry about but I would like to speak to you. Please call me." That was weeks ago, and having heard nothing back from Jessica by the time they set off on their family holiday, she imagined possible explanations for her silence. Perhaps she had upset her by not taking her advice about when to tell Rob about the nursing course? Or maybe Jessica had just decided that they had nothing in common and was bored with the friendship. "Whatever the reason," Zena concluded, "I am not going to hound her. I don't want her to think I only phone her when I need something. She must have got my messages and if she wants to speak to me, she has my number."

As Rob had predicted, Lawrence and Zac loved The Narrow Escape. And lying in bed each night, Zena found great comfort in the close proximity of her sons, tucked up in their cabin only a few feet away. An added bonus was that Rob did not expect his marital rights when the boys were within earshot. In fact, they were sleeping in separate berths in the rear cabin, having given their bedroom to the boys so she and Rob could watch TV and use the galley in the evenings without disturbing them. Zena had waited so long for the summer vacation to start, thinking it would never come, but now it was here she feared the weeks would pass by so quickly that the Autumn Term would be upon them before she knew it. Although she valued Jessica's opinion, she had chosen not to follow her advice but to let the boys have one more family holiday before telling Rob. The awful row that would inevitably follow her disclosure was something that could wait until September when the boys went back to school. And then her term would also be starting so she could move out immediately. Rob had been pushing her for an answer to his idea of having another baby and she had begged him to give her time to think about it. She knew there was little chance of salvaging the marriage and had been frantically saving enough money to enable her to get by on her own if necessary. Her own generous clothing allowance for the previous month had remained untouched. Rob had not noticed that she had changed to a cheaper hairdresser and was manicuring her own fingernails. Neither had he noticed her careful budgeting of the housekeeping money as she used slow cooking methods to disguise the cheaper cuts of meat. The kitchen cupboards, usually crammed full of luxury items, were almost bare, but Rob had seemed content with her explanation that she was running down old stocks so that she could replenish them with fresh items when they returned from the boat. These measures had allowed her to save enough to pay the deposit on the student accommodation that she had secured but she knew there would be much wrangling over money if she left Rob. To her relief, the evaluations she had already obtained on her most expensive items of jewellery meant that she could afford to pay her rent and other living expenses for several months at least, which she hoped would buy her enough time to sort out her finances. However, she was still anxious about moving away on her own to a place where she was a complete stranger and was keen to meet more of Jessica's friends who lived in

Oxford. Michael was very cute, she thought, and it would be lovely to get to know him properly if she left Rob. She wanted to call him but there were so few opportunities to have a private phone call now the boys were on the boat as well.

Chapter 17

"You can't insure against the future, except by really believing in the best bit of you, and in the power beyond it." D.H. Lawrence (Lady Chatterley's Lover)

Arriving back at the moorings at Castle Gardens by mid-morning on Friday, Jessica visited a nearby launderette and wondered how to pass the time until she could walk to the station to meet Michael. Having stocked up at the supermarket the previous day, her fridge and cupboards were crammed with more than enough food for a week. Still smarting from Barbara's comment about her boat being a pigsty, she spent the afternoon cleaning. By the time she had finished, the brasses twinkled in the late afternoon sun that was streaming through the spotless windows and her kitchen sink was shiny enough to impress even her mother. While she scrubbed, she hoped desperately that Michael had been able to leave work early and she repeatedly checked her phone for messages. She finished cleaning and sank down onto the sofa to wait for him to call. Studying her phone she was consumed with concern. Why had she not noticed before that she had no signal? Michael could have been trying to contact her all day. Perhaps he had even phoned to say he would not be coming after all or maybe he was already at the station waiting impatiently for her to arrive? She hurriedly locked up Ragamuffin and headed off towards the station, worrying all the time that Michael may have given up waiting and caught a train home again. Her phone picked up a signal as soon as she reached higher ground and she discovered a message from Michael. "Hi Jess, I am on the train. Will be arriving just before six. See you at the station?" Glancing at her watch, Jessica was relieved to see that it was now half past five. Perfect timing - she could breathe again. Once she had calmed down she realised how silly she had been to panic. She knew that Michael would not have caught a train back but would have used his initiative and walked to the canal to find her. As she replied to Michael's text she decided against signing off with her usual xxx as she generally did to her friends but settled for a simple, matter-of-fact message. "Just on my way to the station now. See you soon."

Their first afternoon and evening together passed incredibly quickly. Jessica shared with Michael the wedding photos she had taken on her phone and they reminisced on what a wonderful day it had been, agreeing together that Karen and Jack were made for one another. Jessica then told Michael about the disastrous visit from her parents and he understood why she missed her Auntie Joan so much. "Talking of Auntie Joan, I have a picture of her here, when she was young." Jessica produced the photos of her aunt and the other girl.

"See that girl she is with? She looks just like pictures of my grandma when she was young," Michael remarked casually.

"She wasn't called Gloria by any chance, was she?"

"Well actually she was. How did you know?" Jessica wanted to show Michael the letters but this seemed like too much of a betrayal to her aunt so she simply told him a little about them.

"But I'm confused," she said. "That can't be Gloria as they had split up before that picture was taken. And your grandma can't be her either because this Gloria married a doctor."

"Ah, that explains why you asked me if Grandma married a doctor. Well I suppose Gloria was a common name at that time. And the girl in the photo reminds me of Grandma because they had the same hairstyle and the same clothes but of course that was the fashion then. It's all just a coincidence," Michael concluded.

On their second day, they travelled through some stunning countryside between Leicester and Foxton. They established a good rhythm, taking turns in steering the boat and working the paddles until one particular lock threatened to disturb the harmony. Jessica brought Ragamuffin up to the gates to wait under a bridge that was just downstream of the lock while Michael raced up the steps to open the paddles. He was feeling confident and energetic and he worked the windlass quickly to raise the first paddle. As the water was released it passed under the boat and sucked it forward, forcing the bows to crash against the lock gates. Although Jessica attempted to reverse Ragamuffin back again, the power of the water was greater than that of the engine and she had no control of the boat. After the initial surge of water, the current eased slightly so she jumped down to the path, intending to tie the centre rope around a bollard. But as she jumped, Michael was already lifting the second paddle and once again the boat was sucked in by the force of the water. The rope was jerked out of Jessica's hands and Ragamuffin backed away beyond her reach. She screamed to Michael to drop the paddle again and Ragamuffin headed downstream and even further away from the side where Jessica watched helplessly. As she had jumped ashore, she had left the engine in reverse gear. Without the current from the emptying lock to suck her back, Ragamuffin was gaining speed. Michael ran down the steps to join Jessica and together they watched as Ragamuffin came to a halt amongst the roots and branches on the far side. Although Jessica was distraught, Michael could see the funny side of the situation. "Don't worry. She's not going anywhere now," he laughed. "The current will bring her round." And he was right. The water flowing downstream soon brought Ragamuffin across the canal so the bow rope was within Michael's reach. Jessica clambered aboard and fought her way through the foliage to the stern deck. Before long, she had manoeuvred the boat into a more dignified position. "Should we try that again?" Michael suggested. "But this time I suggest we tie her up first."

Jessica found that going back up the Foxton staircase was very easy with another pair of hands on board. It was a sultry afternoon as they made the ascent and Jessica was grateful to sit on Ragamuffin and watch Michael doing all the work. She admired the ease with which he wound the paddles and how comfortably he chatted to other boaters and the lock keeper. Jessica had found his company especially welcome after her experience with Barbara and her subsequent time alone. She found him so easy to get along with; if it had not been for her stupid inhibitions back in Abingdon all that time ago they could have been a proper couple by now, she told herself.

Although Michael had only been invited to stay on the boat for four days, he had in fact taken a whole week off work, hoping that romance might blossom between him and Jessica. Their friendship grew during the course of his visit and on his third night on the boat, when Jessica shared with him the letters between Joan and Gloria, he knew he had won her trust. He had so far refrained from questioning her about Steve but now the time seemed right to broach the subject. He was dismayed to learn that

262

Steve and his children would be visiting Jessica when she returned to Milton Keynes. She assured him that the affair was definitely over but she was worried about the children. They were not safe with their mother and she was helping Steve to get custody of them. As soon as that happened, she said, she would cut all ties with Steve. Michael swallowed his disappointment; Jessica was clearly not ready for a serious relationship with him and he could not ask her to sacrifice the children's welfare on his account. He would have to trust her - if she had said it was over with Steve, he had to believe that she meant it. He would wait.

The long lock-free pound after Foxton seemed less monotonous to Jessica on the way back. She pointed out to Michael the spot where she had broken down and told him all about her friend Sue. Michael amazed Jessica with his knowledge of wildlife, showing her the best places to look for kingfishers and giving names to the flora and fauna that she had previously admired but not identified. As he talked about Rosebay willow herb, sedge warblers and brown hawker dragonflies, Jessica guessed Michael would be able to answer her question about why there seemed to be no male mallards around after the baby chicks were hatched. She told him of her fanciful notion of the males all disappearing off on a holiday leaving the females to do all the work. Michael explained that the ducks were unable to fly during the season of their feather moult. By losing their coloured plumage, they would be better camouflaged and safer from predators. "But my explanation was more imaginative," she replied. Michael laughed.

"Yes, and much more fun than my stuffy account of the facts," he agreed amiably. "I hope I haven't been too much of a bore."

"No, not at all, its refreshing to learn new things," replied Jessica, returning his grin. She realised she still had much to learn about her environment, despite all that Auntie Joan had told her, and hoped Michael would be around to teach her.

They approached the main line of the Grand Union at Long Buckby and Jessica noticed the changes that had taken place in the countryside during the short time since she had travelled this way. At Watford locks, a buddleia bush that she had not noticed on her way up was now in full bloom, its purple flowers almost hidden behind a creamy cloud of butterflies. The blossom on the horse chestnut trees had already been replaced by the spiky green fruit that later would be prised apart by eager children in search of conkers. Jessica thought back to all the things that had happened since she was last here and observed that it was not just the countryside that had changed. She remembered how she had been struggling to put Steve out of her mind and realised how far she had come since then. No longer did she long for him. In fact the truth was she dreaded seeing him; she would be quite happy if she had nothing to do with him ever again. She was relieved that he had not phoned her at all during Michael's visit and pondered on the irony of all those wasted hours of her life waiting for Steve to call her. She was bitterly regretting having agreed to spend a whole day with him and the children and wondered how he had managed to persuade her that she would be able to put on a sufficiently convincing performance. Nobody must suspect that the affair was over when the children were questioned about "Daddy's new friend". It was going to be a terribly long and difficult day, she thought. She would much rather be spending more time with Michael. She feared that she might have ruined everything by telling Michael of her decision to help Steve get custody of the children. As she waited in the locks, watching him once again operate the paddles, she wondered what he really thought about her decision. He had refrained from passing judgement but if she was right in believing that he wanted more than just a friendship, why had he not at least tried to persuade her to change her mind about seeing Steve?

As the Narrow Escape slid into a space below the locks at Braunston, Zena jumped off and tied the centre rope to the bollard. "We should wait for another boat to go up with us," Rob shouted. "How about a cuppa while we wait?" Lawrence and Zac were by now so proficient at helping Zena with the locks that the three of them could have managed quite easily on their own but Rob thought the lock keeper would probably tell them to wait in order to save water. He also fancied the company of another boater; it could be very tedious stuck on the boat on his own whilst Zena and the boys worked the locks together. He decided that on their next trip he would teach Lawrence to steer the boat - that way he would eventually be able to leave Lawrence on the tiller and get off and do some locks himself.

By the time their tea was drunk, Rob was getting impatient. He was about to tell the lock keeper that they had waited long enough and would be going through the locks alone when another boat came in sight. Zena and the boys rushed off to prepare the lock and Rob waited to speak to the crew on the boat as it pulled in beside them. He hoped there would be somebody intelligent on the tiller - this trip had been very interesting so he had plenty to talk about. As the boat drew level, the helmsman called to Rob, "Hey mate, thanks for waiting but we're travelling with the boat behind us, so you go on ahead." Rob was peeved.

"Half an hour we've waited and now you're telling me we have to go on our own anyway? Well, thanks for nothing," he muttered.

On the whole, Zena thought, the holiday had been a great success for everybody. The boys had loved the fishing just as much as Rob had enjoyed teaching them. She had been able to relax completely, secure in the belief that Rob would behave himself in front of their sons. But arriving at Braunston reminded her just how close they were to the end of their journey and the beginning of her new future. With each passing mile the knot in her stomach grew until it choked her. The time for procrastination was almost over and she would soon have to confess to Rob what she had done. Maybe she should just accept the inevitable undeniable probability that Rob would never accept the changes she was forcing upon him. Perhaps she should just tell him straight out that she was leaving him and dedicate herself wholly to her studying. But she had to decide when would be the best time for her revelation. Should she wait until the boys were back at school or should she get it over and done with as soon as they arrived home? She knew that he would be expecting the babymaking to start on their first night so she resolved to tell him as soon as they got home and the boys were in bed. But how should she tell him? How would she find the right words? All these questions left Zena in a panic, her confusion like the fog of diesel fumes hanging in the air at the mouth of the Braunston Tunnel. As they once again entered the darkness she began to despair. She put her arm around the shoulders of her youngest son who was sitting with her in the bow of the boat and pulled him into a hug. He did not object to having cuddles with his mum when nobody else could see. Lawrence was on the stern deck with Rob, trying his hand at steering. Every so often, the boat would scrape along the rough brickwork of the tunnel and then hit the opposite side on the rebound as Lawrence tried to straighten her. Zena imagined how hard it must be for Rob to hold back and let Lawrence steer; but then he always had so much more patience with the boys than he did with her. She wondered how they would manage to resolve custody and access if they were to separate. It was going to be so painful for the boys as Rob would almost certainly use them as a weapon to punish her. An oncoming boat grew near and Zena guessed from the way The Narrow Escape slid gently to the side of the tunnel that Rob must have once again taken control of the tiller. "What's the matter, Mum?" Zac asked as the headlight from the approaching boat revealed the wetness on her cheeks.

"Nothing, baby, I'm fine."

"But your face is all wet."

"That's nothing, it was just water dripping from the roof. Look in front - can you see the light? Is that another boat coming or is it the end of the tunnel, do you think?"

They moored in a quiet spot just beyond the tunnel in a thickly wooded cutting that clothed The Narrow Escape in dappled green light. Rob was strangely agitated and Zena guessed there must be an issue at work that was bothering him. As soon as the boys were settled in bed, Rob told her they needed to talk, and Zena could tell that something was seriously wrong. Rob paced up and down the cabin as he spoke. "Lawrence said something today that I need you to clarify for me. It may be that he was mistaken in his interpretation of your position. I sincerely hope that is the case and I am giving you an opportunity to explain yourself." Zena wished he would stop talking like a lawyer and just tell her what was on his mind.

"What is it Rob?" she demanded.

"He told me that you promised him and Zac that you would visit them and phone them next term without my consent." Zena felt sick. For a moment she considered lying to Rob and telling him that Lawrence must have got it wrong. But it was finally time for honesty - that much was clear. First, though, she needed time to gather her thoughts - once she had made her confession there would be no going back.

"That's right Rob, I did say that to Lawrence and I will explain why. But first we need a drink; this is going to be a long and difficult conversation and we need to stay calm. We also need to wait until the boys are properly asleep." So while Rob was opening the wine, she slipped through into the next cabin and sat with her sons. Zac was already fast asleep but Lawrence was still reading. "Time for lights out," she whispered and he grudgingly switched off his light. Then she asked him if she could sit with him while he went to sleep like she used to do when he was little.

"Why?" he asked.

"I want to spend time with you while I can. The holiday is nearly over and I miss you when you are at school."

"OK then," he replied sleepily and for the next twenty minutes she sat on the floor with her head resting on the bed listening to the breathing of her boys. Zac was snoring very softly and Lawrence pulled the quilt over his head and sighed. She waited until she was sure her eldest son was asleep before raising her head to look at him. He had rolled on to his back and his mouth was slightly open.

"Goodnight baby," she whispered, kissing his forehead softly. There was no response and Zena tiptoed out of the cabin to face her future.

Jessica and Michael stopped at the top of Long Buckby for their final night together. From there it was possible to walk to the station but, as the walk involved a busy road, Michael had booked a taxi to collect him from a car park near to where they were moored. He almost asked if he could stay for another few days until Jessica met up with Steve in Milton Keynes. But any longer in her company and he feared that he would irreversibly ruin the trust that was slowly building between them. He would not be able to help himself - the urge to beg her to keep away from Steve was growing stronger by the minute. He must not allow his impatience jeopardise their future. Just as they finished securing the mooring ropes, another boat pulled in behind them. Jessica recognised the boat as Ruby and memories of her mishap filled her with embarrassment. Roy and Margaret waved cheerfully to her and she felt obliged to go and talk to them while they tied their ropes. She introduced Michael as her friend and explained to him that she had met Roy and Margaret when she was in Milton Keynes. "No more watery adventures I hope?" laughed Margaret.

"Oh no. Nothing like that," replied Jessica, changing the subject quickly. "So did you get to Stratford?"

"No we're just on our way there now," Roy told her. "We had some engine trouble." Margaret meanwhile had been studying Michael.

"I hope you are taking good care of her. Don't want any more accidents. Gave us quite a fright she did."

"I'll take care of her if she'll let me," replied Michael. "But the trouble is she's too busy taking care of other people's problems."

Back on Ragamuffin, Jessica had to own up to Michael about how she had fallen into the canal and how Roy and Margaret had helped her. He did not seem surprised by her story and told her how worried he had been when she had not answered her phone and how he had feared for her safety. To change the subject, Jessica brought out Auntie Joan's diary. "I thought you might like to see this. It will help you to understand why I am so keen to find the mysterious Gloria." Michael read some of the extracts from the diary and said,

"You know, it all seems to be too much of a coincidence. Do you mind if I talk to Grandma about it?"

"No not at all. If she does turn out to be the same Gloria I would love to meet her, if she wouldn't mind."

"I'll find out as soon as I get back and let you know. But don't be too disappointed if it turns out to be a coincidence. Actually though, I would like you to meet my Grandma anyway. She's an amazing woman and I think the two of you would get on well." Jessica, knowing how much Michael cared for his grandmother, was flattered. She turned to face him and smiled warmly.

"I'd like that very much."

Michael insisted on doing the cooking that evening. Jessica found it strange to have somebody else taking control in her galley and she hoped he would not attempt to reorganise it as Barbara had done. But Michael would never be so presumptuous. She slumped slothfully on the sofa, wine glass in hand, studying him as he moved easily around the tiny space. It was such a treat to be waited on, she thought. His meal was a simple but delicious spaghetti bolognese and Jessica remarked on how much better things always taste when somebody else has cooked them.

"Well it's your turn to visit me next time. Just wait and see what I can conjure up when I'm working in my own kitchen."

Jessica and Michael were both up at first light the next morning. They had a few hours before the taxi was due to arrive and chose to spend it walking along the towpath beside the locks. It was a glorious morning with the delicate mist like a veil of secrecy over the soft surface of the still water. The air was full of birdsong and scent of flowers from the cottage gardens. It was going to be unbearably hot again later and even at this early hour it was horribly humid. On the way down the locks they avoided the subject of Steve but he was ever present in both their

271

minds. Jessica was becoming increasingly anxious about the visit - how were the children going to react to her? Karen had said they would never accept her and she was probably right. It was going to be uncomfortable but she could live with that. It did not even matter if they hated her since she would not be staying with Steve any longer than was necessary. She reminded herself that what she was doing was for the good of the children. It was not nice but necessary. Michael was equally lost in his own thoughts. He guessed Steve would try to persuade Jessica to get back with him and began to doubt her resolve. He trusted her intentions; as far as she was concerned it was all about rescuing those children from their alcoholic mother. But she had not thought it through. Extricating herself later from the situation may be more complicated than she realised. Surely it would be even more difficult to leave Steve if she had formed an attachment with the children? And what damage might she do to those children in the process? And then, for all Michael knew, Steve may actually be a worse parent than their mother. In Michael's opinion, the whole sorry business needed to be investigated by people who were qualified and experienced in such affairs. He believed Jessica should leave it to Social Services and the courts to decide what would ultimately be best for the children.

They stopped about half way down the flight where one of the old side ponds had been converted into a nature reserve and they sat together on an old wooden bench to soak up the stillness and beauty. As they sat enjoying the birdsong and welcome shade from the early morning sunshine, Michael knew that he could keep quiet no longer. Jessica might not welcome what he had to say but what sort of friend would he be if he did not speak out? He had to at least try to protect her from making what might be the biggest mistake of her life. He tried to make his voice both gentle and assertive. "Jess, you're not going to like this, but as your mate I've got to say it. Are you sure that this little deception Steve has worked out is really such a good idea?" Jessica immediately went on the defensive.

"Look Michael, don't put pressure on me, OK? You know the situation and if you can't handle it, please don't say anything. I'm going to help Steve until those children are safe and there is nothing you can say that will change my mind." Michael could see the stubbornness on Jessica's face and was afraid to push it any further for fear of once again jeopardising their embryonic relationship. He sighed.

"Perhaps it's time we started to head back. My taxi will be here soon anyway." They returned to the towpath over the heavy lock gates and on the way Michael looked down at the dark water in the lock. Since no boats had passed through since the previous day, the surface was as still as a swimming pool full of inviting ice-cold water. If he did not know better he would have been tempted to dive in and clear himself of the oppressive heat and frustration.

On the walk back, the silence between them was as stony as the path along which they stepped. Jessica felt bad about snapping at Michael but concluded that if he was a real friend he must understand that she had no choice but to help those children. His judgement was clouded by his antagonism towards Steve, she told herself. As they reached the pedestrian tunnel just before the top lock she turned to him and said gently, "I'm sorry, Michael. I shouldn't have spoken to you like that. You are a good friend and I know you meant well."

"You're forgiven. Let's not spoil our friendship over it. I'm sorry if I spoke out of turn." He smiled sadly at her. They emerged from the tunnel into the brightness of the morning sunshine and caught sight of the waiting taxi, which had arrived early. Michael called to the driver to say he would be just a few minutes and they hurried off to collect his belongings. As Michael climbed into the taxi he said,

"Thanks for a lovely few days, Jess. Come and see me soon in Oxford."

"Yes I will. I can't wait." She stood watching as the taxi pulled out of the car park and disappeared from view. She wanted to run after it to ask Michael to stay with her until Steve and the children arrived, believing that his company would have given her the strength to face the unwelcome task ahead. But it was too late - he was gone and she was alone. Again.

Chapter 18

"What was he to do? He dared not go near her; her anger might leap out, and make a new barrier. He walked backward and forward in maddening perplexity." D.H.Lawrence (The Rainbow)

As soon as Michael's taxi disappeared from view, Jessica made her lonely way back to her boat. Another boat was approaching in the distance and she set the lock ready to steer Ragamuffin in. She counted her blessings that another boat had come along so quickly and she would be able to get these locks out of the way before the heat of the day became too oppressive. Once through the Buckby flight, she would have miles of lock-free cruising so she would make rapid progress. By rapid, she meant a speed that was slightly faster than the average walking pace, but on the canals that was something of a sprint.

Standing in the shadows on the blustery station platform, Michael shivered. His mind was in turmoil. Why had he simply not sent the taxi away and stayed for a few more days with Jessica? With more time, he was sure he could have persuaded her to think again about the foolishness of Steve's plan. As he boarded the train, disturbed by Jessica's dilemma and his failure to do the right thing, he dropped dispiritedly into the nearest available seat. He was annoyed with himself for not having put a proper argument to Jessica instead of backing off so quickly. "What a wimp! I must have one more try before it is too late," he berated himself. Snatching up his rucksack, he disembarked from the train and strode out of the shadows into the sunshine. The taxi was long gone but it was not too far to walk and he guessed Jessica would still be where he had left her. As he raced along the busy road, he ran through in his head what he would say to Jessica when he finally arrived. After about fifteen minutes he reached the canal and was able to get off the busy road and follow the towpath for the rest of the way.

While Michael was making his way back from the station, Jessica moved quickly through the locks. The man on the boat alongside her was rather sullen but she did not mind as she herself was in no mood for talking. Like Jessica, he was travelling alone so there was no crew to help the two of them, but it was still faster than it would have been if she had had been single-handed. They quickly got into a good rhythm of taking turns to operate the locks; while one went back to close the gates behind them, the other would go ahead to set up the next one. As they met just a couple of boats travelling upstream, most of the locks were set against them and it was physically very demanding. However, these were deep locks and waiting for them to fill gave Jessica plenty of time to recover from the exertion and also the opportunity to think. She wondered what Michael would have said to her about Steve and the children if she had not stopped him. If only she had let him speak. It would have been useful to get a different perspective on the situation; Michael might even have given her a reason that would justify her backing out of the arrangement. The closer she got to Milton Keynes the more she dreaded the prospect of pretending. Deceiving children did not feel right.

Jessica said goodbye to her travelling companion at the bottom lock and set off ahead of him. But the familiar sight of the words Mucky Duck caught her attention and she pulled in and tied up at the next available space. Sue was nowhere to be seen and the doors to Mucky Duck remained tightly closed when she knocked. She guessed that Sue must have crossed at the lock gates to the other side of the canal. She bumped into her at the door to the chandlery. "Hyup me ducks!"

"I thought you would be on your way up the Thames by now. What are you doing here?" Jessica squealed.

"Well, I had a call from Carl. They've asked me if I can moor my boat a bit closer to them for a few months. It appears that Emily's having twins and they'd like me around to help her during her pregnancy and when t'babbies arrive. There's a marina about five minutes away from their house and Carl has booked Mucky Duck into it fer a whole year from the beginning of September."

"That's great news Sue! But what about Bath?"

"Oh if it's lasted since the Romans I expect it will still be there next year." Sue was radiant; despite her love of travelling about the country on Mucky Duck, she looked like she had been given a new lease of life. Jessica was delighted for her.

"Are you in a hurry?" she asked. "Because it would be lovely if we could hang around here for the rest of the morning. I don't have to leave until after lunchtime."

"Good. Let's have lunch together. Your boat or mine?"

Rob watched his wife and sons as they prepared Buckby Top Lock, observing how

277

efficiently they worked as a team and how effortlessly Zena remained in total control. He knew he should have waited for another boat to join them through the flight but he was in no mood for conversation and he wanted to get back to the marina as quickly as possible. He could not believe Zena had applied for that nursing course without consulting him or how well she had concealed her excitement when she had been accepted. It seemed as though she had it all worked out and he would have remained in total ignorance until the last moment if Lawrence had not given the game away. He felt as if he no longer knew her - how could she contemplate breaking up their marriage and jeopardising their sons' happiness? The reason for her lukewarm reaction to his suggestion that they should have another baby was now painfully clear. But he was proud of the way he had reacted when she had told him what she had done; there had been no angry scene and although she had deprived him of all power at least his dignity remained intact. He had to admire her style. Her absolute ultimatum left no room for negotiation; he must let her study as a nurse and have as much contact with the boys as she wanted or else she would leave him. It was as simple as that - take it or leave it. He already knew what his answer would be but by keeping her waiting for his response he was beginning to restore the balance of power. He knew he could not live without her but he would at least make her suffer for a while before he told her. The skilled negotiator in him still hoped to achieve some sort of compromise.

Had Michael arrived at the canal just a few minutes' earlier, he would have seen Jessica come past this spot on her way down the flight. But unaware that she had already set off from her mooring, he headed upstream. Emerging into the sunlight from the pedestrian tunnel at Buckby Top Lock he stopped for a moment to catch his breath. He recognised Zena immediately but was in too much of a hurry to stop and speak to her and hurried past the lock before she noticed him. Ruby was still moored next to the empty space where Ragamuffin had been and Roy and Margaret were on the front deck. "How long ago did she leave?" he called to them.

"Not sure. About half an hour ago, I think. There was another boat went with her. She'll be near the bottom of the flight by now," Roy informed him.

"I'd better run then," he said and set off again, wishing his rucksack was not so heavy.

"Good luck," Margaret called after him. "If you keep going you'll catch her. There's only one way she can have gone."

While Michael was starting to retrace his steps, Rob was just bringing The Narrow Escape smoothly into the lock. He steered remarkably well considering he was on the phone having a heated discussion with one of his colleagues. After closing the gates behind him, Zena and the boys went to the far end to release the water. She caught sight of Michael as he arrived beside the lock. "Hello Michael," she shouted, waving her arms to attract his attention. Pretending to have neither heard nor seen her, he dashed down the steps of the pedestrian tunnel until Zena's scream arrested his descent. He went back up the steps to see Lawrence on his knees, peering desperately over the edge of the lock and for a moment it looked as though he were about to topple in. Michael remembered Jessica's story about

279

Winston the cat who had fallen in at this exact lock but Zena's screams made it clear that more than a cat had gone in this time. He looked to the stern of the boat and saw the empty deck where Rob had been. Seizing the life buoy from the roof of the boat, he hurled it into the water near the spot where Lawrence was staring. When the boat drifted across to the far side of the double lock, Zena was able to jump aboard and cut the engine. Michael searched for signs of Rob in the churning depths below. The lock was by now about three quarters full. Should he leave the paddles open so the lock would continue to empty or close them to slow down the current? Deciding that Rob would be long dead before the lock would have had time to empty he released the catch on the paddle and called to Zac to do the same on the opposite side. There was a harsh rattling from the paddles before the deafening roar of emptying water subsided. But the silence was deceptive as the turbulent tossing of the life buoy demonstrated the immense energy of the residual currents in the lock. There was no sign of Rob, and Michael wondered if he could possibly have been sucked through to the canal below. Or perhaps he was under the boat somewhere? He quickly pulled off his shoes and jacket and scrambled down the ladder into the water. "No Michael, it's too dangerous!" Zena screamed. But either he could not hear her or he chose not to listen as he dived into the blackness. Zena felt helpless, standing there on the boat doing nothing, convinced that both Rob and Michael would be drowned. She contemplated throwing a rope to Lawrence so he could pull the boat over to his side but decided it was best to let it drift rather than risk trapping either Rob or Michael between the boat and the wall of the lock. After another minute that lasted an era, Rob's head broke the surface of the water behind the boat. Lying face down across the stern deck, Zena reached down and grabbed his collar but not even the adrenalin pumping around her blood could give her the strength to lift him. She did however manage to keep his head above water until he got one foot on the propellor and with her help he heaved himself aboard, screaming in pain all the while. Lawrence meanwhile had reached across for the centre rope and was pulling The Narrow Escape into the side. Zac had climbed onto the back gate to get a better view. "Michael. Where's Michael?" The hysteria in Zena's voice silenced Rob.

"It's OK mum, he's there," shouted Zac, pointing to the ladder on the far side of the lock where Michael was hanging on to the rungs. He was deathly white and heaving for breath and Zena feared he was going to pass out and fall back into the water. However the customers of the pub alongside the lock had by this time appeared on the scene so there were numerous hands reaching out to Michael, helping him up the ladder and then sitting him at one of the pub tables to recover. On the boat, Rob was making enough noise to satisfy Zena that there was not too much wrong with him so she turned her attention to Zac, telling him to come off the lock gate and wait with Lawrence before there were any more accidents.

The ambulance arrived not long afterwards. Still screaming with the pain of his apparently dislocated shoulder and with a huge gash across his forehead, the paramedics decided Rob needed to go to hospital. Michael, on the other hand, felt fine and assured them that he did not need any treatment. Turning to Zena he said, "Don't worry about your boat. I'll move her out of the lock and moor her safely if you and the boys want to go with your husband?"

"No thanks, he's in good hands. We'll stay here with you," she replied and Michael marvelled at how calm she was.

While Michael had a hot bath, some of the other boaters helped Zena and the boys to bring The Narrow Escape out of the lock and moor her next to Ruby in the space recently vacated by Ragamuffin. Margaret came aboard with mugs of tea for Zena and Michael and sweets for the boys. She wanted to know all the details; this was a story that she would be retelling many times on her journey to Stratford. Lawrence and Zac soon grew bored sitting with the adults so Zena suggested that they do some fishing from the front of the boat. Eventually Roy came to collect Margaret, leaving Zena and Michael in peace. Zena phoned the hospital and learnt that Rob's head injury was considered minor and that he was still waiting for his shoulder to be reset. She turned her attention to Michael. "So, tell me Michael. What are you doing here, apart from diving into locks?"

"I was visiting Jess. She has gone on towards Milton Keynes and I was supposed to be catching a train home but I changed my mind and came back. There is something I need to talk to her about." Zena studied Michael's face, trying to establish if he wanted to tell her more. Well aware of her growing attraction towards him, she needed to understand the nature of the relationship between him and Jessica. She decided there was no other way but a direct question. "So are you and Jess together now?"

"No. When I first met her, I fancied her like mad. But she's made it clear she was not interested and we're just friends. Although I don't think I have been a very good friend to her today. I just wanted to talk to her to try and stop her from making a big mistake. But she'll have got so far ahead by now that

I suppose I won't catch her up today. I'll just have to phone her instead."

"Does this big mistake have something to do with Steve, by any chance?"

"Of course. Who else? For such an intelligent girl it's amazing how stupid she can be."

Their conversation was interrupted by a phone call from Rob. He hoped to be discharged within an hour or so and planned to get a taxi back to the boat. "But whether we will get back to the marina before dark is debatable. I don't think Lawrence is up to steering the boat into the locks and you certainly can't do it. I really needed to get back to work tomorrow," he complained.

"Hang on a sec - I think I may have the answer," Zena replied and she asked Michael how confident he was at steering and if he felt like helping her take the boat back. When he readily agreed, Zena told Rob of the plan. He was unsure at first but Zena explained that Michael had been steering Ragamuffin for the past few days and Ragamuffin did not even have bow thrusters. Zena guessed Michael's boatmanship skills were not the only thing on Rob's mind. "It's OK Rob, he's Jessica's boyfriend and the boys are here too so there's nothing for you to worry about. Yes, get a taxi to the marina and we'll meet you there." Michael gave Zena a quizzical look as she ended the call. "He gets very jealous," she explained.

"I know, Jessica told me. She can't understand why you stay with him."

"Then she'll be very pleased to know that I'm leaving him. What has happened today has shown me that's the only possible way forward. When Rob was under the water today, I was scared. I wouldn't have wanted him to die like that, especially in front of the boys. But I was nothing like as relieved as I should have been when it turned out he was all right. I was just irritated by all the fuss he was making. It was as though I didn't really care one way or the other whether he had lived or died. And that proves it's right to leave him."

A fine lunch was created with bread, cheese and wine from Sue's boat and Jessica's supply of cold meat and salad. The two of them sat on the front deck of Jessica's boat, eating, drinking and catching up with each other's news. Sue leaned back in her seat, stretching her arms above her head. "Well, I don't know about you me ducks, but I'm too hot and too tired t'move anywhere today. I think I'm going t'stay put until morning."

"Well, I don't need to leave just yet but I really should do a few more hours. I need to be in the centre of Milton Keynes by first thing on Saturday morning," Jessica sighed.

"What's t'hurry? Ah, yer've got a date, haven't yer?"

"No, nothing like that. Absolutely not," said Jessica emphatically.

"But there's a man involved?" Seeing that Sue was intent on finding out about her personal life, Jessica unburdened herself of the whole sorry story. Sue listened patiently, her face becoming steadily more serious as the tale unfolded. In the end, she shook her head at Jessica and sighed. "I can see you don't approve," said Jessica.

"No, I don't. I think yer made a big mistake t'begin with and I'm glad yer saw sense and got yerself out of it. But why the dickens are yer getting involved again now?"

"Because of the children," Jessica explained. "I need to help Steve to get them away from their mother."

"But surely that's up to Social Services, not you. And what happens when the kiddies realise their daddy tricked them? I know yer mean well but I think yer making a big mistake, me ducks. I think yer might end up making t'situation a whole lot worse instead of better." Sue could see the tears forming in Jessica's eyes and her lip beginning to quiver. She moved across to the towpath side of the boat and sat on the bench beside Jessica, putting an arm gently around her shoulders. "I'm sorry I were so blunt," she continued, "but I couldn't just sit back and listen to yer talking 'bout doing summat yer'll regret fer t'rest of yer life."

"I must admit, this idea has never has felt quite right," Jessica admitted, "but Steve was so sure that it was the only thing to do."

"I have generally found that when things don't feel quite right, there's a very good reason for it," Sue said. "It usually isn't right. And when yer deceive somebody, yer hurt not only them, yer hurt yerself an' all." Jessica lost her battle with the tears. She did not know what she was crying about - whether it was the end of her relationship with Steve, or her anxiety about seeing him and his children or a

285

mixture of the two. But regardless of the reason, once she started to cry, she just could not stop. Sue stayed with Jessica until she was less tearful, only returning to her boat when she was sure that her young friend would be all right.   After she had gone, Jessica thought hard about all Sue had said to her. It made a lot of sense and was probably what Michael had been trying to tell her if only she had given him the chance. Her hands were trembling as she dialled Steve's number and left him her brief message.

"Hi Steve. It's Jess. I won't be able to come and meet the children with you after all. Sorry to mess you about, but I can't do it. I'm sorry." She was relieved that Steve had not answered; he would only have tried to persuade her to change her mind again. He always could persuade her, it was as if she had no free will of her own when he was around. She wondered if she would have allowed herself to agree to his scheme if she had not been feeling so alone when he had called her in Nottingham. If she had not had that falling out with her mother, she might have been stronger. And once she had agreed, there had been no going back. Since there was now no reason to reach Milton Keynes in a hurry, Jessica realised that she need not travel any further that day. So she decided to clean herself up and go and see Sue. She was a good friend and a good listener, very much like Michael, the only difference being that Jessica had allowed Sue to speak her mind.

Jessica's phone rang while she was coming out of the shower and she guessed it would be Steve. She refused to answer it. When she was dry and dressed, she discovered that she had a voicemail message. She ignored it; the last thing she needed was to hear Steve's voice begging her to reconsider, for the sake of the children of course. She deliberately left her phone on the boat while she went to enjoy an evening with Sue.

Michael was rather apprehensive about steering The Narrow Escape and was relieved to see that the boat accompanying them down the Long Buckby flight was also in such a pristine condition that its owner was unlikely to bump into The Narrow Escape as they went into the locks. It would have been very unfortunate if they had been joined at this point by one of those characters who gaily banged their boats into the lock sides and into other boats and cheerfully shouted, "Well, it is a contact sport, isn't it?" These people were usually in hire boats. Fortunately, the owner of this boat actually turned out to be very helpful and, when Michael explained the situation to him, he was only too happy to advise him on when and how to use the bow and stern thrusters. Meanwhile Zena and the boys worked the locks efficiently with the woman from the other boat, raising the paddles very slowly to avoid strong currents that would toss the boats around excessively. By the time they came out of the bottom lock, Michael was enjoying himself immensely and was even a little disappointed that he would have no more locks to go through before they reached the marina. Zena and the boys came aboard at the foot of the last lock. "Boys, I'm going to stay on the back to help Michael. Be good. You can help yourselves to drink and ice cream if you like."

"Thanks, Mum. Can we have the TV on?"

"You won't get a signal as the aerial is down. But you can use the iPad." Confident that her boys would be happily occupied for at least half an hour, Zena joined Michael on the large cruiser deck. "Well done Michael. You steered so well! Not a single bump," she beamed, giving him the high fives.

"Well it was a great team effort," he replied. "We work well together."

Zena felt the fire burning inside her and wondered if Michael was feeling the same way. Soon she would be free from her husband and she felt as if she would explode with excitement. "Yes, we do," she murmured, stepping off to untie the mooring rope and climbing gracefully back on to the stern deck, allowing her body to brush against Michael as she bent under the tiller. Tentatively she put her hand on Michael's steering arm and looked up at him. Michael switched the tiller to his other hand and moved to stand next to her, draping his free arm casually around her shoulder. He was already alive with the excitement of having steered The Narrow Escape through the locks; this unexpected turn of events aroused another sensation within him. He rationalised his emotions. "Why wait any longer for Jessica when I can have this beautiful girl who is on the point of leaving her husband and moving to Oxford? Surely this is what is meant to be," he told himself. "Especially as Jessica will almost certainly end up getting back with Steve. I'm just wasting my time there." He pulled Zena closer. They were both so absorbed in each other that neither of them noticed Ragamuffin as they cruised past.

Chapter 19

"She was no longer struggling against the perception of facts, but adjusting herself to their clearest perception." George Eliot (Middlemarch)

"Well, those two haven't wasted any time," gasped Jessica, as she stood on the towpath and watched The Narrow Escape disappear into the distance. She staggered in disbelief towards Sue's boat and the tears started again as she knocked on the door.

"Oh, Jessica. Whatever is the matter?"

"It's my two friends. I introduced them to each other and I so much wanted it to work out between them but now it has and they didn't tell me and I feel so stupid and let down. He could have told me instead of pretending he was catching a train," Jessica gabbled incoherently.

"Oh dear, come aboard me ducks. Tell me all about it." Sue took hold of Jessica's arm and shepherded her into the cosy front cabin. She sat beside her, holding her hand and waiting for the tears to subside.

"Oh, Sue I'm so sorry. You must think I'm such a wimp. Believe it or not, I don't usually cry. I don't know what's got into me recently," Jessica sobbed.

"Well perhaps yer just need a good cry. Don't yer worry about me - just let it all come out. Maybe yer've been bottling up too many things fer too long. But I'm a bit confused about what's upsetting yer this time."

"It was seeing Michael and Zena together on the boat. I wanted them to get together but I didn't expect them to hide it from me," she wailed. "I feel so stupid. And angry. I was only with Michael this morning and he told me he was catching a train to Oxford. Why did he have to lie to me?" Then Jessica saw Sue's knowing look and remembered their earlier conversation. "Yes, you're right. You said it hurts when you're deceived. And the way I am feeling now is exactly how Alice and Tom would have felt if they'd found out I'd been pretending to be their Daddy's girlfriend."

"Sounds like yer've changed yer mind then?"

"Yes and I have phoned Steve to tell him. And I was so pleased with myself that I was on my way to ask you if you'd like to celebrate with me when I saw them go past." Jessica held up the bottle of Merlot.

"And now it seems like yer need someone to help yer drown yer sorrows instead. Well, I can do either." Sue reached up to the top shelf for a couple of wine glasses and took a second bottle of red wine from the cupboard under the sink. "Although I think one bottle won't be nearly enough after the day yer've just had."

As Rob thanked Michael for his help in bringing The Narrow Escape back to the marina he resisted the temptation to inspect the paintwork for scratches. He was tired anyway and just wanted to get back home.

"We're going to have a slight detour via Oxford," announced Zena, before closing the passenger door for Rob and checking the boys had their seat belts on. "After all Michael has done for us today, we must at least take him home."

"No, just drop me off at a station. I'll be fine," interrupted Michael. "Rob looks shattered and you should get him home as quickly as you can." But Zena would not hear of it and announced that she would drop Rob and the boys off at home and then drive to Oxford with Michael. Rob had never seen his wife so assertive before and it amused him to see how she resembled the bossy nurses he had seen at hospital that morning. He began to picture Zena in a nurse's uniform. Although he had previously resisted the idea of her going out to work, he was beginning to understand that if she was boring it was because she was bored. By insisting that she stayed at home he had denied her the opportunity to grow into anything other than a housewife. She was a clever girl and as her husband it was his duty to provide all the assistance she needed to succeed at college. By the time they arrived home, he had already sketched in his mind a detailed plan of the extension he was going to have built on the back of the house where Zena would have her own private study overlooking the garden. As soon as she returned from taking Michael to Oxford he would tell her of his decision to support her through college and of all the things he was going to do to help her.

Sitting in the back of the Lexus, Michael was considering what he should say to Zena after they had dropped off Rob and the boys. She would be expecting something; the first tentative moves towards a relationship had been made and there was a definite spark between them. He reminded himself sternly that just because Zena was so obviously attracted to him that did not mean he had to jump into bed with her at the earliest opportunity. He remembered how he had got it so terribly wrong with Jessica and did not wish to make the same mistake again. He must be patient. He wondered what Jessica would think if she could read his mind now. He laughed to think what a hard time she would give him if she knew he was contemplating an affair with a married woman. He wondered where she was at this moment. Moored somewhere near Milton Keynes no doubt. He desperately hoped she had changed her mind about meeting Steve and his children. Once again he felt the guilt of his failure. He should have tried harder; if it had not been for Rob's accident at the lock, he would have caught up with her and she might have listened to reason. He sent her a text. "Hi Jessica. Can you give me a call tonight if it's not too late when you get this? Or in the morning. I need to speak to you. All the best, Michael."

As she drove, Zena contemplated the possibilities that lay ahead. She had allowed herself to fantasise about Michael while they were together on the back of the boat, safe in the knowledge that nothing would happen while the boys were there. But now it was decision time. When Jessica had asked her all those months ago what it was that she needed, she had no idea. Now she knew what had been missing. It was not just the boys and a career that she had yearned for - she also wanted passion and tenderness and sexual gratification. She wanted somebody who would love her for who she really was, not just the perfect wife that Rob had created. She wanted Michael. The experience of driving Rob's car while he sat helplessly beside her gave her

292

an unfamiliar sense of power. She thrilled with the idea that her potential lover was occupying the car seat immediately behind her husband; it was ironic that after all his earlier jealous outbursts, Rob now had absolutely no idea of how she was feeling or what she was planning. Within a couple of hours, in the very seat where Rob was now sitting, it was possible that she and Michael could be making love. The thought excited her but at the same time it terrified her. She had never been with anybody other than her husband and they had only once done it in a car, many, many years ago. Although she yearned for excitement she did not want to tumble into something torrid and tawdry. She hoped Michael would take things slowly and let the relationship develop at its own pace. She wanted romance more than sex, she decided. Just a kiss tonight perhaps and no more?

Rob totally surprised Zena when she arrived home. With the boys' help, he had cooked dinner and had not made a bad job of it either, with the limited range of ingredients he could find in the freezer and kitchen cupboards. The boys had laid the table beautifully and they were all waiting for her to arrive before they ate. As soon as she walked through the front door, Rob sat her down at the table with a large glass of Chardonnay. She took it without looking at him, inspecting her fingernails as she spoke. "You shouldn't all have waited for me," she said. "I'm sorry I took so long. The road was closed due to a bad accident and I had to follow a diversion."

"You must be shattered," he said, "after the day you've had and then all that driving on top of it all."

The boys were excited about getting back to their own rooms again and went to bed immediately after dinner. As soon as they were alone, Rob came straight to the point. "Zena, I've been thinking about what you said about being a nurse and you're right. You should go to college." Zena was quiet. What could she possibly say? The last thing she wanted was for Rob to start being reasonable now that she needed an excuse for leaving him. "And about the boys," Rob continued. "If you really need to see them more often, I'm sure we can arrange a compromise." Rob wished Zena would reply. How could he negotiate with silence? He sat down on the sofa beside her. His voice was unusually tender. "Zena?" She was staring down at the floor so he moved to sit at her feet where he could see her face. Still she did not speak. As a tear landed on his arm it dawned on him - He had left it too late. He stood up angrily. "Zena, for Christ's sake, say something!"

"But I don't love you any more, Rob. I'm sorry, I can't go on pretending any longer. It's over."

Stumbling aboard Ragamuffin in the early hours, Jessica checked her phone to discover there were twelve missed calls, one voicemail and two text messages. "Persistent bugger, I'll say that for him," she muttered. "Well, it can just wait until the morning. I need my sleep." She undressed and clambered into bed, without bothering to wash or to brush her teeth and switched out the light. But as she lay in the darkness, curiosity took hold and she knew there would be no sleep until she had checked her messages. As anticipated, the missed calls were all from Steve. She found the text message from Michael and decided to ignore it. She did not want to hear any of his excuses. Although Sue had urged her to give Michael a chance to explain himself rather than jumping to conclusions, what could he possibly have to say that would justify such deception and hypocrisy? To think that he had even had the nerve to criticise her for having an affair with a married man! The other message was from Steve. He told her he understood that he had asked too much of her but he still needed to see her. He told her he was coming to Milton Keynes without the children and would be there on Saturday morning as arranged. The first of the voicemails was just a repetition of this message. "Oh no you don't," said Jessica to her phone. "You can come to Milton Keynes if you like but I certainly won't be there to meet you." The second voicemail was harder for her to ignore, however.

"Jess, you can go on refusing to answer my calls and messages as long as you like but you will not get rid of me that easily. I need to see you and I will see you. I am bringing my bike to Milton Keynes and I plan to ride along the towpath for as long as it takes. I'll cycle all week if necessary but I will find you." Listening to the harsh tone of his voice, Jessica wondered how well she knew Steve. She had never denied him anything or done anything to make him angry during their time together. She had never before thought him really capable of violence but now realised that she did not know him - it was only ever a part-time relationship after all. There must have been some reason why his wife had turned to drink. She felt a desperate need to escape. At least by not having continued her journey towards Milton Keynes she had a bit of distance on her side.

But he could travel so much faster on a bike than she could on the boat so she was still not far enough away. She agonised about what to do. If she turned around and headed back north, she would come to a junction at the top of Long Buckby. If she went from there towards Braunston she would meet another junction and if she were then to travel in the direction of Oxford, she would pass that other junction towards Warwick near where her alternator belt had broken all those weeks ago when that lovely guy had towed her. Working out the odds of Steve taking the correct turn at each junction, she calculated he would have only a one in six chance of finding her if she went towards Oxford. Alternatively, she could pay for a month's mooring in the marina and hide in there amongst all those other boats. It would be like looking for a needle in a haystack. Although Steve knew her boat was called Ragamuffin, he had never actually seen it. Perhaps she could just paint out the name and change it to something different? (Needle in a Haystack perhaps?) Jessica knew that her mind was rambling - she had drunk far too much wine to think straight. She considered the braver option of taking Ragamuffin towards Milton Keynes and facing Steve. Surely she was strong enough to resist him, she told herself. Then she remembered how desperate he was to get custody of his children. She considered locking up Ragamuffin and going away, catching a train to visit somebody - her parents perhaps. Or perhaps not - she was not yet ready to face Barbara again. She could go and stay with Karen and Jack, but that might mean seeing Michael. "I don't know what to do! Why is everything so complicated?" she screamed, clenching her hair with her fists in frustration. Her head was spinning and she was too tired and too drunk to make a decision. She could not do anything until the morning anyway. For the second time she switched off her light and tried to sleep.

Michael woke with a start. He knew he had been dreaming but could not recall what the dream had been about. He lay in bed thinking about the previous day's events. That awkward parting from Jessica, his frantic dash back from the station in the heat and then the accident at the lock. He wondered what had made him dive in to the lock to help Rob - somebody he did not even know and who from all accounts was not a very pleasant person. He guessed he did it for Zena. Ah Zena, what a girl! He had certainly been tempted. It would have been so easy to invite her in for a coffee before she drove home again. Then one thing would almost certainly have led to another. He had lectured himself firmly in the car, reminding himself that she was still a married woman and in any case Jessica was the one that he really wanted. He had been quite cool with Zena after they had dropped off Rob and their sons, not wanting to continue the impression that anything might happen between them. When they had pulled into the space outside his flat he had moved quickly and was out of the car before there could be any question of a goodnight kiss. "Thanks a lot. Drive carefully home now," he had said, closing the car door purposefully and walking away without a backward glance.

Jessica was up early the next morning, despite her hangover and her tiredness. She had not slept; whenever she had managed to get Steve out of her head, Michael had taken his place. In her drunken paranoia, she had imagined him and Zena spending the night together, possibly even talking about her and laughing at how cleverly they had deceived her. She was not too drunk to recognise that her anger came from jealousy and she reminded herself crossly that she had had her chance with Michael and had chosen not to take it. Why was it that she only wanted something when she could not have it? Perhaps that was what had attracted her to Steve - would she have wanted him so much if he was not married? As soon as it was light, Jessica sat up in bed and pulled back the curtain to watch the towpath waking up. She saw sparrows busily catching insects in the hedgerow and a blackbird tugging a worm from the ground. The worm stretched like a piece of elastic and Jessica expected it to snap at any moment, hitting the blackbird in the face like a balloon bursting when it is blown too big. But the blackbird was an expert and soon the worm stretched no more. She noticed too the berries that were beginning to form on the creamy white umbrellas of the elderflower blossom and was instantly taken back to Auntie Joan's kitchen that summer when she made elderberry wine. "Oh Auntie Joan, how I miss you."

Jessica was ready for action after a shower and some coffee. She could not face Steve - she was quite certain of that. Running away seemed to be her only option. She had reluctantly accepted that the supply teaching would have to wait until she was sure there was no danger of Steve coming looking for her in Milton Keynes. Instead, she was going to head back to Napton where, back in April, she had been offered a job as a barmaid. Although the summer was nearly over, there might still be the possibility of temporary work in the pub until it was safe to return to Milton Keynes. She hunted amongst her things and finally found the card that the landlord had given her. It was dog-eared but the number was still legible. "Probably a bit too early in the morning to call but I'll try later. Whether or not there is a job, I'm going that way anyway." She drank another cup of strong coffee and then marched down the towpath to look for signs of life aboard Mucky Duck. Sue was just drawing back the curtains when she arrived and she poked her head out of the front door. "How's the hangover?"

"No worse than you'd expect," replied Jessica. "How about you?"

"Bad. I'm getting too old fer this. Yer don't recover so quickly when yer get old, yer know. Even so, I think yer look even worse than me. Yer look like yer didn't sleep a wink."

"I didn't, but never mind - I'll have an early night tonight. I've decided to turn round and go back to Napton. I was wondering what time you were planning on going up through the locks. We could perhaps do them together?"

"Aye, that 'ud be grand. Can yer give me half an hour?"

Jessica walked back to Ragamuffin and sat on the front deck, watching an extended family of Canada Geese. They swam along in procession, with one pair of adults at the head of the line, closely followed by seven goslings and behind them another pair of adults, with another three goslings bringing up the rear. She wondered about the pecking order of this family and pitied the little gosling at the back. Her phone rang while she was watching and, being distracted by the geese, she answered it absentmindedly. "Hi Jessica, it's Michael."

"Oh....... Where are you?" she spluttered.

"I'm at home of course. Where else would I be?"

"Where else indeed? And is Zena with you?" thought Jessica. She was furious with herself for answering her phone. Although she did not want to speak to Michael, it would have been a hundred times worse if it had been Steve who was calling. Whatever was she thinking of?

"Are you OK? You seem a bit quiet. Talk to me Jessica, I'm worried about you."

In her head, Jessica replied, "It looked like it. So worried that you needed Zena to comfort you." But she kept those thoughts to herself and replied casually, "I'm fine. By the way, I saw The Narrow Escape come past yesterday."

"Did you see me at the tiller?"

"Yes, you and Zena together. Where was Rob?" Jessica attempted to keep the edge out of her voice.

"In hospital. It's a long story. I was really on my way to see you. I needed to talk to you so I got off the train and came back to the canal but you had already left by the time I got there," Michael continued. Jessica noticed how uncharacteristically rapidly he was speaking - he was usually so calm. "I wanted to have another go at persuading you not to meet up with Steve. I know you don't want to hear it but...." Jessica interrupted him.

"It's OK, Michael you can stop there. I've already told Steve I am not going to do it."

"Oh really? Cool! I'm so relieved."

Jessica asked why Rob was in hospital and Michael told her an edited version of the story, not admitting that he had dived into the lock or how close he had come to having an affair with Zena. Jessica was similarly selective in her recall of events; omitting to reveal how angry and upset she had been to have seen him and Zena on the boat together and how unbelievably happy she was now she knew the real reason why he had been there. Instead, she just said how lucky it was that he was on hand to help take the boat back to the marina. "So how did Steve take it when you told him?" Michael asked.

"I haven't spoken to him, just sent a message. But he's texted me back to say he's coming here on his own, without the children. He is determined to change my mind. He's going to bring his bike so he can travel along the towpath and find me. I'm going to turn round and head in the opposite direction and hope he doesn't catch me up," Jessica explained, trying to hide her fear behind a false cheeriness.

"And if he does catch up with you?"

Jessica could hear the concern in Michael's voice and let down her guard. "I don't know. I don't want to see him but he's not the sort of guy to take no for an answer. To be honest Michael, I'm a bit scared of him." Michael's anger and protectiveness were hidden behind carefully chosen words and slow, deliberate speech.

"Look Jessica, I really don't want to interfere and you can say no, but would you mind if I came along and gave you some moral support? I could be there tonight or in the morning." He heard the sharp intake of breath followed by a long pause as Jessica struggled with her emotions. Of all the many possibilities that had spun around and around in her head during the night, this was certainly not one of them. And she could never have predicted the shiver of excitement that ran through her body at the thought of seeing him again. What was it that Sue said about the unexpected things in life? "Yes please, Michael. I can't think of anything I'd like more."

Chapter 20

"It's no good trying to get rid of your own aloneness. You've got to stick to it all your life. Only at times, the gap will be filled in. At times! But you have to wait for the times. Accept your own aloneness and stick to it, all your life. And then accept the times when the gap is filled in, when they come. But they've got to come. You can't force them." D.H.Lawrence (Lady Chatterley's Lover)

For a week, Rob tried to persuade Zena to change her mind, but once he realised that he could not stop her from leaving him there was such a violent argument that Zena was let in no doubt that the marriage was well and truly over. She fled with the boys to her parents' house only to be told by them that she should go back to Rob to try and work things out between them. Her mother reminded her of her marriage vows and accused her of giving up too easily. Her parents agreed to look after Lawrence and Zac until the start of term but did not want her living there too as that would be seen as taking sides. Still having a week before she could move into her student accommodation, Zena phoned Michael in the hope that she might stay in his spare room. There had been no contact between them since she had dropped him off at his flat that night and he had run off so quickly without even a proper goodbye. She had concluded that he did not want to get involved with her because she was still married. But now she had left Rob, everything was changed and Zena hoped Michael would see that. That moment on the back of The Narrow Escape was not just something she had imagined – there was definitely some chemistry between them. A few nights alone together in his flat would be enough to rekindle the flame between them, she promised herself. Consequently she had a nasty surprise when she made the phone call, only to

303

discover that Jessica answered it. She was already occupying not only Michael's spare room but also his affections. 'Isn't it exciting?' Jessica squealed. "We're both starting our new lives in Oxford. Oh, I'm so glad you can finally follow your dreams!"

"Well, not all of them," Zena thought sadly. Alone for the first time in her life, she was terrified of the prospect of being without a man to sort things out for her. She began to wonder if she was strong enough to survive on her own. But at least she was not going to be homeless. As Jessica was already spending most of her time in Michael's flat, she had offered her Ragamuffin as a temporary home.

The dancing reflections of the vivid blue sky and brightly painted boats brought a blaze of colour to the Oxford Canal, where Michael and Jessica walked hand in hand along the busy towpath. Jessica could not believe her luck that a residential mooring site about three miles north of the city centre had become available. The mooring fees would be a wise investment, she decided. Having made up her mind to look for a part-time teaching post in Oxford, her only remaining concern had been what to do with Ragamuffin. It would have been impossible to constantly move her from one mooring spot to another but she was reluctant to sell her. That would be like throwing away all chance of escape. Not that she believed she would ever want to escape from Oxford. She did not know if it would last with Michael, but she was content for the moment to suspend her travels and see what happened. Her lonely journey was over; having learned how to be alone she was alone no longer. She had arrived safely at the other side of her solitude and not only had she found Michael, she had also found herself.

As they walked past the area of Jericho, Michael explained that it had recently become a conservation area. There were once iron and brass foundries there, he said, which were conveniently located next to first the canal and then the railway. The original tenements and industrial buildings had been cleared and replaced with Victorian and Edwardian housing. Jessica admired the ornate church tower. "That looks more like it should be in Italy than in Oxford," she observed.

"Oh yes, the church of St Barnabas. It was inspired by a campanile in Venice," replied Michael. Once again Jessica was impressed by his knowledge. Was there anything this man did not know? As they approached the mooring site, she noticed the drooping petals of a flag iris on the bank. "Ah, the last of the yellows," she thought sadly, "but it's going to be a beautiful autumn." Her thoughts were interrupted by a familiar voice.

"Hi you guys. I've just locked up and I'm on my way to meet Dad. He's taking me to see the boys."

"We won't hold you up," said Jessica. "We're on our way to see Michael's grandma anyway but we just wanted to make sure that everything was all right with you."

"Yes, it's cool."

"And the boys?"

"Mum is spoiling them rotten. Apparently they went to stay with Rob at the weekend and he was in a foul mood. They phoned Mum and asked if they could return to my parents' house early. I spoke to them last night and they said that although they were happy at Mum and Dad's house, they can't wait to get back to school." Jessica could see Zena's relief at having come to the end of her nightmare without losing her boys. She still looked stunning despite her lack of make-up and her clothes being somewhat rather the worse for wear. She was positively fizzing with vitality - so different from the vulnerable girl she had been when Jessica first met her. Jessica studied Michael's face for a reaction. He sensed her watching him and grinned, pulling her closer to him for reassurance.

As they resumed their walk along the towpath, Jessica commented on the change in Zena. "Don't you think she looked better without the make-up?"

Michael paused and looked at Jessica. "Er, what can I say to that question? That's not fair," he moaned.

"Well, I expect you would say she's absolutely gorgeous either way," Jessica told him. Michael laughed.

"And how would you feel about that?"

"Fine as long as you're not regretting missing your chance?"

"I love you, you silly girl. Whatever would I want to be with her for?" Michael pulled Jessica close and kissed her, causing a passing cyclist to veer out of the way, almost falling into the canal in the process. Michael shouted an apology to the cyclist before resuming the kiss. Although his words of reassurance were comforting, they were unnecessary; Jessica knew there was no doubting Michael's loyalty or sincerity. Ever since that moment when he had firmly told Steve that Jessica was with him now, she had felt the weight of the world fall off her shoulders. And afterwards, when he confessed how close he had come to giving up on her, she knew how happy he was that he had waited.

They continued further along the towpath, stopping to pick blackberries along the way and feeding them to each other. "It seems like Zena is getting on better with her parents now at least," remarked Michael casually. "It's such a shame when families fall out." Jessica knew what Michael was getting at; he wanted her to try again to patch up her quarrel with Barbara. Her mother had stubbornly refused to speak to her since her parents' unfortunate visit to the boat, despite her father's efforts. Jessica knew that once Barbara heard about Michael she would be so desperate to meet him that she would be able to keep up the silence no longer. However, Jessica wanted to keep Michael to herself for just a bit longer. "I'll phone next week, I promise," she said.

Gloria greeted Jessica with a big smile before ushering her and Michael into the cosy sitting room. There was a smell of stale tobacco on her clothes and Jessica held herself stiffly while Gloria hugged her. She really did not want to be hugged by this woman, the same woman who had written that brutal letter which must have broken her aunt's heart. But it was difficult to dislike her - she was after all Michael's grandmother and she had willingly agreed to meet Jessica to answer her questions about Joan. Michael had already warned Gloria that they had read her letters. She had every right to refuse to talk about such private matters. Yet here she was, carrying in a pot of tea and a plate piled high with homemade cakes. Gloria settled herself in a large armchair opposite her grandson and said, "Now, what is it you want to know?"

"Well, first of all, Grandma, can you tell me if this is you in these photos?" Michael pulled out the 1946 photographs of Auntie Joan and the unknown girl. Gloria put on her reading glasses to study them.

"Yes, that's Joan and me. Oh, that was a lovely summer, that was." She smiled happily and closed her eyes, obviously enjoying the memories. Jessica waited until she was ready to continue the conversation before she spoke. She felt guilty to be interrogating an old lady like this but Michael had assured her that Gloria was more than happy to talk to them.

"But I'm a bit confused Gloria. I thought you and Auntie Joan had split up by then. As you know, we've read the letters and in one of them you told Auntie Joan that you were going out with a doctor. That was when the war was still going on." Gloria leant forward to pour the tea and Jessica noticed her hand shaking. She added gently. "But you don't have to talk about it if you don't want to. It's really none of our business." Michael passed a cup to Jessica.

"Yes honestly, Grandma, we don't want to upset you. Only talk about it if you want to."

"Well, I think it's best if I start from the beginning. Have some cake, please. It's a long story.

Joan and I were very young girls when we first got together. We started off as best friends but quickly found a very strong bond had grown between us. We were full of curiosity - you must understand dear, that there was no such thing as sex education in those days. So girls would talk about it and we learnt from each other what a man did with a woman. We thought it was really disgusting and rather funny as well. But we were scared we would not know how to kiss properly, and that was how it started you see, with us practising kissing together.

When the war started, Joan and I both lived in London. We had been friends since school, even though Joan was in the class ahead of me. I was working in a sweet shop before the war, but there weren't many sweets when rationing started and the shop had to close down. I managed to get myself a job cleaning in a hospital then. Joan's family was better off so she did not paid employment. But she was always doing voluntary work of one kind or another. When we were eighteen we could sign up for proper war work. Joan's birthday came first, in March, and she saw an advertisement in The Times for women to train on the narrowboats. Her mother was most disapproving but Joan was frightfully excited about the prospect. The plan was that I would join her as soon as I was old enough. They worked in teams of three, with one woman sleeping on one boat and the other pair on the other boat. We could have worked it so we shared a cabin and then we really would have been together, which was what we had always dreamed of. Joan was forever saying you should follow your dreams. But when I saw the boats and realised just what it would be like, I was more than a bit scared. I knew I'd be sure to fall in - I was never very good at balancing and to make matters worse I couldn't swim. And then before my birthday came it was winter and I could tell what an awful time Joan was having. The tarpaulin that covered the load would be frozen stiff and almost impossible to roll up. And they still had to run along the top planks and the gunwales even when they were icy and slippery. I would have surely fallen in then even if I had managed to keep my balance before. Joan never complained but when she described how they had to break the ice on the lock gates, I just decided that I was not up to it. I was never as strong as her, you see." Gloria stopped for a moment to sip her tea, and to ask if this was the sort of thing they wanted to hear. Michael told her it was fascinating and to go on if she did not mind talking about it. He poured out a second cup of tea for her.

"So where was I? Oh yes, I'd turned eighteen. I still wanted to be with Joan and I tried my hardest to persuade her to leave the boats and come with me to work in one of the munitions factories. She told me that because they had spent two months training her, followed by several months' valuable experience, it wouldn't be right for her to leave. She was by then experienced enough to train other girls and it was her duty to stay. You see, there were only about thirty of them and the work they were doing was very important. Without the coal and aluminium and all the other things that the boats carried the factories wouldn't have been able to continue. We had a bit of an argument and I went off to Coventry in a sulk. But we still wrote to each other - well, you know all about that. I wouldn't mind seeing those letters again if you still have them."

"Of course, I've got them here. Please, keep them if you like," urged Jessica, laying the bundle of letters on the coffee table. She also showed Gloria the diary and invited her to borrow it. Gloria thanked her and resumed her narrative, telling them all about her work in the munitions factory and how Joan had managed to visit her once. She had brought her boat to Coventry and it was not due to be loaded up until the following day, so Joan had stayed overnight in her hostel. Jessica thought what an amazing woman

310

Gloria was, in her eighties and still able to remember all the details of her youth. What was even more remarkable was her openness; she could easily understand why Michael was so fond of her.

"But things started to go wrong after a while. We hardly ever saw each other and the loneliness was getting me down. A lot of the other women were courting and it felt like I was missing out on all the fun. I also began to think that I'd like to have a baby when the war was over. You see, things were very different then - women were supposed to get married. Nowadays, a couple of women can live together and even adopt children but that didn't happen then. So I was getting quite moody and when I found out that Joan had told the other girls on the boat all about me, I was very cross. It was like she had betrayed us. Joan never cared a jot what other people thought but I did. So when I met Walter, I thought "What the heck, I deserve to have somebody who loves me." You see, working in the factory was hard, and to get by you had to have something to look forward to."

"And Walter was the doctor who looked after you when you hurt your hand?" interrupted Michael. "But that wasn't Grandad, was it?"

"No, I hadn't met your grandad then. Walter was very kind and he made me feel sort of special. And because I was still angry with Joan I agreed to let him court me." Joan then described how good it felt to be with Walter and how she thought she might marry him. When she explained how she had written to Joan to tell her it was over between them, Gloria began to cry. Michael left Jessica's side and put his arm around his grandma. He spoke softly to her.

"You don't have to tell us if it's too painful."

"But I want to. Apart from your grandad, I've never told anybody about this and I think I should explain it to you before I die. But just give me a moment and then I'll tell you the rest." So Michael made a fresh pot of tea and he and Jessica ate some cake while Gloria had a cigarette. Then she resumed her story.

"When Joan got that letter she told the authorities she needed to take some leave to attend to family business of a private nature. She came to Coventry and demanded to see me. She was desperately sorry to have given away our secret and she begged me not to end everything. I finished with Walter and we both managed to arrange some leave so we could be together for a few days. We went to stay in a hotel and pretended we were sisters. The war ended very soon after that and we moved together to the south of London. We had a lovely holiday in Brighton once. Look, you can see us in this photograph. We were so happy."

"So what happened?" asked Jessica, eager to find out which of them had ended the relationship. Gloria explained that they had been too young when the affair started and their friendship had been strengthened by the excitement of doing something secret, something a bit shocking even. Once they were able to spend all of their time together, the excitement faded and they slowly drifted apart. They had both begun to realise that they were no longer in love with one another when Joan fell for a young girl who she had met at work. "Weren't you terribly upset?" asked Jessica.

"No, not really. I knew it was coming to an end between us. It was just a matter of time before one of us found somebody else. And I was beginning to get desperate for a baby as well. So when

312

Michael's grandad came along soon after that, well....
you know the rest."

Jessica thanked Gloria for telling them the
story and they reminisced fondly for a while about
Joan. It appeared that the two women had remained
as friends for many years afterwards. Every year they
used to send each other a long letter with their
Christmas cards and Gloria knew all about Jessica as
a young child. "She used to adore you, you know.
She lived for the holidays when you visited her. You
were such a funny little thing. I even met you once."

Jessica was amazed. "Did you?"

"Yes, you had decided to cut your hair one
day. You made such a mess of it and it reminded us
of the little girl in "The Mill on the Floss". Your
mother was absolutely furious."

"I can just see you as a little Maggie
Tulliver," teased Michael, ruffling Jessica's hair. She
poked him in the ribs and Gloria laughed. She could
recall the incident with the hair but had no memory
of Gloria having been there.

"And the things you used to say. I'll never
forget how amused Joan was one time when you
asked her if doodlebugs were like bedbugs. You
brought her a lot of happiness, you know, which
made up for her being on her own. She did have a
number of girlfriends over the years but she never
did manage to find a lasting relationship like I had
with Michael's grandad. I was the lucky one. She
trained to be a teacher when she was about thirty - it
was something she had wanted to do since she was
on the boats."

313

Jessica interrupted at that point. "I remember reading in her diary how she used to enjoy helping some of the boat people with their reading. None of them had really been to school, or at least not for very long, so they were very grateful when she and the other women helped them."

"Yes she used to love helping people. And she was a really good listener. She was so kind to me when Michael's grandad died. I'm sorry that we sort of lost touch with each other over recent years. I should have made more of an effort to contact her while I still could. I was so sad when Michael told me she had died."

When Michael said it was time for them to leave, Gloria fetched a little wooden box and handed it to Jessica. "Here, you have this. I'm sure she wouldn't have minded." Jessica opened the box, which was full of letters. She recognised Auntie Joan's handwriting immediately. She certainly wanted to read them but it seemed too cruel to take them away from Gloria.

"Are you sure? Don't you want to keep them for yourself?" But Gloria was adamant that Jessica should keep the letters. She also gave her a little silver chain and locket. Inside the locket was a sepia photograph of a young man. "Who is it?" Jessica asked, as she gazed in confusion at the picture.

"That was Joan's father. He died in the war, just like my dad did. She said she was worried that she might lose it on the boats so she asked me to look after it for her. She could have left it at her home but I suppose that leaving it with me was like giving me a token of her love. I put it away in a safe place and then we both just forgot about it. It turned up years later when my mother's house was sold. I've been feeling guilty that I never returned it to her. I know she would have wanted you to have it."

"Thank you. I'd love it, if you're really sure."

That evening in Michael's flat, which already felt like home to her, Jessica finished reading Auntie Joan's letters. She sighed with contentment; Auntie Joan was a strong woman whose life had been lived to the full. She had been alone at the end but Jessica doubted if she would have done things any differently if she could. It was comforting to have heard from Gloria that she had brought pleasure to her aunt. Jessica looked up to watch Michael, busy in his kitchen creating something fabulous for dinner. It was such a miracle that Auntie Joan and Gloria had split up, she thought. Otherwise, this beautiful kind man would never have been born. "What are we having?" she asked.

"You'll have to wait and see," he laughed. "What did your friend Sue tell you about the unexpected things?"

Printed in Great Britain
by Amazon